Heat of the Moment

Heart of Vallantine Book 2

Kelly Moran

CHECK OUT BOOK ONE NOW!

Praise for Kelly Moran's Books:
"Breathes life into an appealing story."
Publishers Weekly
"Readers will fall in love."
Romantic Times
"Great escape reading."
Library Journal
"Touching & gratifying."
Kirkus Reviews
"Sexy, heart-tugging fun."
USA Today
"Emotional & totally engaging."
Carla Neggers
"A gem of a writer."
Sharon Sala
"I read in one sitting."
Carly Phillips
"Compelling characters."
Roxanne St. Claire
"A sexy, emotional romance."
Kim Karr
"An emotionally raw story. A compelling read."
Katie Ashley
"I devoured the book!"
Laura Kaye

Dearest Visitors,

Welcome to Vallantine, Georgia, where the only thing sweeter than the Belle Peaches we're famous for are the patrons.

Founded in 1870 by William & Katherine Vallantine, our cozy, picturesque town is home to 2500 residents, and pocketed between Statesboro and Savannah. Quaint Vallantine is nestled beside the Ogeechee River. We have 3 inns and 2 B&Bs for convenience, or a hotel just outside the city limits. There are several family-operated restaurants for your dining pleasure to suit your palate or fancy.

On your visit, be sure to check out our main square. There're over 45 locally owned independent shops along the old-world cobblestone streets. Take a riverboat dinner cruise at sunset or a horse-drawn carriage ride through the historic district. Enjoy a walking tour of the Vallantine Cemetery or Peach Park, where multiple statues stand in remembrance of important figures in history, and stroll among the hundred-year-old oak trees teeming with Spanish moss. You can even view the original library, which is under renovation, that William built in 1875 for Katherine, who loved books. Some say she never left, that her spirit can be caught reading one of her favorite volumes between the shelves while she idly waits to assist all who enter seeking knowledge.

You may have been drawn here for our annual Peach Festival or Pecan Fair, but our southern charm will make you never want to leave. Hospitality is our middle name. If you're so inclined, before you do depart, go say hello to Miss Katie—the first Belle Peach tree ever planted in town, named after the one and only Katherine Vallantine. It's legend around these parts that doing so will bring you good luck and a lifetime of love. She's also been known to grant a wish or two if she's in the mood.

Y'all come back now, you hear!

Gunner Davis, Mayor of Vallantine

Chapter One

With one side of her face smooshed in her pillow, Scarlett Taylor groaned at the insistent knocking on her bedroom door. One day. Just one day to sleep in. Was that too much to ask? The Rover wedding she'd hosted at her estate last night had gone past one a.m. Cleanup had been another hour beyond that.

The banging commenced.

A moan, and she prodded one eye open, glancing at the clock on her nightstand. For crying out loud. It was only eight. She had no appointments until noon. She knew that for a fact because she'd scheduled it that way. On purpose. So she could sleep in.

Sunlight smacked her in the face as she turned her head. She'd forgotten to close the drapes before crashing last night. Dust motes clung to the air and wafted through the balcony doors.

Cotton, having assumed she was getting up, rubbed his white furry face against her neck and purred loud enough to shake the foundation. Absently, she petted him.

More banging.

Fiddlesticks. "What?"

"Are you decent?"

The rumbling, deep, aw-shucks timbre could only come from one person, and she wasn't in the mood.

"No."

The knob turned anyway, and her ornate heavy door cracked open.

In strode Aden pain-in-her-ass Abner wearing a pair of well-worn jeans, a white t-shirt which emphasized his biceps, and the charming grin every debutant in all of Vallantine swooned over. His disheveled sandy blond hair was growing slightly too long on top, as was the matching five o'clock shadow on his jaw.

Using her bedroom door versus climbing up the rose trellis outside her balcony was a recently new venture that began roughly three years ago when she'd sold him part of the Taylor estate to open his horse-drawn carriage ride business. The barns and horses he adored were included in the deal. She wasn't sure why the sudden change in entry route, but she thought she preferred the balcony. He'd been doing it since they were kids for varying reasons, stemming anywhere from thunderstorms that made him twitchy to her parents had made her cry again. Things were always changing, and though she respected progress, some things she wished would stay the same.

Still prone, she narrowed her eyes at him. "I said I wasn't decent."

"You lied." He walked closer and sat on the edge of her bed, the mattress dipping with his weight. He held out a steaming mug of coffee. "You pause before answering when you're gearing up to lie to me."

Rolling her eyes, she sat up and took the coffee. The red and gold bedding fell to her waist, exposing her in nothing but her black lace nightie. His quick aversion to stare at the ceiling instead made her grin. Served him right.

"I don't lie." She took a sip of coffee and nodded. One cream, two sugars. Aden had his moments.

"Not usually, no. Except to me."

She thought about a retort, but snapped her mouth shut. She did tend to stretch the truth around him. Nothing hurtful. Just in the areas where sanity needed to be maintained. Like how he always smelled like fresh cut grass, and how it had been one of her favorite scents since childhood. Instead of saying that, she'd scrunch her nose and claim he smelled like the outdoors.

And she never got away with it.

"Cover up, darlin'."

"They're just boobs, Aden. I'm wearing a nightie."

"That nightie is wearing you, and I'm done talking about your...breasts."

"My swimsuit covers less."

"I'm aware."

Cotton meandered over to Aden, the traitor, and climbed in his lap for proper petting. Aden obliged while still keeping his gaze heavenward.

Frowning, she drew the covers to her chest and held them in place with her forearm. For all his womanizing, he was a good ole southern gentleman. Whom she lived for taunting.

"You don't like my boobs?"

He pinched his eyes shut and heaved a sigh. "Gonna be the end of me, woman."

"Hasn't happened yet." She took another sip of coffee. "I'm covered. You can open your eyes now."

A glance at her, then away. He seemed to be taking in the details of her room and foraging thought. Walnut bedroom set, four-poster bed, art of various flowers from the vast gardens out back, deep plush carpet. He appeared to be focusing on the balcony doors beside her bathroom longer than was necessary.

"What for you wake me from my slumber?"

His bluer than blue crystalline eyes shifted to her as he cocked his head. A criminal waste on a man, those eyes. "Darcy Lynn Freemore's mother is downstairs, insisting on speaking with you immediately. Charlene was attempting to wrestle the badger when I arrived. Told her I'd get you."

Charlene was Scarlett's assistant, and Darcy's wedding wasn't until next month. What could possibly be so urgent that the bride's mother needed to drop by at stupid o'clock on a Sunday?

"Did she say what she wanted?"

"Nope, but she's got her nose up about something."

Swell. Shoving the covers aside, she rose and headed for the bathroom, sipping coffee on the way.

"I guess you weren't lying, darlin'. You're not decent."

"And you're not the first guy to check out my rack or my ass, Aden."

"I wasn't..." He let out a gale force wind. "I'll feed the cat."

"Thanks."

She shut the bathroom door, relieved herself, brushed her teeth, and since there was no time to shower, she threw her hair into a high ponytail. She spent solid time on cosmetics, something her mama had hammered into her since puberty, and left the bathroom to check out wardrobe selections in her walk-in closet.

She had a meeting at noon for a baby shower—the joys of starting a thriving event business on her family's estate—so she opted for a yellow sundress because she might have to tour the grounds. July in the great state of Georgia was not kind. The toads would be fryin' on the pavement by midday.

Satisfied, she slipped into a pair of black flats, grabbed her phone, and left her bedroom to deal with Mrs. Freemore.

Scarlett loved her home, and she never took it for granted. Ever since Miss Maureen, her grandmother, had passed, leaving the entire estate to Scarlett, she tried to spend every moment she could appreciating it. Her folks had been avidly upset the grounds had been willed to her, but Miss Maureen didn't mince words or feelings. Her grandmother had been richer than an oil tycoon, but she'd never treated others as less than, and she made no secret of her displeasure in how snobby Scarlett's parents behaved.

Inside, there were thirteen furnished rooms, five of them on the main level for events. The second floor Scarlett had kept as her domain, turning one room into a private kitchen and another into a living room. The rest were guest rooms and a library. Polished, gleaming hardwood and vaulted coffered ceilings throughout. Each morning, as she departed her quarters for the day, she smiled. She was blessed to own a place so rich in history and share it with her small town of Vallantine for hosting.

Rounding the banister, she descended the grand mahogany staircase into the foyer, where a flustered Charlene was repeatedly smoothing her tight blonde bun with one hand and waving the other. Scarlett felt bad she'd taken too long upstairs, but seeing guests while not properly put together was a crime against the Taylor name. Her mother would never let her hear the end of it. Mrs. Freemore, donning a plum pantsuit and not one brown strand of her bob out of place, frowned at Scarlett's assistant as royalty might a peon.

Off to the side, Aden had his arms crossed, leaning against the doorway to the Myrtle Room, watching the exchange. The tick-tick of his jaw only proved he was barely keeping his mouth shut, and only out of courtesy to Scarlett.

Game on.

"Mrs. Freemore, how lovely of you to pay us a visit, and so early on a Sunday." Scarlett plastered on a smile, the one she reserved for condescending bitches. It was no wonder the woman had been friends with her mother for decades. Peas in a pod. "How may I assist you today?"

The woman sniffed. "You can start by telling your staff where their place is."

So, it was gonna be one of those mornings.

Whereas Charlene was technically staff, she helped keep Scarlett's business in order, especially with fine details. She certainly didn't deserve the snide comments.

Taking a shallow breath, she turned to Charlene. "Would you be ever so kind as to prepare some cucumber water for our guest? Please ensure the kitchen has made enough for our noon meeting."

Eyes wide in relief, Charlene nodded and did an about-face toward the kitchen.

Aden straightened, but Scarlett subtly shook her head. She had this, and Mrs. Freemore hadn't appeared to notice him, though Scarlett appreciated the backup.

Smile cracking, she faced the mother of the bride. "I'll remind you not to be crass coming into my home or place of business and speak ill of anyone, whether they be friends, guests, family, or my staff. You will give them the respect they deserve." She straightened her shoulders, ignoring the proverbial smoke coming out of the woman's ears. "Now, what can we assist you with today?"

"Honestly, Scarlett. As if we haven't known your family for—"

"Last warning, ma'am. You showed up before business hours and without an appointment, and you were rude to my people."

A huff, and she waved her hand. "Fine. I need to move Darcy's wedding reception from the Willow Room to the Azalea Room. Several of the extended family have responded *yes* at the last minute, and we need more space."

Scarlett tilted her head. This event had been booked for eighteen months. They'd already moved it from the Magnolia Room, a medium-sized venue, to the Willow, their second largest. They never scheduled other events on weekends when they had weddings because all the rooms were accessible through the main foyer. They simply locked the doors to the other rooms. Weddings often occupied Friday nights for the rehearsal, Saturday for the actual wedding, and Sunday for gift opening. Mrs. Freemore's request was doable, as the other rooms were open, but to pull this a month before the wedding was pushing it. There were other factors like seating, flowers, and catering to consider. Not to mention, she wasn't asking, she was ordering, and that was after she'd stormed Scarlett's castle, acting high and mighty.

"Let's head to the office."

Without waiting for an answer, Scarlett turned and went down the hallway to the left of the staircase, her flats shushing on the black and white checkered tile. The small space had once been an unnecessary hall closet which she'd converted into an office for herself and Charlene. It was just spacious enough to hold two desks facing one another on opposite walls.

Mrs. Freemore followed her inside and sat daintily on the edge of an embroidered leather chair across from the desk.

Scarlett plopped in her chair and booted her computer. "How many more people are we expecting?"

"Fifty, give or take."

Geez. Alrighty. The wedding was already set for one hundred and fifty. The Azalea Room, their largest, was only licensed for two hundred. They'd have to move the venue outside if the number rose again, a fact which she'd stressed to Mrs. Freemore upon booking.

"Décor won't be an issue. We have more than enough stock of cloth napkins and such in her theme color." Chartreuse. Blech. "However, there is going to be an upcharge to change rooms."

"That's fine."

Damn right. "I'll have to add additional servers and food for catering. I can probably get the table flower arrangements to stretch, but that's dependent on supply. I'll call Bloom Boutique to see if they can get more in time for the day. If not, I can try Betty at the Garden Club, but I make no promises."

"We ordered white roses and yellow asters."

"Yes, but that was fifty people ago. You're talking an extra five to eight tables, not accounting for the aisle and arches."

"I expect what we paid for."

Sugary smile in place, Scarlett blinked. "You'll get what you paid for. It's the additions you haven't paid for yet that might be problematic last minute. I'm telling you upfront there might be a snag."

"I want everything perfect."

Scarlett hated to tell her, but there was no such thing. "We'll get it as close as possible." She did some math and wrote down a number. "That's the difference you'd be looking at."

"That's absurd. I won't pay it."

This family was as well-off as her own. They could afford it. And she was the one who wanted the adjustment a mere thirty days before the big one.

Scarlett stood. "Then I suggest you tell the extended family they should stay home. We'll keep you in the Willow Room and everything else as planned."

A huff. "Well, I never."

Scarlett believed it. People like her rarely got told *no*.

Opening her pocketbook, Mrs. Freemore extracted her checkbook, snorting and scribbling. She tore off the check and handed it to Scarlett. "Highway robbery, if you ask me."

"I didn't ask you, and these are services for your daughter's wedding. We dedicate a lot of time and effort into making these special. It will be a beautiful day."

Mrs. Freemore rose, turning to leave.

"Next time you'd like to make a change or discuss something regarding the wedding, please call to make an appointment first. Today was a courtesy."

The angry clack-clacking of heels in the hallway was an unnecessary exclamation point.

After a good ten seconds, Scarlett closed her eyes and dropped in her chair.

Footsteps padded the floor, and she instinctually knew it was Aden. She had no clue why, but he'd been slaying her dragons or watching her rear since before kindergarten. Most of the time, she let him, unless it involved her event business, and she specifically asked.

"I don't know why you put up with their shit."

She shrugged. "Side effect of customer service."

Slouched in the chair across from her, legs spread in typical Aden fashion, he studied her. He did that a lot. She'd grown used to it. Except, for some reason, he had these tidbits of introspection that went beyond mere figuring her out and straight to digging in her brain. The majority of the time, she didn't care. Currently, it was making her curious.

"Penny for your thoughts, Aden?"

Up went his brows. "Is that all they're worth?"

Irritation inched north of her neck. They'd had a love/hate relationship growing up that had bled into adulthood. They'd bicker. They'd make up. Constant butting of horns. Above all, there was mutual respect. But she never, not once, insinuated he was beneath her. That response kinda hurt her feelings.

"Relax, Scarlett. I'm jerking your chain."

No, he wasn't, but why bite his tongue? It was uncharacteristic. "Now who's lying?"

His eyes narrowed, but he gave no other indication to his real mood. "Snobbery is not a side effect of customer service. It's a lack of decency on their part. You grew up having tea and beignets with these people whose outfits cost more than a year of my father's salary, yet they order you around like a peasant."

"I put her in place, didn't I?"

A grunt. "You did. Well done."

Then what in the actual haystacks was his problem?

He leaned forward, elbows resting on his thighs. "No one has a right to treat you that way, least of all your social class."

This again. What difference did it make how much she had in the bank? Human decency didn't have a price tag. And those in her "social class" never bothered him before. He went his way, they went theirs, and no elbows had ever been brushed.

"I have a business to run. I enjoy my job. Sometimes, that involves dealing with a difficult mother of the bride."

"She wasn't difficult, babe. She was a hateful shrew."

Babe? That was a new moniker. Typically, when being sarcastic or exasperated, he'd call her *darlin'*. "Hate to burst your bubble, but she's always been a hateful shrew."

"Not to you." Tick-tick went his jaw.

Ah, so this was a defending her honor thing. "I can handle myself."

"No shit." He rose, shoving his hands in his pockets. He spoke over his shoulder as he walked out. "Doesn't mean I have to like what went down this morning."

Chapter Two

Aden walked barefoot onto his open back deck, handing Forest and Graham a bottle of beer before claiming one of the Adirondack chairs. They'd been doing these impromptu "guys' nights" for a couple months now, and he had to admit, he didn't mind. Just friends shootin' the shit and chilling. It helped clear his head, at any rate. Or was a welcomed distraction.

Forest had grown up with him in Vallantine, but Graham was a relatively new transplant from the north who started out as editor of their fledgling local paper, The Gazette, and had returned it to a thriving business. Well, he and his girlfriend, Rebecca, and as a result, they now owned said paper. Aden liked the guy. He was smart, funny, honest, and seemed to make their Rebecca happy. That's all Aden cared about. She hadn't had it so easy in life, what with her folks being killed in a wreck when she'd been nine, and her grandmother had just passed not four months back. She'd returned from the big city to resettle in Vallantine. They made a great pair.

Stars aplenty winked overhead, unmarred by city lights or smog. Thick green grass and mature hundred year old oaks dotting the estate rustled with mild wind gusts. It was hotter than blazes, but with the sun down, temps were more tolerable. Humidity clung like a crazy ex-lover, rendering it hard to breathe, but the breeze brought relief and the warring scents of blooms from Scarlett's gardens blending with chlorine from her in-ground pool behind the main house.

He glanced in that direction. More than a few acres separated the eastern-facing side of her house and the back of his. Her bedroom light was off, meaning she was either planning away in her downstairs office or watching a deplorable rom-com in her upstairs living room, which was at the rear of the mansion. If she were reading, she'd be on her balcony in the summer. Alas, that wasn't the case tonight.

How many times in how many years had he glanced at that window? It had become some twisted form of a beacon, one he didn't know whether to run toward or away from. And lately, all he could think about was her.

Boy, was he a glutton for punishment.

"The Bookish Belles seem to be making good progress on the library." Graham cleared his throat and picked the label of his beer bottle with his thumb. "Lots of banging going on. Rebecca said the new addition is nearly framed."

Only in a small southern town would you have a trio of females named after literary heroines by their mamas and dubbed the Bookish Belles by the patrons. Like Forest, Aden had grown up with Rebecca, Scarlett, and Dorothy. True to their nickname, they loved all things fiction and had restarted the town's book club after they'd been bequeathed the historical library by the former owner. A good thing, too, because the place was falling apart and had been since they were kids.

"It is coming along nicely." Forest scratched the dark whiskers on his chin. "I was initially nervous about their plans, but they had spectacular ideas for updating while still respecting the original elements. Ninety percent of the plans had been an easy sell to the Historical Society."

"Good." Aden nodded. He'd forgotten Forest was in the Historical Society. "It's a cryin' shame how dilapidated the place has gotten."

No one respected history anymore. It was all about the shiny new gadgets or state-of-the-art upgrades. Roots were important, if for no other reason than to learn from mistakes.

The former Vallantine Library owner, Sheldon Brown, was the last remaining descendant of the town founders, William and Katherine Vallantine. Everyone could tell Sheldon had warred between familial obligations and letting it go, but he'd tried to save the library countless times at great expense. The Belles were doing right by it.

"Agree." Exhaling, Forest glanced toward the barns in the distance. "How's your biz doing?"

"Busy." The summer months always were due to tourism and the Peach Festival. People liked the old fashioned horse-drawn carriage rides through the dated parts of town. Come fall, it stayed steady with spooky season and cemetery tours. "Got another of Scarlett's wedding parties booked for this weekend."

Graham shook his head, his light brown strands ruffling with another breeze. "You have the coolest job."

Huffing a laugh, Aden rested his head on the back of the seat. "Sometimes."

He did love working with his horses. Horses which, if not for Scarlett, he wouldn't own.

For three generations, his family had been employed by hers. Nothing wrong with that. Work was work, and they'd made a decent living. Her grandmother, who'd insisted on being called Miss Maureen, not liking the age affiliation with the word "grandma," had always been kind and fair to him. Despite Scarlett's parents not supporting their friendship, Miss Maureen had wielded her power and had put the bug in Aden's ear about horse-drawn carriage rides. Only a couple townsfolk were doing something close, but not on scale for what his new business had become.

The problem had lain with Scarlett. Or so he'd thought. Once Miss Maureen died, Scarlett had inherited the entire estate. Everything. The mansion, gardens, pool, and stables. She didn't mind horses, but she didn't have a love for them like him. Oh, how he'd vexed about bringing her his plans. Initially, he figured he'd run things from her property if she allowed it. Scarlett had turned the whole idea on its ear. Within hours, she'd had her attorney draw up papers to sell eight acres, the stables, the foreman's cabin, and the grazing pastures to him for pennies on the dollar. With zero interest.

After one year, thanks to his savings and a flourishing client load, he owned it all. Sometimes, he still couldn't believe it. He'd been worried she'd poke fun at him. Instead, she'd handed him ammunition to make his dreams a reality.

"Earth to Aden."

He glanced at Forest, a bottle halfway to his lips.

Damn. The blasted woman wasn't even in his immediate orbit, and she'd been on his mind. Again. It was becoming habit. Come to think of it, he'd probably been born with the addiction.

"Sorry. Zoned out."

Forest grinned, following Aden's line of sight toward Scarlett's window. "Certain belle stuck in your bonnet?"

He wasn't touching that one. "I don't wear bonnets."

"Pity." Graham smirked. "You know, when I first moved here, Rebecca gave me the ins and outs of town. She mentioned your relationship with Scarlett, and I told her it sounded like foreplay."

That would imply there would be play after the fore. Alas, there had never been either, nor would there ever be. Scarlett Taylor had never, would never, look at him as anything more than the occasional friend or thorn in her side. The guy next door whose father had trimmed the hedges and cut the lawn. He was the shoulder she cried on or the mender of boo-boos, and then she'd go on her merry way when all had been righted in her world.

Most of the time, he preferred it that way.

Forest rolled his lips over his teeth, failing to hide his amusement.

A sigh, and Aden eyed them. "Wanna braid my hair? I'll polish your toenails."

They both threw their heads back and laughed.

Conversation over.

Graham nudged Forest with his elbow. "How's your job been treating you?"

"Meh." The humor drained from his eyes. "Boring, but stable."

Aden would be bored to tears, too, if he was a bank manager. Forest had followed in his father's footsteps, but he hadn't seemed happy about it. Life was too short for that nonsense.

"Whatever happened to all that woodworking you used to do?"

Graham's brows rose. "Didn't know you had that talent."

"Yeah," Forest said through a sigh. "Picked it up from summers with my granddaddy. Haven't touched it in years. Not since I went away to college. I've got a workshop out back filled with stuff since the divorce, but I don't know. Hard to make a living off it."

"Not if you do it right." Aden took a swig and swallowed.

Like most of Forest's true friends, Aden hadn't cared for the guy's ex. Graham had aptly named her the 'wicked bitch of the west.' After Forest had returned from college, the uppity elitist had lasted a whopping year in small town America before announcing she had found someone else and had moved back to California. Good riddance. Aden wondered if she had played a part in Forest's mindset about the carpentry interest, though. He used to be great at it. Whittling little figurines, plus he'd done remarkable furniture pieces.

Come to think of it... "Scarlett still has the desks you made in her office."

"Really?" Forest puffed his cheeks. "Wow. That must've been, what, eight years ago?"

"Sounds about right. Think about it, anyway. Tourists would eat that up."

Forest nodded, but his distant gaze implied he wouldn't take the leap.

Far be it for Aden to tell anyone what to do with their aspirations. He mucked stalls, carted around visitors, and was still staring at the girl next door's window like he'd been doing since...puberty. Nah, longer. Conception, probably. She'd had him wrapped around her finger as long as they'd been breathing.

"Well." Graham rose, tossing his empty bottle in the trash. "I got an early one tomorrow. My place next time?"

They nodded, and he left.

"I gotta hit the road, too. Thanks for hosting."

"Anytime." Aden tipped his bottle in a salute.

Once the roar of the engines had departed his driveway, he collected the bowl of chips and went in. Dufus, his black lab, lifted his head from his perch on the floor between the kitchen and living room, but he set it back down again.

"Me, too, buddy." He was tired. His days started at the buttcrack and often ended long after sundown.

Living the dream.

Reaching in the cabinet next to the sink, he poured out two of the iron pills he took for anemia, and downed them with a glass of water. Luckily, his condition was treatable, but chronic fatigue always nudged his peripheral. He couldn't complain, though. Rebecca had been diagnosed with fibromyalgia before moving back to Vallantine, and her symptoms sounded horrible. She'd taken it with grace and strength, like she had just about every other curveball thrown throughout her life. To date, she was still the only person who knew his diagnosis, and he'd only gotten it because she'd encouraged him to go in for testing since his symptoms were similar to hers. Some, not all.

Leaning his back against the counter, he crossed his feet at the ankles and studied the kitchen as he slowly drank the rest of his water. If he didn't down the whole glass, he'd be nauseous from the pills in the morning. The dark oak cabinets were outdated, and he'd been meaning to sand 'em down to re-stain them for a few years. Time hadn't been aplenty, not with running his own business the last couple. The pale yellow linoleum needed replacing, as well. Someday, he'd get to it.

The once foreman's cabin had been part of the buyout from Scarlett. A small two-bedroom, one bathroom ranch that resembled a log cabin on the outside. He could fit his whole house into one of Scarlett's ballrooms. It wasn't much, a thousand square feet, but it was his, and something no other member of his family had achieved. Home ownership. He'd grown up in the house since room and board had been a part of his father's employment for Scarlett's family.

It was a wonder why he still felt like the staff.

He headed for his bedroom down a short hallway, Dufus at his heels, and stripped off his shirt.

His dog sniffed the tee where he'd dropped it on the floor.

"Yes, I saw Cotton and Scarlett today. No, I didn't cheat on you with any other dogs."

Funny. She had a white cat and him a black dog. Even their choice of pets proved how polar opposite they were.

Satisfied, the dog jumped on the bed, circled twice, and promptly went to sleep.

Aden envied the mutt. Exhausted as he was, it would be hours before he slept, if the past couple weeks were any indication. He didn't know what the hell his problem was lately, but he needed to get a grip.

His cell chimed with a text. Pulling his phone from his back pocket, he checked the screen.

Dorothy. Weird, she didn't typically text after business hours. *Payroll scheduled for Friday. Emailed you the monthly report.* Nodding, he thumbed his *thanks* and sent it.

Dorothy, Bookish Belle number three, handled payroll for his few employees, taxes, and accounting for his business, as she did for a number of others in town. Another job he wouldn't want if his life depended on it. Give him fresh air and his hands doing something. The mere thought of crunching numbers made his head ache.

And with that thought, he thumbed another text. *You're awesome, in case I forget to say so often enough.*

A second later, her reply pinged. *LOL. Appreciate ya.*

The exchange made him recall a conversation they'd had in passing a few weeks ago. She'd suggested he have brochures made for his carriage rides. Once the library renovations were complete, the Belles planned on having a rack of local business info for tourists, and hoping to be a hub akin to a Welcome Center since the building was on a noll overlooking town. He'd told her how he thought they were doing a great job, and he'd liked the plans. She'd gotten a strange look on her face he couldn't decipher. When he'd asked, she simply shook her head, mumbling something about *imposter syndrome.*

He hadn't thought much of it at the time, but the phrase was circling his mind now. Had she been doubting her own skills and successes? Feeling not as talented or worthy as others believe, and scared people would realize that? Imposter syndrome could cause real harm if left unchecked. He knew for a fact.

He'd been battling it off and on since he'd signed the papers for the land. After all, what business did a gardener-slash-foreman know about running a company? Especially among Vallantine's elite. He wondered if Dorothy was just that adept at masking her anxiety. He'd never sniffed any indication of it before that day.

Frowning, he thumbed a text to Scarlett. *Dorothy suggested I have brochures made. Can you help?*

She was a Master Jedi at marketing and design, whereas he knew squat. He'd relied on word of mouth and her clients requesting his services in the beginning. Now, they just came to him. She'd designed his website, too.

An icon whirled as she typed. *Absolutely. I'll come take pictures tomorrow after the library meeting.*

Case in point. All he ever had to do was ask, and she'd help. Thing was, at this stage, he shouldn't have to depend on her. He could hire someone else. A professional. Sad fact remained, no one knew him better than her or would capture what he wanted with little input from him. Everything was all so one-sided in their relationship. What did she get out of it?

More guilt clawed his gut.

He typed, *thanks*, and tossed his cell on the nightstand.

Sighing, he walked to his window to stare out into the quiet night. Trees rustled and the long pasture grass swayed. The sound of windchimes from her gardens carried on the breeze. Like an idiot, his wandering gaze landed on her house.

The Taylor mansion had been built pre-Civil War and was impeccably maintained. Two-stories, white siding, and black shutters. Boxy and symmetrical. A true Antebellum southern home with neoclassical Greek-revival architecture, twenty Corinthian columns, and ten Doric ones. There was a cast-iron balcony that wrapped around the mansion's upper level, and the front portico centered the covered front porch, spanning the width of the house. Triangular pediments and detailed dormers. Over thirty acres worth of manicured gardens, gazebos, and an in-ground pool.

He shook his head. She'd been aptly named. Scarlett Taylor was, in fact, O'Hara reincarnated, with less daintiness and better coping skills. Plenty of drama. She lacked the vanity and selfishness of the fictional character, but had double the charm. A witty, social, and gorgeous pain-in-the-ass belle who grated his nerves and scraped his patience on the daily. He'd been using Rhett Butler's line *'Frankly, my dear, I don't give a damn'* on her since he was young enough to get in trouble for saying *'damn,'* but just once, he'd like to mean the words. Sincerely, that was his biggest issue in life. He gave too much of a damn about the girl next door, who was so out of his league, she played for an alternate universe.

And he'd loved her since further back than he could recall.

Sometimes, he waffled between in-love or just affection. He hadn't a clue which was more accurate. Regardless, he'd been wise enough not to pine for what he couldn't have, yet he'd acknowledged the feelings to himself. He'd been with other women. Many. A man had needs. Some he'd even thought about getting serious with. But it always circled back to her. None of them made his heart pound or his brain bleed or his temper flare like Scarlett. He swore, she spouted things from that pretty lil mouth of hers just to see how far his patience stretched before he wrung her elegant little neck and...

His phone chimed.

Deadpan, he stared at it, laying on his nightstand, knowing it was her. No one else texted this late.

Pings followed. Three of them.

Closing his eyes, he counted to five, reminding himself he didn't need to respond.

Ping, ping, ping.

He walked to the side of the bed and snatched the phone, his traitorous heart pounding in concern over the sheer amount of texts. It was hard to tell with her whether she was riding a whim or if something was actually wrong.

Shocker, it was Scarlett.

Why are you still awake?

Want to go swimming?

Which bathing suit looks better?

This was followed by two images of herself she'd taken in front of her vanity mirror, one a black bikini, the other bright pink. Both resembled dental floss and had him swallowing his tongue. She had a great body. Lithe, lean, slightly hourglass in shape, and her breasts were created on God's best design day. An act meant to torture him into obedience.

He thumbed a reply.

I don't know.

No.

Both.

There. That should suffice. She'd probably leave him alone to...

Pretty please?

He dug his thumbs into his eyes. There was no cure he hadn't tried for insomnia, but she was the cause.

Aden looked at his dog, laying on his back, legs in the air, tongue lolling from his open mouth. "Want to go swimming?"

In less time than it took for Aden to blink, Dufus jumped from the bed, launched into the hallway, and had skidded to a halt in front of the back door.

Right. He replied to Scarlett.

Fine. Be there in five.

She sent a gif of an emoji with dancing heart eyes.

Walking to his dresser, he pulled out his trunks, donned them, and slid into his flip-flops.

He and Dufus made their way across the yard toward the back of Scarlett's house, grass shushing with their footsteps and humidity coating his skin. Crickets chirped a sing-song while fireflies danced. An owl hooted from the general direction of the barn, and he hoped it wasn't nesting. Last time they'd tried to make a home in the loft, the calling had spooked his youngest mare.

Scarlett's in-ground pool was a freeform with wavy edges and a small waterfall at one end, designed to hide the filtration system. It wasn't large by comparison to others with her level of wealth because she'd wanted something intimate. She'd had it installed the year before her grandmother had passed. It was surrounded by an eight-foot black wrought iron fence and pruned juniper bushes. The encasing deck was brushed concrete with a small corner bar, pool house, and tanning chairs. Overly large pots along the fence contained palms, azaleas, and decorative grass.

As he approached, he found her sitting on the edge of the deep end, long legs dangling in the water, and sipping a cocktail that looked like a mojito. She glanced up and smiled at Dufus as Aden opened the gate, but the smile didn't reach her eyes.

"Who's the best doggie? You are."

Dufus licked her face, offering a full body wag.

She laughed. "Yes, you can get in now."

Without further ado, the black lab dove into the water, splashing like an idiot as he swam.

A roll of his eyes, and Aden limbered to sit beside her. "So, what's wrong? Why are we night swimming?" Though they'd done it a handful of times, it was not their norm.

She tucked her long, wavy chestnut hair behind her ear. Like silk, her tresses. "Eh, couldn't sleep. I—"

"Tell me or don't, but don't lie to me." He was overtired, hot, and irritable. He'd known her his whole life. She was like an extension of him, enough so that he could read her every nuance. The dimming in her beautiful golden eyes and slump in her shoulders spoke volumes.

A long-winded sigh, and she waved her hand in submission. "Mama called."

Ah. Okay, then. Nothing else needed to be said. Her mother was a walking, talking, belittling bitch, who harped on her daughter every second she got despite having raised—through no aid of her own—the most courteous, stunning, brilliant creature in all the land. He'd rather chew glass than be in the woman's presence.

He nodded to her cocktail. "Want something stronger?" A mojito wouldn't cut it for him.

"Nah, but thanks."

He was going to regret asking, but... "What did your mother want?"

Eyes on the dog swimming merrily, she shrugged. "You know, the usual. How she ate small children for breakfast. How her staff missed a speck of dust on the entryway table, proving no one wants to earn a wage anymore."

Translation: Scarlett had done something that wasn't up to par in the woman's eyes. She could cure cancer and solve the energy crisis, and her mother would complain she hadn't put enough makeup on while doing so.

She tilted her head, swinging her legs in the water. "Mrs. Freemore apparently had a lot to say about the way I handled this morning. She failed to invite Mama to brunch with the ladies."

As long as he lived, he'd never comprehend rich people. "Sounds like a *her* problem, not a *you* problem."

"Don't you know, Aden, all her problems are because of me."

"Horseshit."

"Yeah, well, tell her that."

He'd love to, but for Scarlett's sake, he'd always kept his trap shut. "I don't understand why you let her get to you." She was smarter than that and had ten times more character.

"Breeding and grooming, Aden. Breeding and grooming."

Now, that he could attest to. As a kid, she'd not been allowed to get dirty, sit without her knees glued together, or speak without the utmost in old southern hospitality. It had carried over into adulthood. What he wouldn't give to see her after a hot round of sex. Hair mussed, chest heaving, sweaty in all the right ways...

"How was guys' night? Did y'all properly grunt and scratch?"

"We did a lot of belching, too."

"Excellent." She offered her mojito, half gone already.

He took it and downed the contents. He preferred beer, but whatever. After he set it aside, while she was distracted, he wrapped an arm around her waist and tilted forward, plunging them both in the water.

She came up sputtering, eyes narrowed on him.

Treading water, he grinned. Mission accomplished. She wasn't thinking about her wretch of a mother.

Damn, but she was something. There hadn't been a day gone by in their twenty-eight years where he hadn't seen her or been in her presence. Day after day. He knew every curve of her, each freckle, right down to the interpretation of her expressions—all nine million of them—but sometimes, she still smacked him upside the head.

Her hair was so long, the ends floated on the surface of the water. Thick chestnut waves he'd maim to wrap around his fist. Her lips were still bright red from her lipstick, but her mascara had smudged the tiniest bit under her eyes. *Uhn*, her eyes. Golden brown. He'd heard other men refer to the color as aged whiskey, but to him, it was more amber. Reflective, and full of fire, framed by long dark lashes that could create a hurricane.

Forest had once said she looked like she'd been Photoshopped. An accurate description.

"Why are you looking at me like that?" She crossed her arms, pushing her breasts higher.

"Like what?" He knew he'd been staring. It was rare she caught him. Or noticed.

"I don't know."

"If you don't know, there's no point to the question, darlin'."

Eyes narrowing to slits, she heaved a sigh. "Never mind."

Perfect. Problem averted.

He sank underwater and swam to the other side of the pool. The cool water was refreshing against his skin as he made his way back. The heat and humidity had been a scorcher today.

She was playing with the dog when he returned. She laughed at Dufus's happy barking, and he was glad he'd succumbed, once again, to her demand since their visit appeared to have cleared her distress from earlier. He vaguely wondered why she hadn't called her besties.

Climbing the steps, he grabbed two towels from the pool house, and dried off with one, leaving the other for her on the chair.

"You good if I head home?" Drinking plus night swimming equaled problems.

Dufus got out and shook off, throwing water everywhere.

"Yes, thanks." She looked at him and did a double-take. "I'm fine. I only had half a cocktail."

Good. He was just checking. A nod, and he turned towards the gate.

"Aden?"

He paused, glancing over his shoulder. She was still in the pool, but sitting on the steps.

"Why don't you climb up the rose trellis to get into my bedroom anymore?"

He almost flinched. Regardless, if she'd offered to trim said roses, he would've been less surprised. There were a thousand answers to that question. Because they had a business relationship now. Because the act of climbing in her window bordered on romantic like the movies she watched. He settled on a vague one.

"We're not kids anymore."

The twist of her lips and overall expression indicated she wasn't satisfied with his reply, but he didn't care. It was time to go back to his world.

He whistled for the dog, and left.

Chapter Three

Late as usual, Scarlett climbed out of her car in the library parking lot to the sound of hammering and the whine of saws. Work trucks were parked all over the estate overlooking town, and several contractors were milling about. Sunlight beat down as the scent of cut grass and fresh chopped pine rode a breeze.

Not seeing her friends for their weekly meeting, she navigated around the side yard toward the back where the new addition was being framed. She should've worn flats instead of heels. Scattered sunlight reflected off roofing nails littering the lawn, and she shutter-stepped around them best she could. At least it hadn't rained the past few days to make the grass soggy, but a thin sheen of sweat coated her skin as scorching rays fried her where she stood.

Sighing, hands on her hips, she glanced around. There used to be at least half an acre of knee-high grass and weeds between the library and the tree line at the rear of the estate. It had been bush-hogged and leveled for a concrete slab to house the new addition. Lots of potential usable space, which she was grateful they were able to talk the Historical Society into utilizing. She had plans to put out a few picnic tables in the remaining part of the yard with umbrellas, along with a gazebo. Aside from the workers, there was no one else back here, and they'd finished framing. Electricians were setting up outlet boxes while other contractors were drywalling.

"Alrighty." She made her way to the front of the building and realized the front door was propped open. She'd missed that upon arrival.

The library was a severely dilapidated two-story old colonial-style building with a tiny parking lot out front, large enough to hold a handful of cars, hers being one of them. Plans were to add a parking lot on the side of the building where there was nothing but grass. The library's white exterior wood siding had been repainted many times, but it had been years since then, and it was flaking off in chunks. The shutters were gone. A small concrete porch held no furniture or coziness, and only a few holly bushes lined the stairs, overgrown and gnarled. She couldn't wait to fix that. Two Greek support columns flanked the front overhang on either side of the door, and another two at the corners of the porch. A gabled roof, rectangular shape, and symmetrical windows were classic staples of the architecture, but it also had trace design elements like dental moldings along the eaves and pedimented dormers. Luckily, they hadn't been rotted through.

Despite its state, it was really a Vallantine focal point, due in part to its history, and because it rested at the tip of Main Square, overlooking the shops as if protecting them. Behind it were the roads that led to older areas of town like the cemetery and her estate.

By the looks of it, the roof was finally getting replaced, which was a week early, and boded well since they couldn't do much inside until that had been knocked off the list. At least ten guys were standing on the stiff peaks, scraping and pounding. Dorothy had been handling the contractors and that schedule, so this was news to Scarlett.

Climbing the porch steps, she went inside. Forest, Rebecca, and Dorothy were at the podium—an ivory marble counter in the center of the room—glancing at a folder, their backs to Scarlett. Mr. Brown used to sit there when they were girls, working on manuscripts while they read, gossiped, and dreamed about the future. He was the last remaining descendant of the Vallantines, and she still couldn't wrap her head around how he'd bequeathed the library to her and her besties. It had never been out of heirs' hands.

Electricians worked along the far wall and contractors were doing something with the Greek pillars holding up the loft overhang. A large stained-glass window depicting a book lying in the grass under a peach tree allowed filtered light upstairs, which bled partly into the main room, and consumed nearly the entire rear wall of the loft. It was breathtaking, having been designed by the town founder William Vallantine himself when the library had been erected in 1875 for his wife, Katherine.

Gosh, the place smelled the same, though. Aged paper, old wood, and a trace of dust.

Square footage on the main level was roughly twenty-five hundred square feet, and about half that for the second story loft. The new addition would be approximately a thousand square feet. She loved the wide-open floor plan. So much potential. A wrought iron set of curved stairs led to the upper area with a matching railing. The loft was empty, but soon, they'd turn it into a bookstore. The ceiling was coffered with copper plating, and it was on the schedule to be cleaned. An enormous lead-glass chandelier overhead had cobwebs forming their own cobwebs. The original cherry floorboards would get refinished. Wall-to-wall, floor-to-ceiling bookcases lined the left and right walls, and were a hideous green color. They would get painted white, thank gawd. The shelves were empty now, which made her sad. Dorothy said many of the books were in a storage room in back. Mr. and Mrs. Brown had only taken the family volumes with them. Still, there was nothing more pitiful than a vacant bookshelf. Maybe she was crazy, but she was most excited about adding a rolling ladder.

There was an errant scent of dust and mildew that stung her sinuses. A testament to time marching on and taking no prisoners. It made her wonder, though, if the rumors of the place being haunted were true. They'd never experienced anything as young girls.

Legend was, Katherine Vallantine loved books. It was why her beloved husband had built the library for her in the first place. Somehow, through the years, word got around she haunted the place after she'd died, that she assisted all who entered seeking knowledge. Scarlett supposed anything was possible. Mrs. Brown had mentioned once that Katherine's journal had appeared to her and Mr. Brown before they'd married ten years ago. Rebecca, at a crossroads in her life this past spring, had found hundreds of her old blog pages she'd written as a teenager. In both cases, the materials had seemingly appeared out of nowhere.

"Look who finally made it."

Scarlett glanced at Rebecca and shook her head to clear it. "Sorry I'm late."

Dorothy shrugged. "You have your own time zone. We're used to it."

Har, har.

Scarlett walked closer and glanced at the folder in Forest's hands. "I see the roof is getting done. Yay. What else do we have?"

"Well," Dorothy said through a sigh. "The roofers were able to fit us in early due to a cancellation, and thus, the present contractors were able to jump ahead. I'm waiting on the plumbers and HVAC to get back to me."

Rebecca ran her fingers through her long blonde hair, a habit she did often when distracted. "Remember how we thought the loft overhang pillars would have to be replaced?"

"Yeah." Scarlett and her besties had been avidly worried screwing with them would mess up the loft's structure. That, and the Historical Society said replacements would have to match, meaning they'd need to have them custom made. No one around here did that kind of thing.

"Well, we were right. They're going to use jacks to hold up the frame while they remove the old ones."

Crap. How were they supposed to have new ones designed and built if no one...

"Forest is going to make them for us." Dorothy fanned her face with a stack of papers, her auburn strands flying around her cherubic cheeks.

Scarlett glanced toward the back of the library where men were doing just what Rebecca had mentioned. Five jacks were in place, holding up the loft frame. There were only two posts, Greek in design.

"I didn't know you were doing woodworking anymore." He'd been really great at it once. She looked at him, dark strands ruffled and his button-down business shirt damp from sweat. His cheeks were slightly pink as if embarrassed. "It sure would be a load off. Thank you so much!"

"Happy to do it." He cleared his throat, casting his gaze at the old columns coming down. "You'd be hard-pressed to find someone who can recreate the style. Not to mention, to be on the safe side, we're going with four columns versus two."

Eesh. Yeah, the price would be astronomical for custom work. She'd hit him up later and arrange payment so it wouldn't have to come out of the allotted funds.

"On behalf of the Belles, thank you."

He huffed a laugh, and she was reminded of the former jovial high school football star he used to be before life, the wrong woman, and obligations had stolen his thunder.

Dorothy glanced at her notes. "Electricians are going to put in the recessed lighting above the bookshelves once the roofers are finished, which will probably be tomorrow. Drywall has begun in the new addition."

"I saw that. It's coming along nicely." Excitement bubbled in her chest. It was happening. Their wistful childhood dream was becoming a reality.

They chatted a bit more about design features, but everyone had to get back to work, so they departed.

Once everyone had left, Scarlett stood outside her car, trying to understand a text Aden had sent.

The mayor wants to see us.

Was that the equivalent of being sent to the principal's office? If so, what had they done wrong?

Climbing in the car, she started it and blasted the AC while calling Aden.

"What's up, Scarlett?" He sounded as amused as dirt.

"Why does the mayor want to see us?"

"Hell if I know." The whir of his old pickup roared in the background. "I made the mistake of saying I was free today when his secretary called, and that you'd probably be done with your library meeting soon. He took that opportunity to summon us immediately to his office. I'm nearly there."

She really wasn't in the mood. It was hot and she had stuff to do. And the mayor was a blowhard. Since he was technically still a practicing attorney, Gunner Davis's legal office was off the main strip on Belle Street near some physician practices and accounting firms. However, most of his clientele had been in their prime during Vietnam, so he hadn't practiced much in the twenty years since becoming mayor. Thus, he primarily worked out of his mayoral headquarters in the courthouse, which was just behind the library, halfway to her estate.

"Okay, I was just leaving the library. I'll be right there."

Swinging out of the lot, she drove a block up and hung a left. Halfway down on the right was the courthouse, a two-story cream-colored brick building reminiscent of colonial design with ornamented terra cotta trim, bulwarks around the roof line, arched windows, and a round cupola centering the roof. The historic structure stood out from old British plans by having a column-less portico and Beaux Arts vibes. Two mature palm trees flanked the corners with a flagpole in a tiny courtyard. In a town as small as Vallantine, it rarely got used outside of misdemeanors or traffic violations, but it was a neat place.

A quick check of the side lot only showed a dozen cars, so she parked close to that entrance a couple spots down from Aden's truck.

She couldn't recall the last time she'd been inside the courthouse, so the jitterbugs in her belly made zero sense. She wracked her mind for what the summons could possibly entail, but she drew a blank.

Inside, she went through the security check and headed for the marble staircase ahead. The main level held two large courtrooms and three small ones. In the basement were holding cells, which probably had been used a whopping ten times in the building's history. The second floor was mainly register of deeds, clerks, the district attorney, public defenders, and the city's tax office. At the top of the steps, she made a right and went into the mayor's office.

Gunner Davis's secretary waived Scarlett through, and before she could open her mouth, he rounded his massive oak desk, swept past Aden in a chair waiting, and pumped her hand in his beefy one. His thinning, neatly combed white strands didn't budge with the vigorous handshake. He wore a white polo stretched across his paunch and khaki pants barely held in place by a belt.

"So glad you could make it, Ms. Taylor."

She didn't realize she had a choice, but manners lifted the corners of her mouth. "Of course."

While Gunner returned to his place behind his desk, she quickly took in the details of his office. Thin burgundy carpet, a hideous floral settee by the window, matching oak bookcases, and a nauseating amount of photos from his career on the walls.

Yup. Blowhard. It also kind of looked like 1985 threw up in here.

Aden seemed like a cross between bored and irritated as he slumped in a black highbacked chair and raised his brows at her. He wore a white, grass-stained tee that stretched across his biceps and well-worn jeans. His sandy blond strands were disheveled like he'd just climbed out of the barn.

Why that was suddenly attractive, she hadn't a clue.

Perturbed, she claimed the other chair. "What can we do for you, sir?"

"Whelp, my dear, I have an idea."

Great. Ideas from Gunner Davis meant he'd made plans that had yet to be enacted. She and Aden were about to become pawns.

Aden, knowing this as well as she did, rubbed his eyes with his thumb and forefinger.

"The annual Peach Festival is coming up, and I'd like to add certain activities. We just got word that Southern Hospitality Magazine is going to do a feature on our town and the festival."

"Wow." She straightened. That would do wonders for the tourism market. The magazine was distributed to multiple chain stores in the south. Plus, it had millions of online sub-scribers. "That's amazing news. Congratulations, sir."

Wait. What activities was he wanting to add?

"Thank you. As you know, all the restaurants and shops along Main Street are prepared to stay open later by having staff on location, but will also have vendor booths in Peach Park. We have the usual peach pie contest, fireworks, the parade, and a few kiddie rides set to go. Hank has agreed to run more riverboat cruises during the week. However..."

Aden groaned.

Scarlett's stomach churned.

Gunner laced his fingers and set his joined hands on his desk as if he were discussing a grave national security measure. "The two local inns are booked solid due to returning visitors. We don't want the magazine staff to have to stay in a hotel outside city limits. It'll ruin the ambience."

She nodded, getting his drift. "You want me to open Taylor mansion to the magazine staff."

"For starters. Since you have events at the estate, it's a more public venue than private residences. Is that doable?"

Tilting her head, she thought over the logistics. The entire second story was her private residence, but she had her own adjoining bathroom. She had three additional bedrooms besides the library and living room, plus two full baths. It was doable, but she'd have to bring on a few seasonal staff.

"How many people?"

"Just two. A writer and a photographer. They're coming from Alabama."

She nodded. "I can swing that. Let me know arrival and departure."

"Thank you. Now..." Gunner leaned back in his seat, crossing his arms over his girth. "Part of the charm of Vallantine is the historical estates. Again, yours is the only public one, and you have the stables."

Aden opened his mouth, but she got the jump on him.

"Aden owns the stables and pastures."

"Right." Gunner shrugged as if that was of little consequence. "Would you be amendable to allowing tours during daytime hours and possibly horseback riding?"

"No." Aden's knee bounced.

A sigh, and she rolled her eyes. "I'm fine with tours of the main house and gardens." She'd have her guests lock their bedroom doors to keep tourists out, and discuss having her assistant, Charlene, do guided tours. The festival was only two weeks away. This wasn't a lot of notice. "It would need to be limited to three groups per day and no roaming."

Gunner nodded, his eyes shifting to Aden as if asking a silent question.

Finally, after a ten second staring contest, Aden leaned forward. "Look, I understand where you're coming from, but opening the stables to riding is not something I'm insured for, nor do I have the staff capabilities. All four of my horses are being used for the carriage rides during the festival."

"Okay." Gunner nodded again. Or still. He hadn't seemed to stop in the first place. "What about timed guided rides to coincide with Scarlett's estate tour? You have two carriages. They can start by Miss Katie, then ride past the library, since we can't open that to the public during renovations, move on to the cemetery, and up to the estate, where they get off, do the tour, and you bring them back where they started."

That was a good idea. It would limit visitors to eight per carriage, and there was room in the courtyard by the famous peach tree named after the town founder's wife to have people wait without crowding the main square.

She glanced at Aden, his profile not giving anything away. He wasn't an extrovert by any stretch of the imagination, but he typically had an aw-shucks to his personality that made people comfortable in his presence. Unless it involved his horses, he was a go-with-the-flow kind of guy. This would bring in quite a profit for his business.

As he mulled over the suggestion, she crossed her legs and addressed schematics. "We would need a booth set up near Miss Katie for people to book the ride and tour to keep order. With two carriages, assuming Aden agrees, it would have to be limited to a maximum of four rides per day, two each, and on a scheduled timeline."

"What she said. And estate tours do not include the stables." Aden frowned like he wasn't sold on the plan, but he'd concede.

"That can be done." Gunner rose as if the conversation was over. "Get prices, times, and directions to my secretary by tomorrow afternoon. We'll print flyers and order a banner. I'll have someone from my office man the booth during the festival. Thanks for coming."

Huffing a sarcastic laugh, Aden rose and strode out.

A smile, and Scarlett followed.

They met up in the parking lot where he leaned against her car, flipping his keys in his hand.

"You gave in too easy, darlin'."

Maybe. "Yeah, but as an event coordinator, I understand his need to add more attractions, especially with magazine people coming. You were going to be doing carriage rides, anyway."

He grunted. "We need to discuss details."

"Alrighty. Come over tonight and we'll figure it out." In the meantime, she had a lot of calls to make.

Sunlight kissed his shaggy blond strands and highlighted his already tanned skin. He stood quiet, studying her in typical fashion, full lips flatlined. Something in his blue gaze forced her to break contact first. An intensity, perhaps. For a moment, she got caught up in the veins bulging and tendons shifting in his forearms. Why hadn't she noticed how large his hands were before now? Wide shoulders. Narrow waist. Flat abs and contours. Dang, but he was a fine specimen. Friend or not, she could admit that to herself.

He cleared his throat, jarring her. "Mighty nice of you to remind Gunner that I own the stables."

That *had* been strange, Gunner addressing mostly her and not Aden. "You do own the stables. It was your call to make."

He bumped his chin toward the building. "Not many around these parts acknowledge that. Seems they think it's your property or I still work for you."

Where was he going with this? "The Taylor estate has been in our family since conception. Try not to take offense. It's just habit. I'm sure they don't mean anything by it. Besides, your family has been tied to mine for generations."

Up went his brows. "Because mine worked for yours. And some think I still do. If not for you, I would still be working for you."

She narrowed her eyes at him. "But you don't, and I corrected him. *You* came up with a business plan, *you* ran it by me, *you* worked your ass off to achieve it, and *you* made it thrive. Why do you care what they think?"

One corner of his mouth quirked in what could pass as a half-hearted smirk. "I don't care."

Except his expression and the entire discussion belied that remark.

He did an about-face and headed for his truck. "Thanks for the acknowledgement, babe."

Confused, she watched him drive off, and emitted a screech of annoyance. What was with him lately? And with the "babe" moniker again?

Muttering to herself, she climbed in her car, started it, and cranked the AC.

On her way back to the estate, she called Charlene, informing her of the plan, and told her to call in all the seasonal staff for a meeting this afternoon.

She'd use her frustration with Aden Abner to focus on getting details ironed out for the festival on her end.

The stupid man.

Chapter Four

In the back of Scarlett's Myrtle ballroom, Aden crossed his arms, leaned against the doorframe, and waited for her to finish her meeting with the staff while Dufus sat at his heels. Mayor Davis's impromptu wrench for the Peach Festival hadn't appeared to ruffle her feathers. Mere hours later, she'd assembled everyone, had created a signup sheet, and doled tasks. When she called, they came because she was a great boss. She treated her staff well, often gave bonuses, and never made them feel inferior.

It was a marvel she was actually a blood relation to her folks.

The smallest of her ballrooms, the Myrtle Room was as elegant as its owner. Scarlett had a knack for decorating, and this was no exception. White wainscoting below a chair rail, delicate lavender wallpaper, and a chandelier that resembled an upside down tree with purple blooms. She'd set out white folding chairs for her staff of about fifty, and if he had to guess, all but a couple were in attendance.

They stood and began to file out. He smiled and nodded as they passed him and petted the dog, but he kept his focus on Scarlett. She was in charm mode while talking to a few stragglers, hands waving excitedly and all aflutter. The southern belle routine, as he'd dubbed it. That part of her was as much a sliver of her personality as the chunks she didn't let others see. In fact, barring himself and her two best friends, her assistant, Charlene, was about the only person she let past her barriers. It was fascinating, really.

Her long, sleek cocoa locks were down, falling past her shoulders in waves reminiscent of the roaring twenties. As per capita, she went heavy on the cosmetics since she was among the public. But the dress? *Uhn*, the dress. She had millions in her arsenal she called a walk-in closet, but this one took the cake. V-neck, spaghetti strap, and knee-length. White with bright red cherries. The irony. It was enough to turn a man into a fruitarian. The fact her full breasts were playing hide-and-go-seek with the neckline wasn't helping his state of turned-on.

He'd punch his own face to snap out of it if he thought it would make a lick of difference.

As the last of her employees left, she met him at the back of the room, bending to pay attention to the dog. "Mind if we hang out and chat upstairs?"

"Nope." He wondered why she still asked. "Go on. I'll lock up."

"Thanks."

He ordered the dog to go with her, who merrily complied, black tail wagging as they went upstairs.

After checking the back door, he made his way to the front and locked the double French entry doors, then set the security alarm. By the time he'd climbed the grand staircase and got to her bedroom, she'd washed off the makeup and had donned a pair of red satin pajama shorts with a matching top.

Which hadn't helped him in erasing memories of cherries.

Dufus lifted his head from her black corner settee and set it back down again, a piece of furniture Aden swore she'd put there just for the dog.

She paused in the doorway to the adjoining bathroom, rubbing lotion on her arms. "How long do you think it'll take for one of your carriages to get from town square to the mansion?"

Thinking about it, he walked to her bed, kicked off his shoes, and flopped on top of her pillowy embroidered comforter. "Eh, roughly thirty minutes, give or take, but that doesn't account for the cemetery. Typically, on tours, we weave through the center path that cuts through the older part of the cemetery."

"Hmm."

She disappeared into the bathroom for a moment and reappeared with a lotion bottle. Sitting beside him on the bed, she proceeded to apply lotion to her legs. Her long, toned, tan legs...

"For the sake of the Peach Festival and people getting the most out of the carriage ride tours, you don't want to drop the cemetery aspect."

He figured she was waiting for confirmation from him, but her legs were distracting, and the damned lotion smelled like her perfume. Extravagantly rich and brooding with undertones of honeysuckle or something sweet. He could point her out of a lineup if deaf and blind.

"So, what? Add another half hour to include the cemetery?"

Fine by him. "Yeah, plus five to ten minutes to get from the gate to the house."

She nodded, setting the lotion on her nightstand. "Which totals about an hour and fifteen. I'm thinking you can drive one group up here, and Gary can get another a few hours later, then switch that to take a group back for the return. Charlene believes a tour of the main house and gardens shouldn't take more than ninety minutes on our end, and that allows for some wandering, too. She said she'd be happy to do them, which is a load off of me."

He grunted his acknowledgement. Gary was one of his staff, an older retired gentleman who was very vibrant. Tourists loved him. That schedule seemed sufficient, and wouldn't stress them or the horses if they stuck to two or three runs a day.

"Works for me." He rolled on his side, propping his head in his hand. "I'd make sure you've got a couple of your security staff around."

She had event security at each affair, just a handful of guys in suits who milled about in case of issues, but the tourists from the Peach Festival weren't her usual clientele. He'd be running the carriage rides, and her being alone didn't sit well with him, even if she did have her other worker bees around.

"Already done." She flopped on her side and mimicked his position. "I can take care of myself, you know."

Yeah, he knew that, but it would only take one asshole to catch her off guard.

Better to goad her instead. "But what if a big meanie pulls your hair or you break a nail?"

Those golden orbs of hers narrowed on him, framed by the longest, thickest lashes known to womankind. It was the re-action he'd been expecting, yet suddenly, he was attuned to every shutter her lashes created, the bow shape of her lips, the creaminess of her skin. She was a gorgeous creature. Always had been. But no one—not her staff, her folks, or her clients—ever got to see her like this. Sans cosmetics, the natural her, laying in bed without a filter.

"How little you think of me, Aden."

Well, shit. She'd sure aimed to maim with that one. He'd be bleeding awhile.

"I think the world of you, Scarlett."

Her expression indicated she didn't believe him. Neverthe-less, she rolled to her back, where her chestnut waves draped across her pillow, and sighed. "I'll have the gardener bring troughs to the top of the driveway, so your horses are properly hydrated in between runs. Anything else? Carrots or apples maybe as a snack?"

And that was the other thing. She was considerate. Nice, even when it wasn't warranted or required. Most people didn't know that about her, assuming she was a snob like the rest of her upper class. They bickered to no end, but at the end of the day, there was no one he trusted more to have his back. He had his parents and great friends, but aside from her besties, who did she have in her life on that caliber? He'd protected her from the sidelines their whole lives, but she'd very rarely needed him.

Or perhaps that's what she'd wanted him to think.

"Is that a no?"

He sighed, attempting to shake his mood. "Carrots and apples would be great. Thanks."

"I'll add them to the list." Her pause was heinous. "I designed and ordered your brochures today. They'll be here next week in time for the festival."

He closed his eyes. Case in point, damn her. Or bless her. Whichever. She chronically did such things for him, asking nada in return.

"Thank you." He could feel her gaze on him, but he kept mum, saying nothing more.

"Aren't you going to ask what they look like?"

"Nope." He knew they'd be perfect, just like the website she'd designed for him.

"But what if I photocopied your face onto a donkey's ass?"

"You didn't." For one, she would never go to those lengths to tease him, and two... "I have horses, not donkeys. That would be pointless."

"I could've made them bright pink with yellow hearts."

"You hate pink."

"True." She hummed in thought. "I—"

"Designed the best brochure in the history of Vallantine, highlighting the carriage rides and business with amazing pictures you took, and painted me in glorified light so I get more customers."

"Okay, fine. You're right. Mark it on the calendar. We'll make it an official holiday."

He huffed a laugh, setting his hand on his abdomen. She was such a brat.

"I also asked Rebecca to mention the tours and your rides in the Gazette to gear up interest for the festival."

Of course, she did. "Thank you."

Another lengthy pause ensued. He watched her cat jump onto the settee, circle the dog, then curled up beside him to sleep. They resembled a living ying-yang.

Scarlett poked his arm. "What's wrong with you lately? You've been...moody."

Abort!

His mouth didn't listen. "Moody?"

"Yes, moody. Do you need to get laid?"

Ha. She walked right into that one. "Are you offering?" He slashed his hand through the air. "Never mind. Not tonight, dear. I have a headache."

"I'm serious! Have you run out of available females in Vallantine?"

"And some unavailable ones." A lie. He'd never get involved with a woman who was otherwise spoken for. "What about you? Haven't seen some of your choices doin' the walk of shame lately."

Why were they talking about this?

She huffed. "I haven't had time. Besides, I'm getting bored with them."

"Then they're doing it wrong, darlin'."

Scarlett was an immensely beautiful woman with allure for days and appeal in spades. Like him, she enjoyed a good romp, no strings attached, and wasn't ashamed of it. Strange though, how it was recently she'd claimed mundanity. Him, too, and he didn't care for the probable reasons.

But seriously. No one would be good enough for her, despite her mother's efforts to get her hitched to a proper gentleman.

"Maybe." She hummed as if thinking. "What do you know about Gregory Cornwall? He works with Forest at the bank."

"Nothing much, besides he was gunning for Forest's job once upon a time." The guy had been a senior their freshman year of high school. He ran in her social circles, but the age gap meant she probably hadn't had much interaction. "Old money and..." Hold the phone. "Why?"

She shrugged. "He's Mama's choice of the season for me. Normally, I'd ignore her, but I ran into him the other day. He's good-looking, and he seemed...nice."

Nice meant boring. She should never orbit nice.

Then again, perhaps he should encourage her to date more. Her mother would never let up until she settled down, and Scarlett could stand some happiness. She'd not actually dated seriously or for the long haul, and if she was finally in a relationship, maybe his stupid, addled brain would get the message that she was well and truly off-limits.

The thought made his gut ache.

"I'll ask Forest." She stretched, causing her shirt to shift, exposing her midriff. A sight not new for him, considering her various pool outfits, but it hit below the belt, regardless.

Glancing at the ceiling, he frowned. "He'd be the better person to ask." Gregory "Nice" Cornwall couldn't handle her, so she'd move on eventually, and the whole convo would be moot, anyway.

The continuous circle.

And why, he feared, he'd not moved on or settled down himself.

At this rate, at the ripe old age of ninety years, they'll be laying in this bed, still single, forever goading one another, having midnight chats, and him wondering what-if, yet not having the courage to act upon it. He'd go to his grave pining for the girl next door.

It was so very easy for him to chastise himself, but there were reasons. Many. Hundreds of reasons why he'd not acted on his attraction. Her parents. Their friendship. History. Personality differences. At the top of the list? She'd not once shown interest.

"Remember that treehouse Rececca, Dorothy, and I built when we were girls?"

He was getting whiplash. "You mean the treehouse you tried to build, and I fixed?"

Lord, that had been years ago. They'd been maybe twelve years old? Scarlett had gotten it in her head that treehouses were romantic, and it would give her and her friends a place to go just for them. Besides the library. They'd used an old gnarled oak at the back of the estate with low branches, hammering pieces of plywood she'd found in the barn. They could've killed themselves. He'd found them halfway through, and finished it. Properly. He'd suspected she'd done that on purpose so he would build the thing for her. To his knowledge, she'd used it twice.

He turned his head, staring at her profile. She had that wispy faraway smile curving her lips.

"That's the one. Do you think it's stable?"

"Dunno." He scratched his jaw. He hadn't thought about it in eons. "Why?"

"One of my brides asked about it. She thought it might make for some great pictures."

He hissed through his teeth. "Let me look at it tomorrow. Not accounting for rot, there's no tellin' what creepy-crawlies might be lurking." It was probably a lawsuit waiting to happen.

"Thanks."

"Yup."

That was them in a nutshell. She had whims of her mood. He catered.

A rich, lazy laugh emitted from her lips, and she rolled on her side once again to face him. "You were fit to be tied about the treehouse. Remember? Stomping your feet and muttering under your breath."

"Uh-huh. You have no business wielding a hammer." She had many attributes. Construction wasn't one of them. Hell, it was barely one of his.

She mocked him in low tones. "Stupid Belles want a stupid treehouse. She's got a damn mansion with a hundred rooms, but no. She wants a treehouse."

He grinned. "You sound just like me." No, she didn't.

"It worked, though. You built it for me."

"And I knew you were manipulating me." He knew it then, and he knew it now. He'd do it all over again if it meant she'd leave it alone or not wind up in urgent care.

She frowned, but it was belied by her smile. "Why'd you do it, then?"

"Can't have you messing up that pretty face. Your mother would have a duck fit."

Her responding laugh was smoke under the doorjamb. "Mustn't upset Mother." She cleared her throat, staring at him like she was reading one of her precious books. "You think I'm pretty?"

"The fairest in all the land." Insecurity and Scarlett Taylor had not been acquaintances, and she'd never had to fish for complements, so he had to wonder why she'd asked such a thing or chose that as the focus. "You already know that."

Her faint smile vanished. A worry line creased her brow. "Beauty is fleeting and subjective." Her golden gaze met his, searching in its intensity. "You've never called me pretty before."

Bull. Surely, that wasn't the case. They'd known each other since birth, and not a day had gone by where they hadn't seen one another. As kids, he'd riled the hell outta her. As adults, he treaded carefully. But somewhere in their friendship, he had to have slipped and said she was pretty. Beautiful. Breathtaking. Right? Her memory was as delible as his, yet her reaction was proving her admission correct, though. At least, in her eyes. Lips parted, brows furrowed, she looked at him as if he'd sprouted horns and said he was the gatekeeper of another dimension.

He had an awful, sinking suspicion his response would change everything.

He erred on the side of caution. "You've never cared what I think, so why start now?"

Her expression didn't change an iota. "Your opinion has always mattered to me."

Alright. Stop this merry-go-round. He not only wanted off, he needed a shot of bourbon and a slap upside the noggin'.

Slowly, he sat up, eyeing her just in case she did something. What, he hadn't a clue. He wouldn't put anything past her.

Up went her perfectly arched brows. "Now what's wrong with you?"

"Oh, I don't know, darlin'. Maybe because you just claimed my opinion matters, despite you doing the opposite of what I say the better half of our lives."

She rolled her eyes so hard, they thunked in her sockets. "And they call me dramatic." She looked at him and did a double-take. "For crying out loud. Of course, your opinion matters. Why would I bother talking to you if not? You know more about me than almost anyone. Our businesses coincide. We've been friend...*ly* since infancy. We practically share air. I trust you. Even your dog knows that." She sat up and glanced around him to the settee. "Right, Dufus?"

His idiot dog barked.

She raised her palm as if to say, *see?*

Elation warred with irritation behind his ribs. He offered a baleful stare.

"This is what I'm talking about." She pointed at him. "You've been weird lately."

"Me?" He laughed without mirth. "You said I matter without a knife to your throat."

"And you just called me pretty without a six-pack prelude."

No, he'd said she was the fairest in all the land, but best to not split hairs. "How does stating the obvious equate to me being weird?"

"When you stating the obvious is a complement."

He sighed heavily and glanced behind her at the French doors to her balcony. Moonlight scattered across the trees, the grass, and her gardens in the distance. Stars winked. Fireflies danced. He used to climb up her rose trellis and onto the balcony some nights for varying reasons. He'd never, not once, found it locked. They'd talk or fight or just hang out in silence. Sometimes, when her mother had been particularly cruel, he'd hold her until she fell asleep. They never discussed it, though perhaps they should have, and such behavior rarely saw the light of day. Somehow, somewhere along the way, they'd formed this strange pattern of opening veins for one another to let the ugly parts of the world escape, only to hide them behind bandages as if embarrassed by them. He didn't know how to change the behavior.

The most ironic part was the balcony doors were unlocked. Habit or on purpose, he didn't know. Two years had passed since he'd quit climbing her rose trellis, but the doors were still unlocked.

Warm, soft fingers grazed the backs of his hands, and he flinched.

She didn't ease away, but took his hands in hers and met his gaze with the tender underbelly of her personality radiating in her eyes. She could slay him where he stood when she looked at him like that, and he'd gladly perish.

"What's wrong, Aden? Tell me, and I'll fix it."

If only.

He'd insult her by not speaking, so he took the coward's way out. "I have anemia." He'd been meaning to mention it to her, and now seemed as good a time as any. "An iron deficiency. It's not serious, but it does make me tired or feel worn out."

She straightened, lips pursed adorably in concern. "How long have you known?"

"A year."

"A...what? Why are you just telling me now?"

Three hundred and sixty five days, and he still didn't know. "Before Rebecca moved back from Boston, her and I were doing a Facetime to catch up. My symptoms arose when we were discussing hers. They were similar to her fibromyalgia ones. A couple, anyway. On her insistence, I saw my doc. Turns out, I'm just anemic. I take iron pills daily and get labs drawn a few times a year."

She stared at him a hot minute, eyes wide. "Do I need to be worried?"

"No." Lord knew, she worried about everyone else too much, Rebecca especially. They all did. "It's manageable. Like I said, I get tired easily."

Everything he'd said was the truth, but he felt like an ass using his condition to scapegoat his inner turmoil. He needed to get over himself. Not an easy task these days. What started out as mere interest or awareness of her had morphed into attraction that was becoming harder to deny, and now she was all he thought about. He had zero clue how it had happened or why the escalation, but he'd sell a kidney to get it to end.

He and Scarlett could never be a thing.

"All right," she said at length, squeezing his hands and releasing them. "But I want you to tell me if the Peach Festival is too much or if I ever need to step in."

"Will do." He won't, not unless absolutely necessary. She did enough for him and had her own business to run.

It was time to go. Intimate moments like this, though few and far between, weren't doing him any favors. Slowly, he rose from the bed and called for his dog.

Dufus rose, stretched, and sauntered over.

At her doorway, he turned. "I lied earlier. You're not pretty. You're gorgeous. I'll see you tomorrow." He cast a quick glance her way, and yep. Worry was still etched in her features. Except now, shock was winning. "I'll reset the alarm."

Chapter Five

At the close of their book club meeting, Scarlett waited for most of the guests to leave the Myrtle Ballroom before rising from her seat to start cleanup. This room was the smallest, and served well for get-togethers like their monthly book club. Since she and her besties had resurrected the club, they'd slowly gained traction, and were now up to over seventy-five members. Once the library renovations were complete, they'd move the gathering there.

Her mother crossed the room toward Scarlett, purpose in her step. Just swell. What now? Had she not applied the correct season's lipstick or crossed her legs like a lady while seated?

Mother's black flats were perfectly paired with a blazer set and yellow blouse. She looked like a demented bumblebee. Not one strand shifted in her coifed, shoulder-length brown bob cut, but her cosmetics were doing little to mask her age. Years of fussing were taking their toll on Collette Taylor through deeper fine lines between her brows and around her mouth.

"Scarlett, a word."

It would never be just a "word," yet she bit back a snide retort. "Yes, Mother?"

"Why did your staff not arrange the fruit platter to something more appealing? For heaven's sake, it was a sloppy mess."

Seriously? Scarlett had hosted a book club meeting, not foreign dignitaries. Mother was going to have an outright cow when club was moved to the library. Things would be way more laid back.

"I'm sorry it wasn't up to your satisfaction. Do try to remember the snacks are merely a courtesy."

Mother sniffed, glancing around, her thousand dollar purse dangling from her forearm. "I see that Aden Abner is still pretending to be literate."

Scarlett gnashed her teeth. Her mother had never hidden her disdain for Aden, and since he'd joined book club after Scarlett and her besties had restored it, she'd found every opportunity to drop insults. It was getting tiresome and obnoxious.

"Considering he runs his own very successful business and actually read the book pick this month, unlike you, I'd say he's more than literate. Don't embarrass yourself."

"A business you gave him," she shout-whispered. "On our family's estate, no less."

This argument, too, had gone stale. "Once more, with feeling, Aden bought that land from me. I didn't give him anything. He earned it." She left out the part where the "family estate" was on Daddy's side.

Mother opened her mouth to, no doubt, harp about something else, but Aden walked past, carrying a stack of chairs.

"Good evening, ladies. Scarlett, do we want the food in the kitchen?"

Mother's frown deepened. "It certainly doesn't go in the sitting room."

Scarlett gave her mother a withering glance. "Yes, please. It just needs to be wrapped. Jasper will be by later to collect it."

"Jasper Morris? From the shelter?" Mother glanced at the small food table, then Scarlett. "Whatever for?"

Aden offered a tight, generic smile. "Scarlett donates all left-over food from events to the homeless shelter because she's a good human." He looked at Scarlett. "I'll go wrap it."

"Thank you." She smiled at him before he strode away, hoping it relayed her appreciation, then slid her gaze back to her mother. "It was lovely to see you. Bye, now."

Leaving no room for argument, Scarlett pivoted and headed to the far side of the room.

She caught Dorothy and Rebecca in the process of folding chairs. "You guys up for a slumber party tonight? I know it's last minute, but I could use girl time." Aden had been acting off lately and if she didn't vent about Mother, she'd explode. It was getting harder and harder to bite her tongue.

Dorothy eyed her, suspicion twisting her lips. "Everything okay?"

"No. Well, yes, but I need to talk out a few things."

"Of course." Rebecca squeezed Scarlett's shoulder. "I can stay. I just need something to sleep in. Or would you rather go to my house?"

"Ditto and ditto. And we're already here. Might as well stay." Dorothy set a folding chair on a stand with the others. "Georgia Sunsets and chocolate it is. I'll bartend, though."

Scarlett laughed. Their customary cocktail, Georgia Sunset, consisted of peach schnapps, brandy, grenadine, and lemon-lime soda. Dorothy claimed Scarlett was too heavy-handed with the alcohol portion, so she insisted on doing the pouring.

"Awesome. I'll be right back." Scarlett left the room and made a right, pushing open the swinging door to the kitchen. Her staff didn't work on book club nights, so Aden was the only one in the kitchen. He seemed so out of place at the center island, fighting with cling wrap.

The kitchen had been renovated after her grandmother, Miss Maureen, had passed. Scarlett had kept the black and white checkered tile, ornate white cabinets, and coffered ceiling, but she'd replaced the old countertops with green granite, the light fixtures with prettier stained glass ones, and outdated appliances with stainless steel. Modern, yet keeping with the turn-of-the-century style. It was a spacious, rectangular room that ran the length of the house, and for some reason, intimidated Aden. She rarely spotted him in here.

His ruggedly chiseled facial features were taut in concentration. Scruff dotted his jaw, but he'd combed his sandy blond strands back, assumingly to create order among the chaos. His work jeans had been swapped out for a pair of khaki cargo shorts and a short-sleeved blue button-down shirt that matched his eyes. Muscles bunched in his arms as he fiddled with the food.

Once again, for reasons unbeknownst to her, she was struck by his attractiveness. The same boy who'd chased her with toads and teased her to no end had grown into quite a sexy specimen.

Oh, gawd. What was wrong with her?

He glanced up at her, then back to his task. "You need an engineering degree to use this stuff."

"Hang on." Laughing, she took the cling wrap from him and went to the pantry. Extracting several disposable containers, she ducked out and set them on the island. "These work better for transport, anyway."

"Thanks," he muttered, transferring cheese and crackers into a container.

She dished the fruit. He moved on to vegies.

As she reached for the desserts, he said, "I appreciate you sticking up for me back there."

She offered him a questioning expression.

"With your mom and my reading capabilities."

"Oh." She frowned, attempting to secure mini-cupcakes as to not squish them. "No thanks needed. She was just being a shrew, as usual."

"I know, but you didn't have to respond. That was nice of you."

His coarse voice rasped across her skin as if he'd touched her. A voice she'd heard nearly every day of her life, yet was suddenly affecting her.

Face hot, she shook her head, pretending to be offended. "You take that back."

"Make me."

Another laugh, and she stacked the containers. "Not a fight I care to engage in tonight." She brushed her hair over her shoulder. "The besties are spending the night. Can you set these on the back stoop? Jasper said he'd be by before ten."

"Sure thing. Want me to set the alarm?"

"No, thanks. I gotta make sure everyone's gone." She watched him a moment, and the weariness in his eyes smacked her in the breastbone. "Not one soul agrees with my mother. Don't let her upset you."

"I don't."

She didn't believe him, but maybe his mood was from his condition. When he'd told her last evening about being anemic, she'd developed an arresting chokehold that had lasted through the night. He was an active outdoorsman and loved his horses. She'd hate for his diagnosis to interfere with activities he loved.

He pivoted, carrying containers to the back door, conversation obviously over.

"I'll see you tomorrow?"

He waved over his shoulder.

Okay, then.

When she got back to the Myrtle Room, everyone was gone except Dorothy and Rebecca, and they'd finished putting chairs away. Scarlett locked the doors and set the alarm before they headed upstairs.

Once in pajamas, they decided on her upstairs living room so they could sprawl out and be vegetative. She had a large plush white sofa facing a gray brick fireplace with matching chairs on each side. She rarely used the flatscreen above the mantel, but the stack of books on the black iron coffee table were well-worn. The space had once been a formal sitting room, but she'd stripped the wallpaper and replaced it with navy blue paint above the white chair rail, adding a few plants to make it more cozy and less stuffy.

Dorothy poured cocktails from Scarlett's corner bar and passed them out. She took the chair opposite Rebecca and blew out a breath. "Your mama was in top form tonight."

"No kidding." Scarlett eyed her cocktail, stabbing a maraschino cherry with her straw. "She gets worse by the year."

"She was intimidating when we were kids." Rebecca cleared her throat. "But since I've been back in Vallantine, she does seem..."

"Bitchier," Scarlett finished for her. "I don't think she tries anymore."

Dorothy nodded, tucking her auburn strands behind her ears. "My mom hasn't spoken with her in months, and even then, it's polite in passing."

"Really?" Scarlett sipped her drink. That news was surprising. Their mothers, Rebecca's included, had grown up together and been the best of friends. Of course, Rebecca's folks had been killed in a wreck when they'd been only nine years old. It had been devastating for everyone. Scarlett had no clue Dorothy's mom had formed distance from her mother, though. She guessed it wasn't all that surprising. "That makes me sad."

"Me, too." Dorothy crossed her legs and leaned back in her seat. "They were as close as we are once upon a time."

"I noticed it after my parents died."

They both looked at Rebecca, who shrugged.

"It was a slow dissent." Rebecca rubbed her forehead, then ran her fingers through her long blonde strands, disrupting them. "Your fathers quit going golfing together. Your moms still hung out, but not as often." She looked at Scarlett, her eyes wet. "Your mother was always hard on you, needing you to be perfect, but after the accident, she got worse. We were just girls back then, and it was a deliberate shift. I don't know how you did it, honestly." Her breath hitched. "She was just so...mean." She shifted her gaze to Dorothy. "And your mom was grieving, having lost one of her best friends, and ultimately lost the other."

"I had Miss Maureen, so it wasn't as bad." Scarlett's chest grew tight. "My father isn't as stuck-up as my mother, but I always had my grandmother. Come to think of it, you're right. Everything did seem to shift about then. It took another slide when Miss Maureen died. She'd threatened to cut my parents out of the will, but they didn't necessarily believe her. She always intended to give me the estate and knew my plans, but it came as a shock to them."

Her grandmother had been a powerhouse. They'd lived here on the estate Scarlett's whole life, and it wasn't until she turned eighteen that her parents had bought a place of their own, but she'd stayed here with her grandmother until her death. She had a vague recollection of hushed arguments between the matriarch and her mother, so Scarlett supposed that had been the reasoning for them moving. Miss Maureen never had tolerated Mother's antics.

Rebecca drew a breath and released it. "She's been gone almost three years now. The buffer is gone."

"Yeah, but I have you guys." Scarlett glanced at Dorothy. "Your mom must be having a tough time."

Dorothy nodded. "She accepted the loss, even though your mother is still around. She has other friends, but I'm sure it hurts."

Irritated, Scarlett rose and paced in front of the fireplace. "What is wrong with her? I mean, seriously. She's isolated herself from everyone in her life with her behavior."

"I know she's your mom, but I don't know how you deal with it." Rebecca set her drink to the side. "I'd give anything to have my parents back, yet yours treat you like this. It's a surprise to me you aren't a headcase."

"She is a headcase," Dorothy teased.

Scarlett playfully narrowed her eyes. "She called Aden illiterate tonight. At a damn book club meeting."

"Um..." Rebecca tilted her head. "Joke's on her, then."

"That's really crappy."

Agreeing with them both, Scarlett reclaimed her seat, gulping half her drink. "It's one thing not to like him, and another to be outright cruel. Worst part is he overheard her."

Rebecca hissed through her teeth. "Is he upset?"

"Yes, but he won't say so. It was just uncalled for. He's not done anything to deserve her ire. Hell, he's not so much as talked back to defend himself. He takes her shit and bites his tongue out of respect."

"I'd let her have it." Dorothy shrugged.

Rebecca laughed. "No, you wouldn't."

"Yeah, okay. Probably not. But even I have my limits."

Scarlett nodded. "At least she leaves you two alone. I just don't get it. No offense to either of you, but neither of your families come from wealth, yet she's indifferent to you. Aden? Nah. So it can't just be her whack version of social order. He's smart. He's funny. He's handsome. He runs a stable business he built himself." She shook her head. "I got nothing."

The room grew quiet. Scarlett stared at her besties, who eyed each other as if having a conversation based solely on facial expressions.

You do it.

No, you do it.

She pursed her lips. "What?"

"Well," Dorothy broached, dragging the word out into five syllables, "you said a lot of nice things about Aden."

The point? "And?"

"And," Rebecca said, "it's just not something you do very often. Not without tacking on *he's a pain in the ass* or something."

"He *is* a pain in the ass, but he's *my* pain in the ass, and she has no right to insult my friends. Or frienemies. Whatever."

"Whew!" Dorothy rose. "Refill time. It's gonna be a long night."

Now what?

Rebecca had her lips rolled over her teeth to obviously avoid laughing.

Dorothy passed out refills, then left the room. She came back moments later with a bowl of popcorn, a platter of brownies, and a bag of chips from Scarlett's kitchen. After setting the snacks on the table, she plopped in her chair. "No one leaves this room until you tell us what's up. We have sustenance. No excuses."

Scarlett rolled her eyes. She was erroneously starting to wonder why she was labeled the drama llama. A thought she'd just had in Aden's presence last night, with the least dramatic person she knew. Up was down. Down was up. Anarchy.

Leaning forward, Rebecca grabbed the popcorn bowl and set it in her lap. She shoved a handful in her mouth and spoke around the kernels. "Dish the dirt. What's going on?"

"I don't know what you're talking about."

Dorothy sipped from her straw, brows raised. "It's Friday. I can sit here all weekend."

There was no sense in being stubborn. Her friends could wait her out. Except, Scarlett didn't know the problem, just that there was one, and she had wanted to talk. A sleepover was her idea.

Rebecca tossed more popcorn in her mouth. "Want us to start guessing?"

Fun as that might be... "No." She huffed. "Things have been weird with Aden."

Dorothy shrugged. "Hate to be the bearer of bad news, but things are always weird with you and Aden."

"True story." Rebecca took a healthy gulp of her drink. "I mean, most of us think so, we just don't say anything."

"How you two bicker like stepsiblings constantly about anything and everything is a tally in the weird column."

"Yet you'd kill anyone who would dare hurt the other."

"You know every sordid mundane tidbit about each other's life."

"And you've got your own language. Ever notice that? Mute mind-reading juju."

"He's climbed onto your balcony since we were kids to sneak into your bedroom, but you never actually get down and dirty."

Rebecca pointed at Dorothy while Scarlett's head swiveled at their back and forth. "Right? Mega weird."

"She's hot. He's hot. Yet no hanky-panky."

"Graham says it's foreplay."

"I always thought so, but this is the longest case of slow burn I've ever witnessed."

"Preach. If this was a romance novel, their editor would kill them."

"Mmm-hmm." Dorothy set her cocktail aside and snatched a brownie. "Worst rom-com movie evah. One star."

Crossing her arms, Scarlett sighed. "Are you two done?"

Rebecca tilted her head. "Are we?" she asked Dorothy.

"Maybe. I feel as if we've only scratched the surface."

Scarlett stared at the ceiling. "Have a sleepover, I said. It'll be fun, I said."

"You love us." Rebecca grinned.

"That I do." Scarlett chewed her lower lip, thinking about how to explain. "He's been quiet lately."

Dorothy grunted. "Are you using grammar school etiquette and giving him a turn to speak?"

"Yes." Scarlett stuck her tongue out. She tapped her fingers on the arm of the couch, but no lightbulb over her head formed. "I don't know how to describe it. He's almost solemn. He's not goading me as much, he's been daydreaming, and he told me he's anemic."

Dorothy straightened. "Like, as in, low iron? Is he okay?"

"He says yes, just tired sometimes. He takes pills." Scarlett glanced at Rebecca. "Apparently, you knew. *For a year.*"

"It wasn't my story to tell." Rebecca sighed. "I wanted to tell you, trust me, but it wasn't my place. We were doing a video chat one night, and he just seemed ragged. In short, I told him what to say to his physician. I didn't think he had fibromyalgia like me, but something was definitely going on. I'm glad that's all it was."

"Me, too." It still didn't sit right with Scarlett, and she'd worry, but at least the diagnosis wasn't worse. "His condition might be part of his strange behavior, but I don't think it's the whole reason. It just started a few weeks ago. I can't put my finger on it."

"Besides being quiet and distracted, is he doing anything else?" Dorothy resettled in the chair. "Maybe he's working something out."

That was the thing. "Normally, he'd talk to me, though."

"Did you ask?" Rebecca put the popcorn bowl back on the table.

Sorta. "I told him he'd been acting strange and asked why. That's when he told me about being anemic."

"Hmm." Dorothy sipped her cocktail, brows furrowed. "I don't know him as well as you. I don't think anyone does. My advice is to just be there for him."

"Agree." Rebecca stood and stretched. "I hate to cut this short, but do you mind if we call it a night?"

Scarlett eyed her bestie, looking for typical signs Rebecca was at her limit. Her condition had a number of side effects like body temperature not regulating, gastro issues, and fatigue, but the worst of them was pain. Her dear Rebecca was always in pain. One would never know it by looking at her, unless they knew her well enough to spot the little signs. And they were there now. A slight flatline of her lips, a grimace when stretching, and drooping eyelids.

"Of course, not." Dorothy waved her hand. "I'm pretty wiped. I'll be right behind you."

Scarlett stood. "The guestrooms are made up. Take your pick. Do y'all need anything?"

Her besties shook their heads, and they hugged goodnight.

Scarlett grabbed the snacks and walked down the hall toward her upstairs kitchen to put the food away. The dark wood-paneled hallway held portraits of her familial line dating back to Beau and Kitty Taylor in 1898. Her grandmother had looked a lot like Kitty in her youth—short black hair and an angular face—but whereas Kitty had a curvy frame, Miss Maureen was slender to the point of fragile. She'd been anything but, though.

She missed her grandmother something fierce. A proper southern matriarch, she was aristocratic in her manners and her tongue could slice if the situation warranted. She was fair, however, never ever treating others as less than, and who would not forget a kind word to those who needed one. She hadn't been overly affectionate like Rebecca's Gammy, but Scarlett always knew she was loved. Some days, the mansion felt like a cavern without her.

Chest tight, she turned the corner for the kitchen. Since it had been converted from a billiards room, it wasn't the largest room in her house, but it didn't need to be with just her living here. She'd opted for dark blue cabinets and white marble countertops with stainless steel appliances. They were much smaller than in the grand kitchen downstairs, but it was all she'd needed.

She put the food away and finished the last of her cocktail. Maybe it was the alcohol, but she was both light-headed and morose. Talking with her friends, getting her concerns out in the open, had helped, yet anxiety still had her on edge, coupled with the dragging sensation of feeling alone.

The estate had been in her family for generations. In her mind, it was silly to have such grandeur without purpose. So much history here that she could almost hear the footsteps of her ancestors. It was one of the reasons she'd opted to open the mansion to guests by way of her event business. She'd toyed with the idea of making it a B&B, but that wouldn't allow for any privacy. Weddings and events were more suited to her. She could utilize her skills, have company, showcase the estate, yet still have it be her home.

Sometimes, though... Well, sometimes it was lonely once the crowds left. It was just her with the ghosts of the past and shadows of what might be.

Sighing, she went to the sink and set her glass down, staring out the window at the gardens. Miss Maureen had designed most of the back estate when she'd inherited the place. The barns and stables were in the side lot, now Aden's, and hadn't been touched aside from maintenance. Scarlett felt the same about her grandmother's work. Why mess with beauty?

Four separate sections had been plotted in the grass. One for greenery and shrubs, another for roses, azaleas, gardenia, and other flowering bushes, one for climbing vines with trellises, and the last was varying perennials like coneflowers, black-eyed susans, shastas, and phlox. Each area spanned a half-acre. They were in a checkered pattern with a large fountain in the center. The dang thing was fourteen feet tall with cherubs spitting water. Pretty, but overzealous. White marble statues of Greek gods were scattered throughout each garden section, along with benches. Its full beauty and design could only be appreciated from above, yet walking through them was like being transported to another place and time where worries and cares didn't exist.

Maybe if she took a walk, her mind would settle. It had worked on many occasions for her grandmother. Toes in the grass, a light summer breeze on her skin, and the scent of blooms in the air.

Nodding, she turned and headed for the stairs.

Chapter Six

With a glass of sweet tea, Aden sank onto an Adirondack chair on his back deck and sighed. A warm breeze wafted in the night, bringing scents of cut grass and blooms. Tipping his head, he glanced at the stars, too many for counting, and enjoyed the quiet.

He loved his job, that he was his own boss, and that he made his own schedule. He even loved that he could interact with people and get out. But sometimes, it got to be too much. Excited tourists and snapping pictures. The questions. Back and forth. The Peach Festival was going to be exhausting. He'd even gotten a kick out of the guys' nights and book club lately.

Until tonight.

His temples throbbed. Though he didn't think anyone had overheard Mrs. Taylor's little tantrum, it still stuck in his craw she felt the need to say anything at all. He got it, okay? She hated him. She didn't want him around her daughter. He was gum on her shoe. It wasn't necessary to beat a dead horse, though.

Over and over.

Year after year.

And it hadn't been doing her any good. He and Scarlett were friends. Had been for ages. That wouldn't change. Nothing she'd tried or said would or had put a rift between them. He hadn't done a thing to hurt her, and he never would. Why couldn't the blasted woman get off his back? She was making her daughter miserable.

Misery loved company, he supposed. He always figured Miss Maureen's will had rubbed Mrs. Taylor the wrong way. She felt entitled to the estate, yet didn't get it. That, and her daughter had quit placating her every demand, becoming her own woman. Scarlett starting her event business had been the proverbial nail in the coffin.

Damn, but she had a way of making him feel so small, so insignificant. He shouldn't let her, but he'd tried over the years with no success to let her jabs roll off his shoulders.

A grunt, and he glanced back up at the stars. They didn't judge or ridicule. They never asked him to be something he wasn't, and accepted him just the way he was, faults and all.

As if sensing his mood, Dufus set his head in Aden's lap, and he laughed. Petting the dog's soft fur, he gazed around.

Horses whinnied and an owl hooted. The barn's exterior light off in the distance cast a yellow glow on the pasture, surrounded by a wooden split rail fence. Two of the posts would have to be replaced this fall. He'd redone most of the fence when he'd bought the property, but the last bit would need it. He added the task to his mental to-do, along with repainting the barn doors. The Taylors had been smart in their barn design, using an aluminum roof and red siding for the one and a half story building. All except the doors. The structure housed ten stalls, but he only had four horses at the moment. Heated, too, with skylights and a grooming station. It was fancier than he would've come up with, but it was all his now.

It was still hard to wrap his mind around that sometimes. The kid who'd mucked the stalls and whose dad had been the landscaper wound up owning the very property they'd been hired to maintain. His own house, land, pastures, horses, and a barn. It was more than any of his kin had before. He'd had a second barn erected next to the original one to house his two carriages, and had mapped out a second pasture. In under a year, he was looking to buy another carriage and hire more staff.

Shaking his head, he refocused on the grounds, listening to the crickets chirp. A few lingering fireflies danced over the grass and leaves stirred in the breeze. He enjoyed the shade the gnarled oaks and maples offered in summer, but the few weeping willows scattered around were his favorite. Droopy, unique.

It was peaceful. Content. He couldn't ask for more. A cold glass of sweet tea, loyal dog by his side, lazy summer evening, and...

Scarlett in a nightgown walking by herself near the gardens. The hell?

Weren't her besties spending the night? This was pretty late for her to be awake, sleepover aside. He'd never known her to wander around the grounds past dark, nor was she prone to sleepwalking.

Leaning forward, he watched her, setting his tea aside. From this distance, there was an acre between them, so he could barely make out her form. It was her, though. Dark hair flowed behind her and her white nightie swirled with her movement. Inground path lights amongst the floral landscape illuminated her form as well as the lampposts that led from her patio to the gardens.

"What is she doing?"

Dufus whined.

"You're right. We should check on her."

It was definitely strange, at any rate.

Rising, he tapped his thigh for Dufus to follow, and descended the back deck steps into the grass. Vallantine wasn't home to the dangers of city life. They didn't have much crime, if any, but that didn't mean it was nonexistent. Besides, the darned woman could create trouble just by existing. His heartrate tripped while he briskly walked across the lawn toward her, wondering what was going on. A quick glance showed all the lights were off in the house. No one was in the pool. Just as he got to the edging around the pool fence and on the other side, she disappeared from sight into the gardens.

"Damn it."

He jogged across the pea gravel walking path, spotting the gigantic fountain up ahead her grandmother had put in ages ago. Its illumination allowed him to navigate without falling, but he didn't have to search for long. On one of the benches near the vine garden was Scarlett, knees drawn to her chest and arms around her legs.

Coming to a halt a few feet away, he took stock. Knee-length white nightgown was not torn or soiled. Hair down. No cosmetics. Barefoot. Zero scratches or bruises on her that he could see. She stared at the fountain, her features illuminated by the soft yellowish light, and she resembled an impish fairy.

Breaths soughing, he shook head. She was fine.

The dog jumped onto the bench beside her.

"Dufus!" Arm around the lab, Scarlett nuzzled the black fur on his neck. "Who's a good boy?"

Her words were this side of slurred. Tipsy, then. Probably from the Belles customary Georgia Sunset cocktails. She'd either had more than one—the lightweight—or she'd been the bartender tonight instead of Dorothy.

"Aden!" Up went her arms as if it were normal for him to walk into them.

He swiped a hand down his face and gestured for the dog to get down. Claiming the seat Dufus vacated, Aden eyed her. She wasn't drunk, but she'd definitely gotten buzzed.

"How's the sleepover going?"

"Awesome. We discussed you and my mother." She frowned, and it would've been comical if not for the words. "Maybe not so fun."

He nodded, despite not understanding at all. He and Collette Taylor should never be put in the same thought, never mind the same sentence. "And what did you discuss?"

"Oh, you know. How she's a bitch, but you're not."

He laughed. "Okay. Why are you roaming the gardens in the dark in a nightgown?"

She glanced down at her plain white cotton nightie. "It was the first thing I grabbed. Dorothy and Rebecca borrowed my pajamas. I never wear this thing."

Yeah, he knew that. She much preferred shorts and a shirt combo. Silk ones. "You skipped the question."

"What question?"

This was like talking to a kindergartner on a sugar high. "Why are you outside?"

"Um..." Her face twisted adorably in thought. "It's a nice night?"

"Are you asking or telling?"

"Both?" She shrugged and rubbed her eyes, then sighed as if contented. "The besties are sleeping. I was restless, so I figured if walking in the garden helped Miss Maureen, maybe it would for me, too."

Alrighty.

"Why are *you* out here?"

"Because you are." What else was there to say? He was worried, so he followed her. "It's not like you to wander around the grounds at night."

"So..." She turned her head, a feat that seemed difficult for her. "You're here to rescue me?"

From herself? Usually. She wasn't a damsel in distress, and he was no white knight. That nonsense belonged in the books on her shelves. But she did sometimes need saving.

Mercy, moonlight and the glow from her inground lights were playing a sonnet with her features. She had an oval face with sharp cheekbones and skin that was like buttermilk. Her typical cosmetics were gone, leaving only the real her. It always felt jarring to him when he spotted this version, no matter how many times he'd born witness. Arched brows. Golden eyes. Thick chestnut waves of hair trailing over her shoulders and down her back.

"You're always coming to my rescue." She blinked. "Why?"

"You were born in need of rescuing, darlin'. Why not me?" Except, at this precise moment, he feared *he* needed the rescuing this time.

"Why not you?" she breathed.

Her satiated gaze searched his facial features, brows wrenched as if she were working out a problem. Or finding a solution. Over his hair, across his forehead, in his eyes, down his cheeks to *his mouth*. Her gaze hovered there, on his mouth, and all the oxygen evaporated from her entire estate.

Poof. Gone.

And then... *Then*, she cupped his cheeks in her warm palms, and he inhaled. Hard.

What in all tarnation was happening?

Inches separated them. Close enough, he could breathe in her lingering sultry perfume and almost taste the peaches from her cocktail. Her soft hands brushing against the scruff on his jaw created a rasping sound in the otherwise quiet night. He became all too aware of her wavering exhale that fanned his lips. Every single muscle in his body locked in some kind of almost painful survival instinct. A warring ensued between his head and his heart.

Close the distance.

Don't you dare.

She ultimately made the choice for them, easing closer. Her eyes drifted shut with a flutter of her lashes.

And he came to his senses. Maybe it was oh-shit, maybe it was self-preservation, but something in him snapped.

Hands on her shoulders, he jerked his head away, studying her, heart thundering in his ears. How it was possible, he couldn't fathom a guess, but he actually experienced withdrawal from something he never consumed. It took her quite a few elongated seconds, but eventually, she opened her eyes. Those enticing, amazing, gorgeous golden brown eyes.

She stared at him, seemingly confused. "You're offended." Matter of fact. Straight to the point.

Was he? Frankly, he wasn't sure.

Come to think of it... "You've known me all my life. You're drunk, and you chose *now* to kiss me. Countless evenings in your bedroom, school dances, horseback riding, hanging out by the pool. At any given time in almost thirty years, you could've kissed me, but you had to get tipsy to try."

"But I didn't kiss you. You stopped me."

Leave it to her to ignore everything but that. "Semantics."

She tilted her head. "Have you ever thought about it?"

Nearly every day since puberty, but he didn't reply.

"Why not now?" Her lips pursed. "I'm single. You're single."

She wanted to play this game? Fine, he'd play. "You're rich. I'm not."

"You're attractive. I'm attractive."

"You own one of the largest estates in Georgia. I muck the stalls."

"My friends love you."

"Your family hates me."

"You want me. I want you."

He nearly died where he sat. On a bench in her gardens, under the moonlight and starry sky, he almost perished from her admission. His idiot heart thundered in glee.

Swallowing hard, he removed his hands from her shoulders and set them on his thighs. "You want a distraction. I want to keep my..." heart "...sanity intact."

She'd just said the night before she'd been bored with her lovers. Maybe she was just testing the waters or scraping the bottom of the barrel, but he wasn't a plaything. He'd do damn near anything for her, but not this. Not screw up a lifelong friendship, a business arrangement, and shatter their world into oblivion. Nope. He was tapping out.

And it hurt. So badly. There were some days he ached to touch her. Actually, physically ached.

She blinked repeatedly as he stood. "What's wrong with a distraction?"

And there it was in a nutshell. "I have too much respect for you to go there." When she just stared in confusion, he sighed. "Come on. Let's get you inside."

She defiantly crossed her arms. "I don't want to go inside."

"Have it your way." He bent and wrapped his arms around her waist, lifting her, and hauling her over his shoulder. "I'm not leaving you half in the bag outside by yourself."

She squealed and kicked her legs. "I'm not half in the bag."

"A quarter, then."

He strode out of the gardens, around the pool, and across the patio to her back door, her huffing the whole way. Opening the door, he let the dog in first, then stepped inside. Through the kitchen they went, and into the hallway to the grand staircase.

"Aden Abner, you put me down."

"Nope."

She screeched. "I don't appreciate this, you know."

Yeah, he knew. She rarely appreciated all the ways he looked after her. This tactic was downright barbaric, but visions of her going for a night swim and not surfacing pummeled his mind.

Instead, he resorted to his usual response in such cases. "Frankly, my dear, I don't give a damn."

"Don't you dare quote 'Gone With the Wind' to me, you brute."

Whew, she was slender, but carrying her through the yard and up the stairs was taxing. He made a left, winded, and strode into her room, where he turned down the covers and unceremoniously dropped her on the bed.

She bounced once, glaring at him, her hair a bird's nest. "Not funny."

"Wasn't trying to be." He covered her with blankets, turned off her lamp, and went to the door. "Goodnight, babe."

She screeched again as he shut the door behind him. Closing his eyes, he slumped against the frame and let out a gale force wind.

Jesus Yosemite Sam Christ on biscuits, he'd almost kissed Scarlett.

After a few seconds, he pried his lids open to find Dorothy and Rebecca in their pajamas, side-by-side outside a guestroom in the hallway, staring at him with rounded eyes. The dog was asleep on the landing.

"Evening, ladies."

"Hi," they said in unison.

"Uh..." Dorothy leaned to the right as if to peer around him. "Everything okay?"

"Peachy. You?"

"Good, thanks." Rebecca scratched her head. "Anything we should know about?"

He jerked a thumb at the door behind him. "Found her out in the garden. How many Georgia Sunsets does it take to make her do that?" Scarlett was a lightweight, but he'd never seen her drunk. This was the closest, and she hadn't been fall-down intoxicated.

Dorothy narrowed her eyes in thought. "Three?" She glanced at Rebecca for confirmation, who nodded. "Three. We were lax, but I wouldn't call her inebriated. Maybe it kicked in later after we went to bed."

"Perhaps." His shoulders sagged, and he suddenly realized he could sleep where he stood. The woman was exhausting. The whole day had been exhausting.

"Do you need to talk about it?" Rebecca's blue eyes met his, concern in their depths.

He opened his mouth to spout an automatic no, but he snapped it shut again. He wasn't a talk-it-out kind of guy, and he really didn't do heart-to-hearts. Damn, but he could stand an ear that wasn't Scarlett's, though.

"We're your friends, too." Dorothy twisted her fingers, wringing them. "I know we're her BFFs, but we're your friend, too."

Rebecca nodded.

"Hell, why not." He turned and quietly opened Scarlett's bedroom door. Yep, just as he thought. She was sprawled out on her stomach, fast asleep, Cotton purring beside her. He closed the door again. "Living room?"

They walked down the hall and into the upstairs living room, where he plopped on his back on the couch. When in Rome. If they were going to talk, may as well be in shrink-office position.

He groaned. "Full disclosure, I'm wiped. I may crash any minute."

"Same." Rebecca claimed the chair to his left.

"I find myself strangely awake." Dorothy took the other chair to his right. "She told us about you being anemic. Are you managing okay?"

He figured she would. "Yeah, I'm good. A few pills a day. I get tired, but eh."

Rebecca cleared her throat. "If you don't mind me asking, why did it take you so long to tell her?"

"Don't take this the wrong way, blondie, but she worries about you a lot. We all do. The time never felt right, and I didn't want to add more to her plate. Her mother does that well enough for everyone."

She snorted a laugh.

Dorothy, however, sighed. "I'm so sorry about what Mrs. Taylor said tonight. It was uncalled for."

He guessed he wasn't the only one to overhear. Just ducky. Emasculation unlocked.

"Thanks, but I'm used to it."

Rebecca shook her head. "One should never have to get used to such a thing. I dealt with petty twats at the newspaper in Boston for seven years. I speak from experience."

Irritation rammed his temples. "Whose ass I gotta kick?"

Her lips curved in a warm smile. "I'm co-owner of my own newspaper. I got my revenge."

"Good girl." He nodded. He owned his own horse-drawn carriage ride business on what used to be part of Taylor land. He could argue he got his revenge, too. Sure didn't feel like it. Then again, he hadn't been after revenge. He'd just wanted to accomplish a dream and make a decent living. "In all seriousness, I wish the woman would leave Scarlett alone. Let her do or say whatever she wants to me, but leave her daughter out of it."

Blondie and red exchanged a look he couldn't decipher.

He shuddered to ask... "Something on your minds?"

Rebecca opened and closed her mouth twice before speaking. "Scarlett mentioned you'd been acting unusual lately. Is it because of your anemia or something else?"

He rolled answers around in his brain until his skull rattled, but nothing was forthcoming. "Both."

"You care about her a lot." Dorothy's soft voice bore no inquisitiveness. She stared at him, her blue eyes intense and acutely aware as if she'd dug in his head for the answers.

He had the acute urge to get defensive, though he wasn't sure why. "Of course, I care about her." Why the hell would he put up with her antics this long if that weren't the case? A sane man would've bolted. "I care about all of you."

Dorothy's gaze never left his. "But not in the same way you care about her."

Closing his eyes, he sighed, pinching the bridge of his nose. All these years, and no one had ever asked him. Not a soul had hinted at what he and Scarlett did behind closed doors or if they should. Hadn't implied or suggested. He'd gotten the distinct impression everyone in Vallantine, including his friends, thought the idea was preposterous. *He* thought it was insane, and he was the one wrangling feelings for her. Had he been so obvious that her BFFs noticed? Had he not been hiding the torment well enough?

Rebecca cleared her throat. "Have you told her?"

Of all the absurdity...

He huffed a laugh, but then it gained momentum until he was nearly hysterical. His eyes watered, and he glanced at both of them. Their distraught and wary expressions had him laughing all over again. His gut ached by the time it finally subsided.

Their expressions hadn't changed, but blondie's brows were raised as if insisting he answer the original question.

"No, I haven't told her." He raised his hand, and dropped it again. "I may be a glutton for punishment, but I don't have a death wish."

Rebecca eyed Dorothy. "He's been around her too long if he's picking up on her drama."

Dorothy morosely nodded.

"Look, I—"

"Nuh-uh." Rebecca leaned forward in her seat. "We've kinda suspected for a while. Scarlett doesn't. Not to our knowledge. What would be the harm in testing those waters?"

"The harm?" He sat up, because no way was he taking this lying down. "Have you met her? Have you met *me*? Her parents? Ain't no way."

"Scarlett's never done what was expected of her." Rebecca lifted a hand when he tried to disagree. "Not when it counted. The debutant routine from her mother? Putting on a class act? Catching more flies with honey? Sure. To an extent. But not when it truly mattered." She ticked off points on her fingers. "Her friendship with you. The company she keeps. Turning the family estate into a business. Selling you land to build your dreams. Overpaying her staff. Cancelling the country club membership. Shunning all potential love matches based on social class."

A huff, and she straightened. "She rebels when and where she sees fit. On the things that matter."

Whereas all that was true, it didn't solve the problem. Any of the problems. Top of the list being... "She has never shown interest, so this is a moot point. I'm not going to jack up a decades-long friendship and our circle because I can't get my shit together."

Rebecca started to speak, but Dorothy made a humming noise in her throat and shook her head.

"Never?"

Aden and Rebecca glanced at her, confusion palpable.

"You said she's never shown interest. I mean, we're not around you two all the time. You have your own friendship separate from ours that's always been tangible, if not intense. All this time, and she's never even hinted?"

Damn. No. Not that he'd picked up on. Not until tonight. And she'd been drunk, so...

He stared straight ahead, lips firmly closed.

"Ah ha," Rebecca sang. "Tell us."

As her best friends, wouldn't Scarlett have told them? Maybe not about this evening yet, but if she'd been thinking outside the friend zone? It only proved his point that she'd been bored and not in her right mind.

"It was nothing." Laying his head against the cushion, he stared at the fireplace, wondering if she'd even remember what happened come morning. In honesty, he hoped not. They could resume as normal. "A spontaneous thing, and one she'll regret tomorrow."

"Tonight?" Dorothy crossed her legs as if settling in for a ghost story. "It happened tonight? In the garden?"

He let out a long, slow exhale. Nothing got by them. He debated saying anything, then said, *screw it*. They knew her as well as him. Perhaps gaining their insight might help him.

"She tried to kiss me."

Rebecca reared.

Dorothy was more subtle, yet her wide eyes indicated the same shock. "Tried? As in, attempted but didn't succeed?"

"Correct. I stopped her."

"Because she'd been drinking?"

"Because she'd been drinking," he confirmed.

Rebecca pressed a hand to her forehead, breathing a laugh. "So that's why she was fit to be tied and carrying on? You rejected her?"

"I didn't reject her. She was inebriated. And I think she was pissed off because I carried her inside."

"Props for respect." Dorothy nodded. "But what happens next time if she's in her right mind?"

There won't be a next time. If she had to be drunk before considering, it won't occur to her while sober. Not accounting for the fact, it took this long for him to even ping her radar.

Silence ensued while he continued not to answer. He was hoping for more insight from them, not the other way around.

"She never talks about it." Dorothy looked at Rebecca. "Have you noticed that? She never discusses her love life, except in passing. We know she has lovers, and none of them are serious, but she doesn't go into detail."

Aden all but swallowed his tongue. "You talk about that. *In detail?*"

Rebecca shrugged. "Sure. Not, like, porno movie deets, but yeah." She glanced at Dorothy. "But you're right, come to think of it. She doesn't bring it up."

They started their own back and forth, and he sighed. It was time to go home. The fair maiden was safe and asleep in her bed, and he'd unloaded some deep thoughts on the jokers to take pressure off his mind. It had half-worked.

He slapped his thighs and rose. "Goodnight, ladies."

They stared at him, but he about-faced and retreated, whistling for the dog.

Chapter Seven

Scarlett drove through the center of town square, mindful of passersby, with large black sunglasses and an extra big travel mug of coffee. Her stomach was still a little queasy, but most of her hangover symptoms were gone. The sunlight was still stabby, though.

It was peak tourism season, so the cobblestone street was packed with people. Flowerboxes beside the old-world cast iron lampposts were teeming with zinnias, cosmos, snapdragons, and petunias, bringing bright splashes of color. Cherry blossom trees, no longer in blooming season, lined the road, creating much-needed shade. Small shop owners had their doors open below their colorful awnings.

It was too packed to park anywhere, so she circled around and headed for the library overlooking Main Street. It was closed off to local traffic, but as co-owner, she could put her car in the lot and walk to meet her dad at What A Pickle deli. She'd thought about cancelling their monthly lunch, but it was the only time she ever got to be alone with him. She parked and got out, snatching her purse from the passenger seat and locking the door.

Holy moly, it was a hot one today. She'd worn a sleeveless lavender sundress with a bow around the waist, but moisture coated her skin immediately from heavy humidity. Wiping her brow with her forearm, she crossed the street and headed for the deli about three-fourths of the way down the block, her white flats clacking.

The wafting scents of food from Pizza My Heart and Guac On didn't make her stomach recoil, so that boded well for actually eating. Gawd, she was so embarrassed. Not only had she drunk two cocktails too many, she'd lost all sense of self-respect and had hit on Aden. Her cheeks heated, and not from the weather. Aden Abner, of all people. Her fulltime friend and parttime frienemy. Bane of her existence and silent white knight. She'd tried to kiss him. In her garden. Under the moon's glow in the middle of the night. He'd come to check on her, and she'd blown their friendship out of the water.

She still had no clue why. Something had just...come over her. He'd said something like, *why not me*, and it was as if dots had connected in her mind. Her tedium with her casual lovers. How no other man's personality seemed to balance hers. How lonely she'd been. And then, there was Aden. Handsome, dependable, gallant Aden. Right in front of her. Why not him?

In the light of day, minus the Georgia Sunsets in her system, reality had dawned. But it was too late, and the damage had been done. His reaction and rejection had pierced her ribcage. The pang was still there. Aching. Poking. Prodding. She had to admit, under the embarrassment, she was surprised it had hurt this much. Through the years, she'd admired his attractiveness, was drawn to his charms, but she'd not once thought of him as anything other than...well, as Aden. Logically, his rejection shouldn't have this kind of effect.

She had no idea how to fix it between them. They lived next door to one another, had a shared business model, he was her friend, yet none of that mattered. She'd crossed the line. Would he laugh it off or would things get awkward? She could always claim she didn't remember. She *had* been drinking. But no, that was deceitful, and she may skirt around the truth with him sometimes, but she never lied to him.

"Scarlett."

Halting, she glanced around.

Her father waved from a few storefronts down where she'd just passed.

She glanced above where she'd stopped. Shearly Beloved, the hair salon. Her father was under the awning for What A Pickle.

Fiddlesticks. She'd passed it while distracted.

"Coming!" She attempted to rush, but in her shoes, just wound up looking like an idiot while shutter-stepping. She wrapped an arm around his shoulders and kissed his clean-shaven cheek, catching a whiff of his expensive woodsy aftershave in the process. "Hi, Daddy. Sorry, I wasn't paying attention. You look good."

He looked the same as he had her whole life, except there was a little more salt to the pepper in his hair. He wore a green polo and khakis, as he usually dressed for casual, unless important business was to be done. Such a lean figure and face, with a wide chin and dark brown eyes. There were more creases around his eyes and mouth, but he'd aged better than Mama, not that she'd say so aloud.

"Thank you. Same to you. I arrived early and got us a table."

"Wonderful!" With as busy as the square was, that had been a marvel.

They sat at a café table by the window. Two sweet teas with lemon wedges were waiting that he must've ordered.

He glanced at the counter, the line ten deep with customers. "What would you like?"

What A Pickle had the best market sandwiches, and suddenly, she was ravenous. She spouted her order, then pulled her phone out of her purse to make sure she had no texts while her father got food. They had a baby shower at the mansion tomorrow, the last of the events before the Peach Festival. No alerts, so her assistant Charlene either had it handled, or everything was good.

A few minutes later, her father returned with two wrapped sandwiches and a basket of chips. "It's a zoo in here. I don't know why we couldn't go to the country club." He reclaimed his seat.

"Because it's important to support local small business."

"Yeah, yeah." He smiled, unwrapping his sandwich. "And what was wrong with the place we went to last month, or the month before?"

"Nothing." She didn't tell her father, but the day before their lunches, she asked Dorothy which locale had the lowest revenue the month before, since her BFF did the accounting for most of them, and that was the place she and her father would visit for their lunches. "It's nice to mix it up."

"If you say so, sweetie." He took a bite and reared. "Hey, this is pretty damn good. I'll have to pop in more often for lunch when I'm at the office."

"What'd you get?" She leaned over. Roast beef and cheddar on rye with lettuce and tomato. "Looks good." She unwrapped her turkey and provolone on wheat, loaded with vegies.

Daddy shook his head. "Yours looks like a salad."

"Oh, but it's better." Laughing, she took a bite. "How's work?"

"Eh." He wiped his mouth on a napkin. "Can't complain."

As he was a real estate investor, she didn't know a lot about what he did, only that it sounded boring. Her parents lived just outside Vallantine in a large mansion community, but her father held offices here in town.

"Your mother wants you to rejoin the country club. I'm supposed to remind you."

"Yeah, well, she can continue to be disappointed." She'd left for a reason, not liking the atmosphere. There was no sense in giving her money to a bunch of hoity toity people who thought they were better than everyone else. She had everything she needed right here.

"It would get her to stop fussin'."

"Ha." She took a sip of sweet tea. "No, it wouldn't. She'd just find something else to harp about. She could make a Happy Meal cry."

"True."

He glanced out the window while he chewed, and she took the opportunity to better examine him. He seemed tired. Or maybe weary was a better term. He'd never been an animated man, sticking more to his proper upbringing, yet through the years, especially since Miss Maureen had died, he'd been morose. Unhappy. She wondered, and not for the first time, if he ever loved Mama. They seemed so mismatched.

"Can I ask you a serious question, Daddy?"

"Of course." He drank from his tea. "I'm not good at science, though, so steer clear of that topic."

She smiled. A joke. How unlike him.

Fidgeting with a corner of her napkin, she scrambled for the right words. "Are you upset Miss Maureen left me the estate?"

He frowned in thought, seemingly surprised by the question. "Why would you ask that?"

She shrugged. "I don't know. It was your family home, dating back many generations. Mama was livid." She didn't really know how her father felt, though. He always appeared more interested in keeping the peace.

"No, I wasn't upset. Maybe a little hurt, at first, but not upset." One corner of his mouth lifted in a quasi-attempt at a smile that never quite made it. "She adored you to pieces. You had a wonderful relationship with her, so I'm glad it turned out the way it did. I just wanted it to stay in the family." He dipped his chin, glaring at her as if over a pair of imaginary glasses. "Your grandmother wasn't very fond of your mother."

"I know." She set the other half of her sandwich aside. "Did they ever get along?"

"Hmm." He leaned back in his seat, crossing his arms. "When your mother and I first started dating, the relationship was civil. I don't think there was any love lost. Right after the wedding, when your mother moved in, I think that's when it went down-hill. Appearances were kept in place for the public."

How sad. "That must've been hard for you." Stuck between his mother and his wife.

He looked at her like no one had ever considered that opin-ion. Brows furrowed, lips parted, he stared as if flabbergasted.

After a moment, he collected himself. "Well, the mansion was certainly big enough. We did all right."

She nodded, understanding he was uncomfortable. She wanted to ask more questions, like was Mother always this mean and why he stayed with her, but she supposed the answers didn't matter.

He folded his hands on the table. "Let me ask you a serious question."

"Okay." She smiled. "But I'm terrible at math, so steer clear of that topic."

He laughed at her twist on his words. "Is there anything going on between you and Aden Abner?"

Criminy. Had someone else spotted them in the garden? "Romantically?"

He nodded.

"No, we're just friends. Why?"

"Your mother came home in a tizzy from your book club meeting, claiming you were taking his side on everything, and he was corrupting you. She insisted something more was afoot."

For crying out loud. "She insulted him to me where anyone could've overheard. In fact, Aden *did* overhear. So, yes, I stood up for him. She was wrong."

Father dipped his head, staring at the table. "His horse business is doing okay?"

"It is."

"I don't know him very well, but his father was from good stock. He did great work until he retired." He huffed as if flustered. "Aden appears to have a solid head on his shoulders. I wish him well. I sincerely do, but do you really think he's the right person for you? Can he offer you stability and—"

"Stop." She put up her hand, palm out. This wasn't happening. "One, we're not dating. I just said we were friends. Two, if we *were* dating, it wouldn't be for you or Mother or anyone to say whether he was right for me. That would be up to me. And three, I don't need anyone to take care of me. In case you didn't notice, I have a huge bank account and a thriving business of my own. If Aden wanted to spend his days twiddling his thumbs and watching grass grow, he could. I could support us. As it so turns out, his business is raking it in, and he works hard."

Halfway through her diatribe, he was emphatically nodding. "You're right. I'll butt out."

"Ah, Daddy." She reached across the table and held his hands in hers. "You don't need to butt out. You just need to trust me. Like Dorothy and Rebecca, I've known him my whole life. He'd never hurt me."

"I trust you." He squeezed her fingers and let go, obviously out of sorts.

"And quit listening to Mother."

Laughing, he stood. "Would you like to take the rest of that home?"

She glanced at her half-eaten sandwich. "Sure." She rewrapped it and rose, grabbing her purse.

"Let's give someone else a chance to sit."

By the time they made it to the door, the table had already been claimed.

Outside, under the awning, she faced him. "It was so good to see you."

"Same, sweetie. I have to get back to work." He offered her a quick hug, and for a brief moment, she was seven years old again, getting a rare bit of genuine affection.

"Me, too." She smiled, watching him walk to his car.

After he drove off, she sighed. She felt better, but was still restless. Townsfolk and tourists passed by her, went around her, and she just seemed...stuck. Rooted, but not grounded. This would not do.

Instead of heading for the library and her car, she strode the other way toward the courtyard. Maybe a short walk and a chat with Miss Katie would help. At the end of the street, she followed the roundabout to the benches in the square.

And there she was, good ole Miss Katie. A black fence surrounded her base with a brick walking path. Smaller lampposts and benches decorated the grassy part of the courtyard around the tree, which had been planted by the town founder William Vallantine for his wife Katherine. Thus, its name, Miss Katie. It had telltale characteristics of Belle of Georgia peach trees with a rounded crown shape on top, upward reaching branches, and dark green deciduous leaves.

A little girl, maybe five years old, was standing in front of the plaque with whom Scarlett assumed was her mother. They had the same ebony hair and wispy frame. She didn't recognize them, but Vallantine was just large enough to not know everyone. Probably tourists.

The woman turned, offering a smile. "Are you from here?"

"Yes, ma'am."

She jerked a thumb behind her. "This is quite a memorial for just a tree."

There was no malice to her statement or in her tone, so Scarlett didn't take offense. She opened her mouth to reply, but the girl tugged her mom's hand.

"Pretty tree."

"She *is* a pretty tree." Scarlett crossed her legs and leaned forward. "Her name is Miss Katie, and she's a modern marvel. She was planted in 1875, making it almost one hundred and fifty years old."

"Wow," the girl breathed, obviously enthralled.

"I know, right?" Scarlett glanced at the woman. "Belle of Georgia trees have a lifespan of fifteen to twenty years. They typically grow to a maximum height of fifteen to twenty-five feet with a span of twenty feet at maturity. They rarely even get that big. She's twice that size. The 1898 hurricane that killed our town founders and took out their mansion left this tree intact. She's withstood countless tropical storms and hurricanes since." Scarlett shrugged. "So, yeah. We're pretty proud of Miss Katie and take good care of her."

"Well, okay then." The woman glanced over her shoulder at the tree. "How amazing."

It was rather amazing.

"And you know what?" Scarlett grinned at the girl. "She grants wishes."

"Really?" Her brown eyes widened to saucers. "Can I make a wish, Mommy?"

The woman laughed, waving her hand. "Absolutely. Make a wish."

The girl squeezed her eyes shut. "I wish to be like Cinderella."

Scarlett shook her head, smiling. To be that young and hopeful again. "Are you kind to animals and do you treat everyone like your equal?"

The girl nodded emphatically.

"Then, I'd say you're mostly there." Scarlett cleared her throat and addressed the mom. "Our Peach Festival is next week. There will be horse drawn carriage rides for a certain princess if you're interested. The booth to sign up will be right over there." She bumped her chin toward the other side of the courtyard.

"Thank you! I'll definitely look into it. We came in town early to get a jump on shopping." She squeezed her daughter's hand. "We should go find your dad. I bet he got in trouble."

Scarlett smiled at their banter while they left the courtyard, but a pang struck her abdomen and a wedge formed in her throat, deflating her smile.

She never gave much thought to having kids. If she did, she did, and if she didn't, it wasn't meant to be. Staring at the duo as they disappeared from view, though, made her realize she did want a family. Children running around the estate and a husband to curl up with while reading. She wouldn't insist on perfection and appearances like how she'd been raised. She'd let them be themselves with no pretenses or requirements to be loved. She'd bathe them in adoration and affection, encourage them at every pass, and tell them they could be whomever and whatever they desired. A boy and a girl, perhaps. Aden could build a proper treehouse this time in one of the weeping willows and...

Merciful heavens, how had Aden popped into a whimsical family daydream? A pretend future she hadn't realized she'd wanted until accidentally stumbling onto the sweetest child.

She narrowed her eyes at Miss Katie. "Trying to tell me something or are you up to no good?"

Now she was talking to a tree. Out loud. In public. Even if it was Miss Katie, this wasn't right.

She glanced at her lap, forgetting she still had the other half of her sandwich. Reaching in her purse, she pulled out a twenty dollar bill and slipped it into the wrapper, then rose and strode the two blocks toward the small underpass that led out of Vallantine.

Just where she usually found him was Vern, reclined on the cement and seemingly enjoying the shade. He was the mailman, Harold's, brother and a Vietnam veteran. He'd been homeless by choice since as long as she could recall because he hadn't acclimated to civilian life very well after med-boarding out of the Army. His hair was nearly as long as hers, stringy and matted. So were his clothes, both dingy and worn.

Not wanting to disturb him, she left the sandwich on top of his duffel bag, smoothed her dress, and headed for the library to get her car.

Chapter Eight

Aden set his phone aside and glanced at the television, mindlessly watching a replay of the baseball game. His team had lost, or so Dad's text had said somewhere around ten o'clock, but it was better than infomercials. He'd cancelled his streaming services since he never used them, but maybe he should rejoin.

Petting Dufus, whose head rested in Aden's lap while they vegged on the couch, he sighed heavily.

This insomnia thing was for the birds. He'd had bouts of it his whole life, but never like this, and never for this long. A month. A month, he'd been unable to catch more than a few hours a night, and that was after doing everything in his power to actually fall asleep in the first place. Medication. Herbs. Headphones. Physical labor. TV. Phone scrolling.

Growling at the top of his lungs.

Maybe he should try bashing his head against the wall.

Two A.M., and he was still up, rewinding that moment in the garden with Scarlett and mentally ticking off things he needed to do tomorrow for the start of the Peach Festival. He was going to be a zombie. Not a good thing considering he had to be his affable self while doing tours and maintaining safety.

What in the actual hell was wrong with him?

Shaking his head, he rose, only to pace the floor. He thought about going out onto the back deck with a beer, but that hadn't helped last night. Or the night before. Or the night before that.

On average, he usually got five hours in. He tried to recall the last instance where he'd had eight solid hours or more of shut-eye, and couldn't. Best he could come up with was the time he'd accidentally crashed at Scarlett's place after her grandmother's funeral. Damn, two years ago? She'd been rightfully upset, and he'd stayed with her, holding her until they'd both fallen asleep. He'd awoken in the morning before her, and to this day, he didn't think she knew he'd been in bed with her all night.

He was just frustrated enough to go over there and do it again.

Not really, but it was better than pacing the finish off the floors while pulling his hair out.

Barely.

Irritation battled against his temples, and he stalked down the hall. Perhaps the act of being in his dark bedroom would prompt his brain to shut off. The dog followed on his heels, jumping on the bed, circling, and laying down. Seconds later, Dufus was snoring.

"Show off."

Hands braced on the pane, he stood at the window, overlooking the yard.

Grass. Trees. Moonlight. Fireflies.

Scarlett's lights were still on. Weird. She'd had no events except a baby shower earlier today. She'd cleared her calendar for the festival. She always did for the Peach Festival and then again for the Pecan Fair in the fall. She was rarely up this late.

Concerned, he went back in the living room to get his phone. Unlocking it, he stared at the screen.

She hadn't texted or called since before The Incident. The one in the garden. Where he'd almost given in to insanity and ten years of hopeless, blanketed desire. *That* incident.

Kinda like the pot calling the kettle black. He hadn't reached out to her, either. Which was highly unusual. They barely went a day, never mind two, without some form of contact.

Was she having a restless night, too? Was she pacing the floors, half out of her gourd, regretting what happened? Embarrassed? Pissed off?

He questioned, and not for the first time, what she'd meant by that move in the garden. She'd been tipsy, but not drunk. She had to have had some wits about her. What, after all these years, had possessed her to kiss him? Or try, at any rate. At the time, he'd figured it had been whimsy or boredom. His plan afterward had been to play it by ear.

But. She. Hadn't. Called.

Phone in hand, he headed to the bedroom once again, debating whether to call her or not. Normally, it would be a no-brainer. But things had changed.

He glanced out the window, and did a double-take.

A shadow moved in the middle of the yard between their houses.

No, scratch that. It didn't move, it stalked. In a tank top and shorts. Brunette hair swirling. Fists clenched.

Stomp, stomp.

Well, there was his answer. Scarlett wasn't embarrassed. She was fuming.

And on her way here.

Closing his eyes, he dropped his chin. Hope and glee coiled in his gut, battling with worry and anxiety. He was shocked he didn't have an ulcer.

The screen door to the back deck opened with a whine of its hinges.

Then the storm door's knob turned.

Dufus lifted his head.

Aden shook his. "You'd be better off going back to sleep. Our belle is fit to be tied."

As if understanding, the dog set his head back down.

"Aden Joseph Abner!"

"Shit," he said to the dog. "She used my full name."

Dufus whined.

"Me, too, buddy."

Alrighty, time to face the dragon. He headed down the hallway, where he found her in the space between his kitchen and living room, arms crossed, and toe tapping.

"Kind of late, darlin'."

"You were awake, same as me."

So he was. Touché.

"Where have you been, Aden?"

He spread his arms, indicating the obvious.

"Two days." She held up her index and middle fingers as if he couldn't count that high without demonstration. "Two days without a word from you."

"Your phone works, doesn't it?"

That was the wrong thing to say. Up went her brows, and she bared her teeth in the sexiest, scariest display of animalistic rage.

"So, what? You avoid me, then? Like a coward?"

Normally, he'd get royally defensive and pissed off right about now. But one, he was beyond exhausted, and two, she was right. He could haul hay from sunup to sundown, sweat his ass off in the blaring heat working the fields, hold his own in a bar fight, or wrangle a stubborn gelding, but this woman brought him to his knees. Every time. Every day. To his knees.

Yeah, he was a coward. He'd rather avoid the conversation altogether than find out, with glaring precision, that she'd never return his feelings. Denial he could live with. Rejection, he wasn't sure. If it meant losing her, then no. Funny thing was, as much as they raked one another's nerves raw, they emotionally relied too heavily on each other to survive. He'd known it all along. He didn't think she'd caught on yet.

Her arms slapped her sides. "It was just a kiss."

"Not quite." There was no *just* about it. The moment was embedded in his brain forever. He remembered every second, even if she didn't.

She rolled her eyes. "An almost kiss, which is even more to my point. I'm sorry. I'm sorry I crossed the line and I'm sorry you were disgusted by it and I'm—"

"What?"

"I'm sorry."

Damn it. "I got that part. You don't disgust me." Seriously, it was a wonder she hadn't caught on to the opposite.

She stared at him, and he could've sworn she saw through him to all the ugly, messed up, crazy shit in his head. Curiosity battled with determination in her gorgeous honey-soaked eyes. Like a switch, she deflated, her shoulders sagging.

She bit her lower lip. "Why are you ignoring me, then?"

He thought about countering with, *why did you try to kiss me*, but he caught himself short. "I don't know. You took me by surprise, I guess. I was working it out in my head."

"And what did you conclude?"

He couldn't tell if she was insecure or genuinely curious. Neither was optimal. Or normal. Not to mention, he had no answer.

"Aden?"

Screw it. "Why did you do it? All these years, babe. Why now?"

She tilted her head, her lashes creating a current with a rapid blink. "You called me 'babe' again."

He straightened. "What?"

"You did it a few nights ago in my room. You've used *darlin'* a gazillion times, usually in sarcasm, but never *babe*."

That's what she took from his question? A moniker? One he hadn't realized he'd said. "Answer me."

In dramatic fashion, she threw her hands up. "I don't know. Why does it matter?"

"It matters."

"Fine." She sighed. "You said, *why not me*."

Talking to her sometimes was like trying to give a pedicure to a rabid badger. "I'm not following."

"In the garden, I asked why you were always rescuing me. You said, *someone has to do it, why not me?*"

"Uh huh." Two plus two was equaling zero at the moment. And she obviously recalled more about what happened than he'd assumed.

"*Sooo*," she drew out, "it made me think." She shrugged as if they were discussing whether to have corn on the cob or green beans with dinner. "Why not you?"

His world came to a careening halt. Just like that.

"Why not me," he flatly repeated. His tongue went numb. He'd never had that happen before.

"Exactly! Why not you? We've never, you know, been anything else. So, I kissed you. Or tried. What can I say? I'd had a couple too many cocktails. You pushed me away like we were ten and I had cuties, plus—"

"Scarlett." Crap, one thing at a time. She'd just shoved them into the deep end. "We already established you're not revolting, so the cuties are moot." He couldn't believe how far this train had derailed.

Her perfect little hands settled on her perfect little hips. "If you're not revolted by me, then why did you act like it?"

"I did not."

"Did, too."

Fuck him. They were back in kindergarten. "You are not disgusting, and I'm not revolted by you." He'd never so much as thought such a thing. "You're beautiful. Everything about you is beautiful. Can we move on from that?"

She reared as if he'd slapped her.

He pressed his palm to his forehead to stop the pounding. "What now?"

"That's twice in a handful of days you've said I was beautiful, and you called me 'babe.' Twice."

They were back to monikers again. "I don't know why I called you 'babe,' other than it was involuntary, but you are beautiful. We discussed that already." He stared at the ceiling a beat. "You're sober now. Do you regret it? Would you have attempted to kiss me if you'd been clearheaded?"

Her lips parted, but no words emerged. A tiny wrinkle formed between her brows.

And there it was, the answer he always knew he never wanted.

"I didn't push you away." He drew a long, deep breath and held it before exhaling. "I stopped you from making a mistake you'd regret come morning." He should've known better than to allow doubt or hope to wiggle in. "It's late. Do you want to stay here, or should I walk you home?"

For whatever reason, she just stared at him. Unblinking, just stared.

Several linoleum tiles separated her from him, and he couldn't tell if it was too many or not enough. The air became saturated with all the unsaid thoughts, but he hadn't a clue what hers were. Time had frozen to some drugging slow-motion reel.

Finally, after too long, she broke the silence. "You never told me about the state of the treehouse."

All right. Okay. Had *he* been drinking?

Without taking her gaze from his, she elaborated. "I asked you if the treehouse was safe. You said you'd look into it."

He'd nearly forgotten. Why was that suddenly important? "It's not safe. I went back there this morning. I'll build you a new one."

"Would you?" Her tone was flat, and her reactions were like that of someone in a trance.

"Yes." Uncomfortable, he crossed his arms. She was behaving strangely, and this felt like an exam he hadn't studied for. What was going on with her? "I'll build you another. I'll build you ten treehouses if that's what you want."

Understanding dawned in her eyes.

Which made one of them. He didn't know whether to check his ass or scratch his watch.

Haltingly, she took a step forward. "You're always rescuing me."

His heart stopped so fast, it left skid marks along the inside of his ribs.

Another step. "We're almost thirty years old, and you'd build me a treehouse simply because I wanted one."

Air trapped painfully in his chest.

"I haven't had a cocktail tonight." Another step, then another, until she was standing in front of him and her scent wove around him. "Why not you?"

A gale force wind expelled from his lungs. "Scarlett," he whispered. It was about all he could manage.

She cupped his cheeks in her warm palms, just like she'd done the other night in the garden, but this time, he had no excuse. None that would come to mind, anyhow. She was touching him. Voluntarily and while clearheaded. His hands fisted at his sides, waiting. It had to be her. He wasn't going to upend everything. She had to be the one who...

Kissed him. Up on her toes, she pulled him toward her and kissed him.

Hesitating, he closed his eyes, her soft as hell lips barely grazing his. Blood roared through his veins with such ferocity, his eardrums had a pulse. A slight wavering exhale left her mouth and caressed his, and that was it. He'd waited a decade for this moment he thought would never come.

Wrapping an arm around her waist, he threaded the other hand in her silky strands and tilted his head. He sealed the gap between them, taking her upper lip between his, then her lower, teasing the ever-living hell out of them both.

Her arms wrapped around his neck. She arched toward him, aligning their bodies and crushing her breasts against his chest. Her lips parted, and without any warning of her atom bomb, she caressed his tongue with hers. Long, slow, languid strokes that nearly buckled his knees.

Angling the other way, he matched her sweet torture with his own, and they all but consumed the other. His fingers tightened in her strands, holding her to him. She was like lightning in a bottle, untamable and erratic. He had a feeling it would be like this between them if they'd ever crossed the friendship line in the sand.

Volatile. Explosive.

A moan, and she lifted her head. Lazily, her lids opened, and he was ensnared by eyes he'd looked into a thousand times in his lifespan. Dark brown around the edges, honey gold toward the center, and the most gorgeous thing about her in a long line of stunning traits.

Her gaze darted between his as if searching for something she'd lost. Or found.

He couldn't regulate his heartrate for the life of him. What happened tonight hadn't been an *almost*. They'd done it. They'd gone beyond what they had been to uncharted territory. He had zero clue what to do.

Sliding one arm from around his neck, she wedged it between them to stroke his jaw. The rasping of his whiskers against her fingers was somehow louder than his heartbeat. She followed the path of her fingers with her gaze, her pouty lips reddened by the kiss.

"Wow, Aden," she breathed.

She had a real way with understatements, but was that a good 'wow' or a bad one? She'd willingly participated. In fact, her heart was thundering against him.

He said the only thing his wrangled mind could come up with at the moment. "You started it."

She huffed a laugh, which gained momentum into her rich, full-bodied one that liked to sucker punch him in the gut. Weapon number seven thousand and fifty she used against him.

"I did, didn't I?" She released a breath which ended in a sigh. "What do we do now?"

He had ideas. Lots and lots of ideas. But it had taken this long to get here, and he wasn't fully certain she knew what 'here' meant.

Tucking a strand of her cocoa locks behind her ear, he eased his grip from around her waist. "I suggest we think about it before anything else happens."

"Thinking is overrated."

He glared at the ceiling, his body tight with need. "Deliver me from evil."

"Okay, okay." She eased out of his arms and wove around him to the counter. "You say the sweetest things." She reached into an overhead cabinet, taking down a canister he'd never seen.

"What are you doing?"

"Making you some tea. You're in an insomnia phase again, right? That's why you're still awake?"

It wasn't the only reason. "I don't have tea."

Setting a kettle to boil, she raised the small cannister. "Chamomile. I brought it over in the spring and told you to make it before bed. I see you haven't."

"The stuff that tastes like dandelions?" He didn't realize she'd left it here.

"How would you know what dandelions taste like?" She added honey to a mug, then turned around and leaned a hip against the counter, watching him. Her gaze ran over his features, and hers slackened in response to whatever she found. "You look exhausted."

He was. Bone-deep exhausted.

"Haven't been sleeping very well." He shrugged, unsure of what else to say.

"How long has it been?"

He scratched his neck. "Since I slept well?" Forever. "A month."

"A month?" Her eyes widened. "Geez, that's a long time. How are you standing?"

Grit and determination.

The kettle whistled. She removed it from the burner and poured water into the mug. Repeatedly, she dipped the teabag into the water to let it steep, a small plume of steam emitting from the rim.

He watched her profile while she was distracted, and his heart waved a white flag. Middle of the night, they both had a big week ahead, and here she was, taking care of him. She did it often in so many tiny ways that no one but him would notice. Always had.

After removing the teabag and tossing it in the trash, she stirred the contents of the mug with a spoon and handed it to him. "Drink."

"Yes, my liege."

While they leaned against opposite counters, staring at one another, he sipped the tea and wondered if the space between them was a literal metaphor. And blech. The crap did taste like dandelions. Regardless, he finished it, setting the mug in the sink.

"Want me to walk you home?"

Shaking her head, she shoved off the counter and went down the hallway.

Frowning, he shut off the light and followed her.

Dufus had moved to the foot of the bed and Scarlett had the covers pulled back.

"Come on." She patted the mattress beside her and reclined under the sheets, turning on her side to face where he usually lay.

They were having a sleepover? This was supposed to help his insomnia how?

He plugged his phone in to charge on the nightstand where he'd left it, then climbed in, laying on his back.

"I snore." He stared at the shadows dancing on his ceiling, wanting so damn badly to kiss her again.

"I know." She made a circular motion with her finger. "Roll over."

Judging by the direction of her gesture, he assumed she meant he should roll away from her, so he did. Tucking the covers around him, he sighed.

Her hand touched his back, gentle and with no hesitation. Then, sweet Lord, she rubbed in soothing circular patterns as if he was six years old and had awoken from a nightmare. Though her movements and gesture were maternal in nature, it was anything but. Her scent invaded his orbit. The sound of her even breathing was new to the confines of his bedroom. Her touch was both a balm and a current.

Damn if his eyes didn't drift shut, though.

Chapter Nine

After falling asleep for a few hours at Aden's, Scarlett stole his phone off the nightstand and went into the kitchen, letting him sleep. While she fed Dufus and the coffee brewed, she went through Aden's contacts until she found Gary.

Connecting the call, she opened the door for the dog and stepped out onto the back deck. Sunrise broke the horizon in brilliant splashes of red and orange.

"Mornin', boss."

"Hey, Gary. It's Scarlett."

"Well, hey, missy." His voice, as usual, was chipper. He reminded her of a summer version of Santa—jolly, but beardless. "Somethin' wrong?"

She waved her hand as if he could see her. "No, no. All good. Did Aden give you a schedule for today?" The Peach Festival was due to start, which meant so did the carriage rides and her estate tours.

"Yep. He's doing the first round, picking up tourists at the booth in the square at ten. I do mine at two. Why?"

"He hasn't been sleeping well. You didn't hear that from me. Would you mind switching times and taking the morning round? He's finally asleep."

"Oh, sure. Not a problem. I'll be there in a jiffy to help you get the carriages out."

"Thank you!"

After disconnecting, she went in and poured coffee. While it cooled a bit, she snuck into Aden's bedroom to snatch a pair of sweats and a tee, since she was not dressed for company in what she'd worn over here last night. Proper enough. His phone in her pocket, she grabbed her coffee, put a lid on the travel mug, and made her way out to the barns while drinking.

Dufus followed on her heels, staring at her.

"I know. It's an unusual morning. Are you gonna help me feed horses?"

He barked, and she laughed.

Aden had four horses, two male black Percherons, and two dark brown female Hackneys. Miss Maureen had acquired them not long before she'd passed, but Scarlett had been used to horse care and maintence having Belgian Draughts, Holsteiners, and Gelderlanders growing up. She didn't have a genuine love or affinity for them like Aden, but she knew what to do.

Setting her coffee on a fencepost, she opened the barn latch and propped the doors open. Hands on her hips, she looked around. She hadn't been in the barn in ages, not since he'd had the second one built to house carriages. Light filtered in from the windows on the far end above those doors. Dust motes clung to the air and wafted. Five stalls were on either side, six of them obviously empty. A grooming station was along the back wall on the left with the tack room opposite on the right.

She hoped the feed was still in the tack room, and headed that way. Sure enough, there it was, along with laminated instructions just in case. And he called her organized?

Once the horses were fed and set out to pasture, she cleaned the stalls, then leaned against a post drinking coffee. It was a beautiful morning. Warm, but not sweltering yet, with a timid breeze. Dew clung to grass and reflected in the sunlight. It smelled like hay and fur with a lingering trace of roses from her gardens.

It was then, while it was quiet and she waited for Gary, that last night fully hit her. Square between the eyes.

She'd kissed Aden, and he hadn't rejected her this time. Criminy, it had been good, too. Like, the Earth shook kind of good. They'd each had occasional lovers, but nothing serious or long-standing. They were free to see whomever they wanted, but did last night mean anything? Pent up steam releasing or something more? She'd be lying if she said she hadn't thought about it, yet a dynamic such as theirs implied nothing more beyond what flirting implied. Heck, they'd barely done that in their friendship.

After he'd knocked her socks off, had she been wearing any, he'd said to think about it. She doubted she'd do anything else. She'd never been kissed like that. Ever. Tender, impassioned. It was as if he'd been telling a story. Not just heat and hormones, but connection. Thing was, if they tried for more, there was a lot to lose if things went sideways. She didn't know how he felt. Until she'd kissed him, she'd been under the impression, based on what had happened in the garden, that he wasn't into her.

She'd talk to her besties about it today. Thinking through a whirl in her head wouldn't solve anything.

Tires crunched on gravel, and she turned her head. Gary's white SUV pulled in and parked outside the pasture fence.

"Come on, boy. Let's help Gary."

Dufus barked and followed her to the vehicle.

Gary lumbered out of the driver's side wearing jeans and a white tee with Aden's company logo. A stocky man in his sixties, he had solid white hair and a cleanshaven face.

He nodded and placed a Stetson on his head. "Hey there, missy. Strange seeing you out here."

"Eh, it never hurts to get dirty once in a while." Her mother would be mortified.

Giving her attire a once-over, he chuckled. "They fed and ready?"

"Yessir." She didn't know the proper gear for the horses and carriages, so she'd leave that to him. "Do you think I need to call Jason or Tom?" They were Aden's other employees who helped with the business.

"Naw." He opened the pasture fence and held it for her. "Tom's going to be up at the main house for transfer of carriages during tours and Jason is manning the booth in town. We can do this." He faced her, pausing his stride. "Are you sure Aden's okay?"

"Yes, just tired." She chewed her lip, worried he'd be angry for stepping in. This was his business, not hers, even if she was trying to help. "Should I wake him?"

"No need." He continued walking toward the second barn. "We have it handled, and all we did was switch schedules."

True.

She carried what he told her to carry and followed tasks per his instructions. While he did his thing, he told the worst dad jokes that had her rolling. No wonder Aden had hired him for tours. He was a hoot.

An hour later, with the black Percherons pulling the white and gold carriage, Gary disappeared down the driveway, and Scarlett blew out a breath.

"Well, Dufus, let's check on our guy."

She closed the barns and rechecked the pasture fence, then made her way back to Aden's house, only to find he was still clocked out. Twisting her lips in thought, she calculated how long he'd need to get ready for the second trip early this afternoon, and set the alarm on his phone. She wrote a note explaining what she'd done so he wouldn't freak out, and put both on his nightstand.

She was supposed to meet her besties around noon, so she told Dufus to stay put, turned off the coffeepot, and made her way back to the mansion. The staff stopped mid-task in the kitchen while gathered around the island, coffee cups halfway to their mouths.

"Good morning, everyone."

"Good morning." Charlene, eyes wide, gave her a once-over. "Are you all right?"

Scarlett supposed she did look a fright in hay-covered sweats and a tee that were way too large. "I helped with the horses this morning."

They nodded in unison as if they understood, but their comically shocked expressions indicated otherwise. Her cook, George, an older Black man who made the best shrimp and grits this side of the Mason-Dixie line, seemed especially distraught as he rubbed his bald head.

"Honestly, y'all. I'm fine. It's the start of the Peach Festival. I just helped out. Which reminds me, have the guests from the magazine arrived yet?"

"No, ma'am." Her housekeeper, Dee, straightened from the counter, unnatural red hair cut in a clean bob. "The Mayor's bringing them any minute. The two guestrooms are made up with clean linens and towels. I put a basket of goodies in each room from local shops as you suggested."

"Grass was mowed yesterday, and the hedges were trimmed." The gardener, Mike, tipped his hat, dark hair poking out underneath. "The troughs for the horses are at the top of the driveway, off to the side."

"And I've got dinner prepared in case they stay in, along with fresh fruit and finger sandwiches for lunch." George tossed a towel over his shoulder. "Eggs benedict for breakfast tomorrow."

Charlene smoothed her orderly blonde bun. "I've got a display in the foyer of brochures for the event business that people can grab as they tour. All the ballrooms have tables set out for appearances with tablecloths and fresh cut flowers. Betty from the garden club brought them over."

What a relief. At least her staff had their shit together. "You're awesome. All of you." She rushed for the doorway, calling over her shoulder. "I'm going to get ready. Take next week off. Every one of you. A paid week."

She left them to their excited muttering and took the stairs two at a time.

Once in her room, she had no choice but to shower or she'd smell like the barns all day. Since she didn't have time for fiddling with her hair, she quickly dried it, threw it in a high ponytail, and applied her cosmetics. Donning a cute green sundress and matching sandals, she eyed herself in the mirror.

Well, it wasn't her best hair day, and her makeup wasn't the greatest, but she was presentable. Hopefully, she wouldn't run into Mama today. With this dress color, she probably should've used the gold eye shadow, but whatevs.

She descended the grand staircase just as Gunner Davis strolled in, followed by a man and woman. She didn't know what she'd been expecting, but the reporter looked fresh out of high school playing in the big leagues with long blonde locks and a black suit. The other person, assumingly the cameraman, judging by the equipment bag, was an older gentleman who was tall and hefty, easily matching Gunner in girth. He had sweat on his brow already.

The woman gazed around the foyer, cooing. "This is so lovely!"

"Hey, y'all. Welcome to the Taylor estate. I'm Scarlett." She shook their hands.

"Miss Scarlett," Gunner gestured at the blonde, "this is Abigail, and the fella over there is Mark."

"Thanks for having us." Abigail grinned, showing a row of straight white teeth. "This is way better than a hotel."

"Pleased as punch to have you. Let me show you your rooms, and then I'll give you a tour."

Two hours later, she was finally on her way to town to meet her besties. If she thought yesterday was busy as a bee, today was the whole hive. The cobblestone streets were overcrowded with tourists, and she barely made it to the library parking lot.

Both Rebecca and Dorothy were already there waiting, leaning against Rebecca's car.

Scarlett grabbed her purse and climbed out. "Sorry I'm late."

Rebecca grinned. "We're gonna have that printed on your tombstone."

"Mmm-hmm," Dorothy agreed.

"Well, I *am* sorry. The people from the magazine arrived today, and I had to be hospitable."

"We're only poking fun." Dorothy tilted her head. "Heard you helped with some horses this morning."

Scarlett sighed. Had to love small towns. Word travelled faster than a hot knife through butter.

"About that..." She flipped her ponytail over her shoulder. "I need to talk to you."

Rebecca nudged her chin toward the park just on the other side of the library. "Let's walk and talk. I need me some peach pie."

Halfway down the block, Scarlett couldn't shut up another second. "He kissed me. Aden kissed me. Well, actually, I think I kissed him. Last night, we had a fight, and it just sorta happened."

Her besties stopped on a dime, speaking simultaneously.

"Oh, my gawd. What?"

"Was it good?"

She threw her hands up. "I know, right? And it was *sooo* good." She fanned her face.

"Never thought I'd see the day." Rebecca shook her head.

Her, either.

"Are you dating? Seeing one another?" Dorothy's expression bordered on concern.

"No." Scarlett pouted. "I don't know. He said to think about it before we decide anything. The stubborn mule kisses me like straight out of a romance novel, then taps the brakes."

"Eh, not a bad call." Rebecca started walking anew. "I mean, you've been friends since diapers."

"Frienemies," Dorothy added.

"Me thinkst Graham was right." Rebecca waggled her brows. "Fighting is foreplay."

That was how it had started last night. Scarlett wiped her brow with her forearm. She needed out of the sun. It was so hot.

They arrived at the park, teeming with booths, vendors, and rides. Excited children laughed while townsfolk chitchatted. A variety of scents from popcorn to barbeque hung in the air.

Rebecca let out a long-winded sigh of contentment. "Peach Festival, how I have missed thee."

They laughed, but Scarlett had missed this, too.

When Rebecca had gone away for college, and then had stayed gone for work, they talked, texted, and video-chatted all the time, but it wasn't the same. As girls, they'd run from one vender to another, eating until they thought they'd puke, then go on the merry-go-round to cool off and rest. After dark, they'd stay for the fireworks, devouring ice cream, and have a sleepover at Rebecca's. Her grandmother would have cookies waiting, and let them gossip all through the night. Sometimes, they'd read poetry to each other from a collection, or watch scary movies that had Dorothy hiding under a blanket. The routine hadn't changed much as teens. They'd just inserted boys into the mix.

Scarlett's folks rarely came to the Peach Festival or Pecan Fair. It was two weeks out of the year where she didn't have to be on her game or put up pretenses. Her throat grew tight. Much as she'd missed those days, few and far between as they'd been, she was just glad to have her favorite people back in one place again.

They started with roasted corn on the cob, parking their butts at a picnic table under a maple tree.

After a few bites, Dorothy wiped her mouth with a napkin, eyeing Scarlett. "Truth. Do you want something more from Aden?"

She opened her mouth, but swiftly closed it again. Her knee-jerk response was to say yes, but there were factors. All the things that could go wrong. What they could lose. They were pretty mismatched.

But, that kiss.

Dorothy and Rebecca shared a look Scarlett couldn't decipher. Something akin to *ruh-roh* with a side of *darn it.*

Finished with her corn, Scarlett tossed it in a nearby trash can and reclaimed her seat. "Out with it. What's going on?"

Rebecca winced.

"Well..." Dorothy wrinkled her nose. "We've been friends since birth, right? And we have our group of friends, separate from our trio, like with Aden and Forest, adding Graham as he came along."

"Uh huh." What was her point?

"It's just...Graham, as a newcomer to the group, may have been on to something." Rebecca set her fully eaten corn on the table. "You and Aden have always been..." She looked at Dorothy for assistance.

"Volatile." Dorothy nodded. "Like you're one side-eye away from killing each other. Except lately, ever since Graham made that comment, we've been watching more closely."

Scarlett narrowed her eyes. "Spying on me and Aden?"

"No." Rebecca *pffed*. "Not spying. Being more observant."

"Uh huh," she repeated, unamused. "And?"

They exchanged a look again, and Scarlett rolled her eyes. Ultimately, it was Dorothy who spoke.

"When you're not paying attention, the way he looks at you is…" She twirled her hands as if summoning the correct term.

"Hot," Rebecca finished. "It's hot. Like how Westley looks at Buttercup in *The Princess Bride* kind of hot."

Scarlett straightened. No way she heard that right. She glanced at Dorothy, who emphatically nodded.

When she could speak, all that emerged was, "Aden?"

"Yeah, Aden," they said in sync.

"Look." Rebecca pressed her palm to the table. "There's not a shadow of a doubt you guys deeply care about each other. We just always figured it was more like siblings."

"Not anymore," Dorotthy added.

Had Scarlett figured this wrong? She'd assumed the whole romantic entanglement had been brought on by her shifting things in the garden by almost kissing him, and that had been the catalyst for the change. Had there been something more going on with him?

"I'm worried," she mumbled.

"About what?" Dorothy tossed hers and Rebecca's corn away. "He'd never hurt you."

"Maybe not, but doing something about this sudden attraction could hurt our friend circle, our business relationship, and what he and I already have."

Dorothy shrugged. "But it could make way for something great and lasting."

"There's another thing you're not considering." Rebecca rolled her head to stretch her neck, something she typically did while trying to get her fibro pain to ease. "In my experience, once something like this occurs, it's hard to go back to normal, anyway. Almost like it's always there in the background, waiting to be acknowledged. If it's not, it could ruin all the things you mentioned without trying. The dynamic will be off until you address it or play it out." She smiled, a hate-to-say-it implication in the gesture. "Things have already changed."

"Gah." Scarlett pressed her forehead to the table.

On one hand, that kiss had been amazing. Chemistry, meet thy minion. On the other, sparks led to fire, and fire ravaged. Just because they had attraction didn't mean it would last or that they were properly paired for one another. Half the time, she wasn't even sure he liked her. Loved? Yes. They had a bond and would do just about anything for the other, but like was a different subject. She had to wonder if what he was feeling was out of obligation or conformity.

Her phone buzzed in her purse. Lifting her head, she dug out her cell and stared at the screen. It was the exact time she'd set Aden's alarm to wake up. Any second now, he'd see her note. She was still a little worried he'd be mad.

"What happened last night?" Dorothy stared at her like she already knew the answer.

Scarlett ran her fingers through her ponytail. "It's like I said, we were arguing, and... I don't know. It happened again, that sensation of an overwhelming need to make a move. He didn't push me away this time, though. My golly, you guys. I thought I was floating."

"Aww." Rebecca grinned.

Dorothy lifted her brows. "And afterward?"

"I noticed how tired he seemed. He gets phases of insomnia now and then. He said this one was lasting longer than normal."

She set her elbow on the table and chin in her hand. "I made him tea and rubbed his back until he fell asleep."

They stared at her, unblinking. It was starting to get on her nerves.

Dorothy whipped her attention to Rebecca. "I never pegged her as this maternal."

"She's way more than I am. She takes care of her people and always did stuff like this for us."

"True, but this is different. She doesn't even seem aware."

Scarlett snapped her fingers to get their attention. "I'm right here, y'all."

"Oh, we know." Dorothy rose. "Let's go hit the barbeque booth."

What? "We were in the middle of a discussion."

"So, let's walk and talk." Dorothy about-faced.

Rebecca followed suit. "She's not ready for our insight yet."

"Nope."

Rolling her eyes, Scarlett followed. "You two are whack."

A few hours later, after sharing barbequed chicken, roasted almonds, popcorn, cotton candy, saltwater taffy, and peach pie with her besties, she didn't think she could walk another step or consume another bite.

They sat in the grass under a river birch in front of one of the stages, waiting for a local band to begin playing. It was great seeing the community come together for festivities and tourists enjoying themselves. There was something to be said for small town life, despite its quirks and idiosyncrasies. Gossip and rumors aside, there was usually a helping hand nearby should one ever need it.

After a rest and listening to some music, they played a few games, then decided to hook up with Graham, since he was finished covering the festival for The Gazette, and with Forest, who'd just gotten out of work at the bank. They claimed spots on the grassy noll by the library to watch fireworks, chatting about Graham's first Peach Festival experience as the sun descended.

And Aden still hadn't called or texted.

"It's insane. I had no clue there were five thousand ways to eat or prepare a peach."

Scarlett laughed, watching the street for Aden. "Eh, more like ten thousand."

Dorothy caught her checking her phone. "Have you tried texting him? He's probably done with carriage rides."

"Who?" Graham glanced between them. "Aden?"

"Yep." Rebecca fed him some of her ice cream. "He always joins us."

A warmth spread in Scarlett's chest watching them. Rebecca hadn't had the smoothest life so far, and until Graham had come along, Dorothy and Scarlett had been worried about her. Alas, they had a great relationship built on mutual trust, respect, and passion. She'd never seen two people more suited for each other.

And if that made Scarlett a touch jealous, then she'd have to get over it.

"Yeah, but he might be behind schedule. I last saw him around six, and he was wrapping up." Forest scratched his jaw. "Want me to head to the booth? See if he's there?"

"No." Scarlett rose, dusting off her dress and smoothing her skirt. "I'll go. I need to make sure the scheduler has proper times for tomorrow anyway." A lie. That had been worked out a few days ago.

"Fireworks are gonna start in an hour." Dorothy smiled. "Better hurry."

"Ha." Rebecca grinned. "She'll make her own."

Hilarious.

Scarlett abruptly turned her back on the guys' confused expressions and headed toward the street, her sandals sinking into the plush grass and a warm breeze caressing her skin.

Chapter Ten

"That should do it." Jason closed the grate overhang for the booth in the town square, dusting his hands together. "You're booked solid nearly the whole week already. We left two spaces open for tomorrow like the Mayor requested on account of those magazine people."

From the driver's seat of the carriage, reins in his hands, Aden nodded. He figured that's how things would play out. Last year, the Pecan Fair in the fall and Peach Festival in the summer had him hopping, but he had to admit, scheduling things ahead of time at the booth made things easier. Passengers wouldn't have to wait in line for a ticket, only to be disappointed because of capacity. They could go about their way, enjoying all Vallantine had to offer. Perhaps he should talk to Scarlett about adding a schedule to his site for the rest of the year.

For now, he bumped his chin toward the rows of shops. "Go have fun, man. You're free."

Laughing, Jason waved over his shoulder as he strode away.

Leaning back in his seat, Aden sighed. They'd gotten back way later on this last trip than he would've liked because the tour group at the estate had been *ooh*ing and *ahh*ing over Scarlett's gardens. Charlene had barely managed to wrangle them into submission. He didn't much like running the carriages at night when they'd been going all day, but he'd reward the horses later.

He was going to miss fireworks with his friends, but he'd shoot for earlier tomorrow to meet up with them.

Townsfolk and tourists bustled about, roaming the cobblestone street, popping in and out of shops. The old world lampposts cast a yellow glow, adding a strange picturesque romanticism to the main square. Soon, the Tipsy Turtle Bar & Grill would start live music after the fireworks, and other shops would close, leaving just the restaurants open. Dusk descended, creating purple and red hues across the horizon.

It was quite beautiful, his little town. He didn't venture out much this time of the day, often missing the highlights. Usually, he was happy on his back deck with a beer, staring at the mansion next door, or hanging out with her at her place while she drove him batshit crazy.

Speaking of. Scarlett hadn't messaged him back. Thanks to her, he'd gotten nine hours of shut-eye. Admittedly, he'd been a little irked at first by her antics, but once the oh-shit wore off, he realized she hadn't been stepping on his toes or messing with him, and she'd coordinated with Gary first.

He glanced at his phone and winced. His text hadn't gone through, either because he'd sent it near the cemetery where service was sketchy or because he forgot to hit Send. Damn, he put it through now.

Thanks for last night and this morning. I appreciate it.

A lump in his throat, he didn't know what else to say to her. Not when he'd thought he'd originally sent the text or now. She'd comforted him until he'd fallen asleep, had arranged his morning to assure he stayed that way to catch up on much-needed rest. Fed his dog. Hell, had fed his horses. Called his staff.

What other woman would do such a thing? The town saw her as the rich girl on the hill, born with a silver spoon in her mouth, and as dramatic as her namesake. They loved her as they did each of their fellow neighbors, but not a patron in Vallantine had a clue about the depths of her soul. The kindness. Empathy. Devotion. Her errant, constant guilt.

He didn't know what to do. After their stop-traffic kiss, one he'd been waiting eons for, he'd told her to think about it. Fact was, if she chose to try, to keep going, it would level him to ash. It was one thing to admire her from afar, play head games with what-if, ponder could-have-beens, and another thing entirely to actually go for it. That Scarlett no one else got to see? He couldn't live without her. Nor did he want to.

Jaw clenching, he stared aimlessly toward the direction of the library. He'd wait a few minutes to see if she would come by to check on him or would reply to his text. If not, he'd head home alone. About now, they'd usually be on the noll by the library with friends, trying to eat ice cream before it melted, and waiting for the fireworks display. That's probably where she was at the moment, so he ignored the disappointment in his gut when she didn't appear.

Just as he was about to lead the horses around to leave, he spotted her halfway down Main Street under a lamppost beside The Busy Bean coffee shop. She had her head down, staring at her phone. A beat later, her shoulders relaxed.

She'd been worried, after all. She'd gotten his thank-you text, way too late, and he'd have to do better. Her guilt this time was on him. Busy or not, he should've made sure she knew he appreciated the gesture.

Lifting her head, she glanced around. Damn, but the soft hue from the lampposts, combined with the vivid colors of sunset, put her in a gorgeous light. She had her hair up in a ponytail, exposing her elegant regal neck, and wore a green dress the color of shamrocks. He couldn't tell from here, but he'd bet his right arm and left leg that her cosmetics still looked flawless. Always pretty as a picture before she left the house.

What he wouldn't give to see her without any of it. The makeup. The dress.

He knew the second she spotted him, as her whole body went still, and electricity zinged in the space between them. She paused a heartbeat, then slowly started making her way toward him, weaving around pedestrians.

His stupid heart pounded in stupid elation. Hope was so damn dangerous.

She stopped beside the carriage, glancing up at him. In her golden eyes was the same guilt and worry he so often found there. He blamed her folks, but when perfection had been hammered into her throughout her entire life, it left a trail of hangups in its place. She overcompensated. She never let herself be true to her nature. She was always in the spotlight. It didn't matter how many times he or her besties tried to relieve her of that, it still clung.

"You mad at me?"

He'd like to go one day, one hour, without her slaying him. "No."

"Are you sure?"

"I'm sure. I didn't realize my text hadn't gone through. I sent it at one o'clock."

"Oh." Lip bite.

"I meant what I said. Thank you for last night and this morning."

"Never had anyone thank me for kissing them." She tilted her head. "Actually, yes. A few times a—"

"You know damn well what I meant." A sigh, and he glanced at the heavens. He'd thank her for the kiss, too, but there weren't words in the English language to properly illiterate that part. "It's a nice evening. Want a ride?"

She linked her fingers in front of her chest like a child begging for sweets. "My own private horse-drawn carriage ride?"

She had a knack for making him feel like an idiot. "Yes."

"My car's at the library."

"I'll drive you to pick it up tomorrow."

"You have a full day scheduled."

"And you have three more cars in your garage at home."

"But if I drive one of them, how will I get that car—"

"Scarlett." He narrowed his eyes on her, teeth grinding. "Get in the damn carriage."

She grinned as if the idea had been hers all along and she had talked him into it. The little minx.

He held out his hand, and she clasped it, setting her foot on the rung to hoist herself up. Stepping over him, she claimed the seat beside him.

"Can I drive?"

"Not a chance, babe." He snapped the reins, and the horses pivoted.

She pulled her phone out of her purse. "You're no fun."

Oh, he'd show her fun. The horizontal kind that left her unable to walk or mutter coherent sentences. But she had to make up her mind first, *and* let him in on that decision. Neither of which he thought she'd do.

She talked as she texted. "You called me 'babe' again."

"Are you going to point that out every time? I told you it was involuntary. How about 'brat'? I'll call you *brat* instead." He glanced at her screen, then ahead to make sure he didn't plow anyone over. "Who are you texting?"

"Our friends to let them know where we are, so they don't think we're dead in a ditch."

Considerate. "Doesn't that go against polite society to admit willingly associating with me?"

"I've never been embarrassed to be associated with you." She put her phone away. "Besides, I told them you kidnapped me."

"Of course, you did."

Grinning, she slouched in her seat and tilted her face toward the inky sky. Fingers laced over her abdomen, she let out a breath that bordered on a contented sigh.

They rode in silence up the hill toward Valantine Cemetery where the wide cobblestone streets changed over to brick-laid curves, and decorative trees switched to giant oaks. Some tombstones were large, baroque, and darkly weathered by time. Others were simple markers with flowers. Moonlight lit them in cerulean hues while Spanish moss clung to branches and swayed in the breeze. Some townsfolk called it black or long moss, but the very older generation, like Scarlett's late grandmother, referred to it as horsehair. Probably due to its resemblance. He supposed it did look like a grayish-green version of a horse mane.

Most tourists and a bunch of residents didn't know squat about it, other than it was pretty. Which was why he often gave a short science lesson about it on tours. Folks were usually surprised Spanish moss wasn't actually from Spain, nor was it moss. It's actually a bromeliad, a tiny flowering air plant that clung to itself as it dangled from tree limbs, gulping moisture or nutrients from the surrounding atmosphere and rain.

During daylight, the wispy hanging moss was reminiscent of romantic days gone by often found in movies. Or so Rebecca had told him once. Old south and its hidden gems. Sitting on the front porch drinking sweet tea and waving to passersby. Not a care in the world, except if it would rain. At night, the moss added a dreary, creepy sensation. Fingers crawling up the spine. Snarled dangling limbs that forever reached. A reminder that shadows hid dangers. It was a highlight in the tours they did for the month of October.

He went past the entrance to Scarlett's estate and around the corner to his driveway. Once they'd made it to the pasture fence, he hopped down and guided the horses beyond the gate.

"Want help?"

Smiling, he shook his head. "I got it, thanks. Stay put."

He disconnected the horses, removed their tack, and set them in their stalls with some words of encouragement and half an apple. Closing up, he shut the barn door behind him, and was this side of astounded Scarlett had listened to him. She was still in her seat in the carriage, staring out into the distance.

Climbing back into the carriage, he sat beside her, glancing in the same direction she appeared to be. The gardens. They were a sight up close, while walking through them, or staring overhead from her bedroom window, but after dark, they took on an ethereal quality that was both tranquil and eerie. The statues were imposing, seemingly watching, while blooms and vines danced in a breeze, all aglow from path lights. Shadows every-where. Miss Maureen had designed most of the space many years before, and Scarlett had made sure the upkeep was pristine in her grandmother's memory.

But he had a sinking suspicion that wasn't what she was thinking about. And it didn't truly matter what her decision wound up being with regards to him and her. They weren't going back. It would never be as it was before. They may, in time, get past it and create a semblance of a new normal. They'd still admire and respect one another, working together when needed. Yet, that closeness they shared, that innate ability to support without speaking or understand without voicing, to completely depend on with a trust which couldn't be bought or bartered, was gone.

He'd known all along it would happen.

"What do you want, Aden?" Her voice, so forgiving, so quiet, barely carried over to him from right beside her.

He considered being a smart ass, but nothing about the situation was funny. "It doesn't matter what I want."

Turning her head, she stared at him, but he kept his gaze ahead. "Why? Because I started it?"

Her mimicking his joke from last night was such a Scarlett move. Dodge, weave. Especially if she didn't know what to say. It didn't bode well for him. If she didn't know whether she wanted him or not after that kiss, then nothing would convince her. It hadn't even been his idea.

"I didn't start it, though, did I?"

What did she mean by that? He studied her profile, but her stoic expression indicated nothing.

Finally, after a heinous pause, she looked at him again. Her stoic gaze swept across his features as if she'd never seen him before. "You've thought about it long before I ever tried to kiss you."

Shit on a shingle. Had her besties said something? Had she caught on herself? Had he been obvious?

His brain scrambled to reply, but it wound up fried. Not sure what to do or say, he broke the intense connection and stared ahead. Mortification battled with penetrating desperation in his gut until his stomach lining ate itself.

"How long, Aden?"

He closed his eyes and wished for death. Anyone else, and he wouldn't care. But not with her. He couldn't do this with her. She was just starting to figure out her self-proclaimed knight in armor had rust.

"Well, Aden? How long?"

How long? Since kindergarten when she'd smacked Joey Smithfield in the forehead with a lollipop at recess because he'd made fun of Aden's grass-stained jeans. Since fifth grade when he struggled to find decent books he was actually interested in for English class and she'd brought him ten, all of which were still on his shelf as favorites. Since senior prom when she'd saved the last dance for him because his date wound up kissing the running back under the bleachers halfway through the event. Since last week when she'd defended him, yet again, to her mother.

There was no logical answer to her question other than to say, all along. That's how long. *All* along.

Jaw ticking, he said, "Long enough."

It would be swell if the ground opened up and swallowed him whole.

Just his luck, it would take her with him.

She turned in her seat, propping her arm on the back cushion, and his last act of bravery was to meet her gaze. It was a low blow, those eyes in the moonlight. There was no confusion, remorse, or pity in her stare, but she did seem to be picking him apart, atom by atom, without saying a word. It was hard to breathe with her in his orbit, especially with her studying him, and her scent was everywhere. Rich and intoxicating.

He wondered if this was it. The straw that broke the belle's back, her finding out he'd had feelings for her that predated their garden moment. Just in case, he drank in the sight of her. Her pretty oval face and high cheekbones. The arch of her brows, shades darker than her cocoa strands. Golden eyes framed by thick lashes. And those lips. They were a shade of red probably named sin. Her kiss was lethal, so it seemed apt. Not only her kiss, but her wit and sass and gumption.

Her brows furrowed the tiniest bit. "Just like Westley. They were right."

"Come again?" Now she was speaking Gaelic for all he understood of that comment.

She shook her head, a barely perceivable motion. "Just something the BFFs said earlier." She drew a deep breath and released it. "Have you always looked at me like that and I haven't noticed, or was it purposely done while I had my head turned so I wouldn't see."

"I'm not connecting the dots, darlin'." Someone help him, because it seemed awfully important to her, but he was lost.

"What were you waiting for?"

The way she phrased that question made it sound like upending everything and making a move on her was as easy as adding ice cream to warm apple pie. Plop. Done. *Tada.*

"You," he said through a sigh. She'd not once in all these years given any indication she saw him as anything but what he'd always been. Why would he say or do something in that case? It wasn't until her blaring revelation after consuming cocktails the other night that this was even a discussion on the table. Leaning forward, he rested his elbows on his knees and his face in his hands, rubbing his eyes. "You, babe."

"So, I ask again, because *it doesn't matter* isn't an appropriate reply. What do you want?"

"You know what I want."

"Say it out loud."

He straightened, glaring at her. Had he not been humiliated enough? Was this some ploy to bolster her confidence? She was gorgeous and smart and funny. She could have any suitor she desired with a flick of her finger. She'd had lovers aplenty. She had more money than half the county combined. She was a successful businesswoman. She had friends who would help her bury a body, no questions asked. Why, on God's green Earth, would she need validation from him? Him, of all people.

Know what? Whatever. "You, Scarlett. I want you. Not sure why we had to ram that home and spell it out, but I want you. Consider me a glutton for punishment."

One corner of her lips curved. "Feel better?"

"Nope."

"Changed your mind now that you've said it out loud?"

He gave her a side-eye. She needed an instruction manual.

"It's a legit question. Sometimes, we have this idea of things in our head, and they don't always translate onto paper. You might've thought you felt one way, but it turned out not to be the case. Or perhaps the feelings weren't there after we kissed and—"

He growled. Literally growled like an animal.

Rising, he turned and slapped his palms on the back of the seat on either side of her and bent close enough to count each one of her million eyelashes. "I have felt this way for a very long time. I didn't say anything because you didn't seem to be onboard and there were too many complications to risk it. I have not changed my mind. That kiss decimated me, thank you very much. You are what I want. Besides world peace and to build another pasture fence, you are *all* I want. Satisfied?"

Several thumps of her pulse beat against her neck. He wanted to kiss her there, but waited. He was getting pretty good at waiting.

"That was really sexy," she whispered, eyes round.

His lips flatlined. He narrowed his eyes. "What?"

"I'm serious. I mean, if you had pulled my hair at the end of that diatribe, I might've climbed you like a tree. Not accounting for the growl, that was seriously the sexiest thing anyone's ever said to me."

"Good God, Scarlett." He straightened to full height, arms crossed. Wait. Had she said... "Pull your hair?"

"Oh yeah."

He not only needed an instruction manual, but one not written in Chinese. And she still hadn't said what she wanted, aside from confusing the ever living hell out of him with statements of sexiness.

Her brows rose. "I made the move the first time, rejection notwithstanding. I kissed you the second time." She set her foot on the rail beside him. "Whatcha gonna do about it?"

Taunting. She was taunting him? He had ten years of pent up frustration and desire splitting his seams.

"Is that what you want, babe?" He wasn't going to mince words. He was a southern gentleman at heart, and she wasn't some romp in the hay for release. He needed her unequivocal consent to fully cross the friendship line because she was correct. She'd made the last two chess moves. If she agreed, then fine. They'd tiptoed around long enough.

"I want you."

Enough said. And mercy, he never thought he'd ever hear those words.

Bending, he wedged his hands under her thighs and lifted her. She let out the cutest squeak of surprise. He turned and plopped on the seat, setting her in his lap. Then, he wrapped the strands of her ponytail around his hand and gently tugged her head back so he could look her in the eyes. She gasped, and he almost came undone.

Through hooded eyes, she stared at him, lips parted and breathing irregular.

"Like that, babe?"

"*Yesss,*" she hissed.

"Say it again." He was astutely aware of every inch of her in direct contact with nearly every inch of him. He leaned in, brushing his nose against hers, their lips a whisper apart. *Please, tell me again you want me.*

A devilish grin had her lips caressing his. "It again."

Well, she wouldn't be Scarlett if she made it easy.

He sealed his lips to hers, and just like last night, they fit. It hadn't been a fluke. It was like combustion in a mason jar. Explosive.

His heart thundered in his chest and his skin heated. She was so soft. So warm. So responsive. He kissed her top lip, then the bottom, slowly and with meticulousness. She opened for him, stroking his tongue until there was no air left. His fist tightened around her ponytail, and he slid his other hand from her side to her back, pressing her closer. It would never be close enough after this. She tasted like vanilla ice cream and smelled like the exotic perfume she often wore. Sultry. Hints of floral.

She cupped his face like he was a treasure to cherish, to behold, and the sentiment tightened his throat. Her fingertips lightly played with the hair on his nape, sending shivers of awareness and need to his entire nervous system. Her kiss matched her personality. Bolsterous and gentle. Descriptive and open. Possessive and giving. All contradictions if one didn't know her as well as him.

Rising on her knees, she angled his head back, assumingly to take more control, and the moment turned from hot to scalding. He broke away, needing air, and latched onto her throat, right over her pulse pounding hard. Head back, she moaned, her fingers clenching his strands as if worried he'd stop. Her breathy sounds were a direct current to behind his zipper, and the ache was profound.

Lower, he kissed, across her collarbone and to the swell of her breasts. But then she arched, rubbing her good parts against his through their clothes, and he pressed his face against her scented skin to gain clarity.

It wasn't working. Muscle locked around bone, and he shook with need. Fervent, desperate need.

"What the hell took us so long?" she breathed, eyes pinched shut, red lips swollen.

That did it. Her words snapped a semblance of lucidity. He'd waited years to have her, not sure if he ever would. Every molecule in his body screamed to take her, to finally obtain what he always desired. But no. Not like this, in his carriage, in the middle of a pasture, a solitary day after she realized she might have romantic feelings for him. She deserved better than this, and he wasn't going to screw this up.

He rested his chin on her shoulder, face buried in the hair behind her ear, and struggled for oxygen. "Go on a date with me."

She resettled on his lap and kissed his forehead. The act nearly undid him, and his already tight throat formed a lump. It was a caring, protective gesture no one had ever done for him. It meant she gave a damn.

A smile, and she opened her eyes. "A date, huh?"

He brushed a loose strand of hair from her cheek. "Yup."

"Haven't been on one of those in a while." Her smile never faltered, but she had the slightest twinge of nervousness in her eyes.

Like a smack upside the noggin,' he realized the levity in not only what she said, but his words, as well. She had lovers. Quite a few. They came and went as she saw fit, but only under the safety of her private kingdom where no one else could see. Dating meant the public. Public meant talk and rumors. She wouldn't risk that for just anyone unless she was thinking of something more serious than sex.

Would she be embarrassed to be seen with him for anything other than friendship?

"What did you have in mind?" She climbed off his lap and sat beside him, taking his hand in hers. "Like dinner and a movie?"

They'd have to go into Savannah for the movie part. Theatres made horrible date venues because you couldn't talk to the other person. Would they need to talk? They already knew intimate details of one another. Flustered, he tried to conjure something appropriate and couldn't. She wasn't just anyone, either.

She made an indescribable noise in the back of her throat. "Second guessing?"

"No." He squeezed her hand. "Just thinking." There was plenty to do in Vallantine, after all. "What about a riverboat dinner cruise?" He hadn't been on one in all the years he lived here.

"That would be fun. You're on. Friday night?"

"Yeah. I'll book tickets." That meant staying in Vallantine for their date. "Are you sure?"

"Yes." She offered him an expression that indicated he may have hit his head one too many times in his youth. "Why?"

"People will see."

She reared. "Embarrassed by me?"

Other way around. "It won't be speculation after Friday. The whole town will know and talk." Including her folks.

A shrug, and she rested her head on his shoulder. "Let 'em talk."

That was exactly what he was worried about.

Chapter Eleven

"I can't believe you're going on a date with Aden Abner." Rebecca sat next to Dorothy on the settee in Scarlett's bedroom and petted Cotton, who soaked up the attention with loud meows and purring. "I mean, it's like the sky is falling."

Scarlett laughed, shifting hangers in her closet to find an outfit. "Dang it, y'all. He's seen my whole wardrobe."

"Pretty sure he'd rather see you out of it." Dorothy grinned. Rebecca high-fived her.

"Funny." Scarlett set her hands on her hips in the doorway. "I should've bought something."

"Girl," Rebecca drawled. "That man doesn't care what you look like or what you wear."

"Yeah, I know. It's just..."

"Just what?" Dorothy took a sip from her water bottle.

Geez. It was Aden, for crying out loud. Scarlett hadn't been on a date in ages, and what he'd said a few nights ago kept sticking in her craw. The people of Vallantine would gossip about this for at least the next week, if not the whole month. Opinions would be tossed around like the spin cycle. Mama would get worked up and make Scarlett's life a living hell. Focusing on clothing options seemed a better use for her anxiety. There was so much pressure on her, she couldn't breathe.

"What if he doesn't like me?" Eyes hot and sinuses stinging, she sat on the edge of her bed. "What if, after all this time, he realizes his feelings were wrong and he actually doesn't like me? Then we blew up the whole friendship for nothing." It had been a very real concern ever since he'd asked her on a date a few nights ago.

"Oh! No, no, no." Rebecca rose and moved to the bed to sit beside her. "Ain't no way that's going to happen. If he didn't like you, he wouldn't have stuck around this long. Besides, who doesn't like our Scarlett?"

Sniffing, Scarlett set her head on Rebecca's shoulder. "Thanks."

"She's right." Dorothy took over the petting of Cotton, setting her water bottle aside. "He waited this long for you. He's sure. There's no one on Earth better equipped to handle you than Aden. I'm kind of surprised it wasn't something we thought about or addressed before now."

Her bestie had a point. "Thanks, guys."

Dorothy sighed, avoiding eye contact and running her fingers through her auburn strands. "Honestly, I'm jealous of you two right now."

They stared at her, but neither Scarlett nor Rebecca seemed to know what to say.

"I haven't had a serious relationship since college. Everyone who we went to high school with sees me as good ole Dorothy. You know, the tubby girl they once passed in the halls who was good at math, but they couldn't remember afterward."

Scarlett's temples pounded. "You are more memorable than for your skills at math, and you're not fat. Knock it off."

"Maybe not now, but I was back then."

Rebecca shook her head. "I never saw you that way, and if anyone else did, that's on them. You weren't fat. You were definitely curvier, but never overweight."

"I agree," Scarlett added.

Dorothy shrugged, her features melancholy with heavy lids and her lips downturned. "Regardless, I always figured I'd be married by now with a kid on the way." She huffed a laugh devoid of humor. "I can't even get a date to save my life."

Scarlett had no clue her friend had felt this way. She was smart and pretty and loyal. Who wouldn't want someone like her to settle down with and start a family? Scarlett and Rebecca had always had high career aspirations. If a guy fell into that, then okay. But all Dorothy ever wanted was the white picket fence, kids running around, a man who loved her, and a dog or two in the yard.

"Maybe we should start setting you up on some blind dates." Rebecca rolled her head to stretch her neck. "It can't hurt."

"No. God, no. But thanks. I just need to shift my goals to something more realistic."

"Love should always be a reality." Scarlett chewed her lip. "You could adopt or try insemination."

"I don't know." Dorothy waved her hand as if the topic could be wiped away. "Enough about me. I'm so happy Rebecca found Graham, because he's amazing, and that you and Aden are starting a romance. You both deserve it."

"You'll get everything you want, Dorothy." Scarlett smiled, hoping to reassure her. "I swear, you will."

And if Rebecca and Scarlett had to intervene, they would. Plenty of people transferred to Vallantine for work or the quiet life who hadn't known Dorothy a long time or saw her as she did herself. Scarlett would talk to Rebecca later about it.

A sigh, and she rose from the bed to retreat to her closet. Her friends were right. Aden didn't care what she wore. She was the one getting worked up over how the town and her family would react to their date. She shouldn't care, but the Taylor name had forever been a staple in Vallantine, and proper appearances had been drilled into her since birth. Perhaps one day she'd break free from the restraints, but tonight wasn't that day.

Grabbing a cobalt blue wrap dress, she stepped into it and tied the fittings. As a V-neck and knee-length, it would accentuate her breasts and her legs. The dress was casual enough to not go overboard with formalities. She pulled a pair of matching sandals from the shelf and stepped into them.

"How's this?" She walked out of the closet.

"Sexy." Rebecca waggled her brows.

"I was going to say pretty, but sexy works, too." Dorothy smiled, but it didn't reach her eyes. "You look wonderful."

"Thanks, guys." She blew out a nervous breath. "There's gonna be talk tomorrow."

"And the day after that." Rebecca shrugged. "Who cares?"

Scarlett's mother, that's who. She'd deal with it later, but wondered if she should give Daddy a heads up. Deciding yes, she went to her nightstand and picked up her cell, texting him.

Just wanted you to know I'm going on a date with Aden tonight. You might want to hide from Mother. I'll tell you more later.

Dropping her phone in her purse, she glanced at her friends. "Any touchups needed?" She'd left her hair down and had used her favorite gray shimmering eyeshadow with a darker plum lipstick shade.

Both shook their heads and stood up. They headed down the grand staircase, where she said bye to her besties.

Father texted his thanks for the warning, but agreed they *would* talk later. Yippee, he was mad at her already, and she hadn't even left the house yet. Her stomach grew queasy again.

Deciding to wait for Aden on the porch, she snatched what she needed, stepped outside, and locked the door. She claimed one of the wooden white rocking chairs and set it in motion with her feet.

She should come out here more often. Miss Maureen had loved lounging on the porch, rocking away, watching the world around her with a glass of mint julip and a smile. They'd chat about the latest gossip, who was doing what to whom and why. She'd crack a dry joke in her heavy twang, and Scarlett would laugh until her side ached.

How she missed her grandmother. Sometimes, the pang of grief came out of nowhere, and it hurt just as much as the day they'd buried her. She'd had a lot of support in her life, from Aden to her besties to townsfolk, but Miss Maureen had been the matriarch, and that carried weight. Her opinion mattered to Scarlett more than she'd realized. She wondered if her grandmother would be proud of the woman she'd become, if she would approve of a relationship with Aden, and if she'd liked the changes Scarlett had made to the estate.

Windchimes sounded from the other end of the porch, and a warm breeze caressed her skin. She rested the back of her head on the chair. It was a pleasant evening. Some of the humidity had faded, but the air was still saturated with summer heat.

The porch ran the full length of the house, perfectly even on both sides with the front door centered. High ceilings had outdoor fans in a leaf shape spinning slowly to circulate air. They weren't doing much, though. A hanging swing on the other end hadn't been used in ages, either, but her staff did a wonderful job about changing out the cushions and making sure the potters got watered. The railings had hanging boxes with petunias and begonias. Above them hung the customary potted ferns. The windchimes had been her personal touch. The melodic sound was soothing.

Beyond the porch, mature crepe myrtles and weeping willows stirred with the breeze. The long, winding brick-laid driveway to her left was lined on both sides with hundred year old oaks. Gnarled, knotted branches made it appear as if they were hugging the path toward the mansion. The circular drive was properly centered with the covered porch, a giant fountain in the middle. Besides the chimes, trickling water from the fountain were the only sounds filling the quiet night. Fireflies danced and stars winked overhead.

Wondering where Aden was, she checked her watch. She hadn't realized it was still early. He wasn't due for another fifteen minutes. Guess she'd been overeager. Then again, like her father always said, *better to be ten minutes early than one minute late.* She was usually late.

Tires crunched in the distance, and she smiled. Aden had taken the phrase to heart. A moment later, headlights cut through the trees along the driveway and his black pickup truck emerged.

She rose from her seat, purse in hand, as he lumbered out of the vehicle. Just like Aden, when he wanted and in his own sweet time. He had on a pair of dark gray slacks she'd never seen on him and a white button down dress shirt rolled up to the elbows. He'd shaved, too, which was a pity. She really liked his perpetual five o'clock shadow. Dark, sandy blond hair stirred in the breeze as he glanced up at her.

She smiled. "You look nice."

In the most aw-shucks move she'd seen to date, he rubbed the back of his neck and sheepishly grinned. "Pretty sure that's supposed to be my line." Climbing the porch steps, he gave her a once-over. "You don't look nice, though. You're beautiful."

"Aww." Well, dang. Her cheeks heated. "Thank you." If he kept this up, there would be no need to get used to their new dynamic. She was already swooning.

He kissed her cheek, and his familiar scent of the outdoors soothed some of her nervousness. It was Aden.

Aden was safe.

Aden always had her back.

Aden would never let anything happen to her.

"Ready?" He held out his hand, and she took it.

They rode to the edge of town toward the riverfront, chatting about the craziness of the Peach Festival and how both were glad it was over tonight. She'd had more than two hundred visitors for tours of the estate, and he hadn't had a moment to breathe because they'd added a third rotation for carriage rides. She felt like she hadn't seen him in weeks when it had only been a few days.

He parked in the gravel lot reserved for the cruises, consisting of crushed clam and seashells. Two large white ships waited, bobbing in the shallow water, their lights a bright yellowish glow against a navy sky littered with stars. One ship was used for dinner and daytime tours, and was two stories tall. The other catered more to nightlife with dancing and cocktails, often booked for weddings or events, and was three levels.

The scent of freshwater and fish rose as they made their way up the dock to wait in line to board. People chatted excitedly. Most seemed like tourists, dressed in t-shirts and shorts. She didn't recognize anyone from town, but she didn't necessarily know everyone, either. A warm breeze wrapped around her to beat off some of the humidity as fireflies blinked in the long grass by shore.

Once onboard, they walked around the lower level, consisting of a gift shop, café, and bar. She'd never thought to do one of the riverboat cruises before, and figured it might make for a great girls' night out later. Perhaps in the fall.

They worked their way upstairs and to a table for two by the window. White tablecloths with lanterns and cloth napkins with silverware were already set up. String lights hung from the ceiling in a cross pattern while decorative nets and anchors hung on the walls. Lots of polished wood and rustic décor. It was nice.

Definitely not what she was used to, and there was absolutely nothing wrong with that.

"It's so beautiful out here." She set her elbow on the table and chin in her hand. "I sometimes forget the Ogeechee River is so close by."

"I don't know what made me think of it, but I'm glad I did."

"Me, too."

A waiter arrived dressed in black slacks and a white shirt with a bowtie. He delivered ice water and asked if they wanted drinks. They ordered colas instead of wine because she didn't want the alcohol going to her head. The boat began moving, so they checked the menu, noting an array of steak and seafood. Ultimately, she settled on grilled shrimp with angel hair pasta and broccoli. Aden got a sirloin with roasted potatoes and collards.

"Heard you gave the staff all of next week off."

She took a sip of her water. "I did. They deserve it. Between the tours and unexpected guests from the magazine, things were cray-cray this week. I'll need them the week after next for upcoming events. It was as good a time as any."

He nodded, admiration in his eyes and in the twist of his lips. "You're a good boss."

"Thank you, but I'm betting you did the same."

His grin decimated her entire existence into shambles. "I did."

Fanning herself seemed obvious, so she cleared her throat and looked away.

"Never known you to blush, babe." Amped grin still in place, he brushed a finger across her cheek.

"Yeah, well. Your smile could level kingdoms. I'm convinced men like you are the reason chastity belts were a thing."

He threw his head back and laughed. "I shall accept your complement and offer you one. Your eyes could make a grown man genuflect."

Jaw dropped, she stared at him, her heart pit-pattering. "Dang, Aden."

His shrug was all, *eh, truth is truth*. "Off topic, how did it go with the magazine people? Gunner was stupid happy about them coming. I kept spotting him around town, showing them this or that. I felt bad for 'em."

Ah, yes. Their good ole mayor. He'd dropped by the mansion a couple times or twenty.

"They were really nice, and appeared happy with their stay. The photographer, Mark, didn't say much, but he now worships at the altar of George. Hand to God, I think he tried levying every recipe my cook has in his arsenal."

Aden tipped his cola and took a swig. "The man is a damn fine chef."

"Word." She leaned back in her seat. "Did they come talk to you? The reporter was asking about the rides. I gave her your brochure."

"Abigail, yes." He shook his head. "A thousand questions. She held us up on day two, but I think she got what she came for." He rubbed his lips like he often did in thought. "She asked when we were getting married."

"Oh, really."

"She assumed we were a thing."

"We are now." She smiled, hoping to ease his mind.

He nodded, but said nothing more.

Sensing his concerns, she crossed her arms on the table and leaned forward. "Terms. We are exclusive to each other. No more itch-to-be-scratched passing lovers. Just you and me until one of us wants to stop. We keep the friendship exactly as its always been and stay honest with one another. And since we're on a date in public, we're out of the closet, per se."

He stared at her for the longest breadth of time. "That what you want?"

"No, I just made it up. I have another date later. In fact," she checked her watch, "I have to be home in an hour."

His expression remained unchanged. "Is that so?"

She sighed. "Yes, that's what I want. No, I don't have another date."

Nodding, he glanced out the window.

Before she could retort, someone called her name. Turning, she spotted Ginny from Bark & Beyond pet supplies coming their way from across an aisle, dressed in jeans and a frilly purple top. Behind her was her husband, looking like he wanted to be anywhere else.

And so it begins...

Rising, she hugged the older woman, catching a strong whiff of patchouli and dog fur. "I'm tickled to see you." No, she wasn't.

"You, as well. We're having an anniversary dinner. We haven't had a date in ages."

The husband, whose name Scarlett couldn't recall, rocked on his heels.

"Happy anniversary! That's amazing. Congratulations!"

"Thank you, thank you." Ginny glanced between Aden and Scarlett. "Are you two—" she dropped her tone to a conspiratorial whisper "—on a date?"

"We absolutely are. I was just telling my Aden that we needed a change of pace. Here we are."

Ginny seemed unconvinced. "I was unaware you were an item. I'm sure I would've heard."

"Oh." Scarlett swiped her hand through the air. "Old news. You look pretty as a peach. Where did you get that darling blouse?"

After a few more diversions, Ginny and her husband reclaimed their seats on the other side of the dining room.

Aden had his head down, pinching the bridge of his nose, when Scarlett sat across from him.

"You're a modern marvel." Laughing, he lifted his head. "Imagine my surprise. It's amazing how long we've been together. Complete news to me. I'm flabbergasted."

The smartass. "It worked, didn't it?" She set her napkin in her lap. "She now believes we've been in a relationship longer than we actually have been, and thus, probably won't make a huge deal about it when talking to others."

He let out a long breath. "It's going to get out. Word is going to spread, darlin'."

Dinner arrived before she could retort, and it was delicious. Afterward, they left the dining hall and went upstairs to the open upper deck, claiming a bench up front.

Other diners mingled about, but it was quiet. Peaceful. A gentle sway from the slow-chugging boat was hypnotic and relaxing. To their left was the shore and glimpses of Vallantine. To the right was a narrow channel of water with cattails, high grass, and water lilies. The riverboat had already turned while they'd eaten and was heading back to dock.

Stars winked in the navy sky, too many for counting, as they sat in contented silence. Aden had never been the type of man to fill the quiet with unnecessary words for the sake of chatter. He had a tendency to say so much without talking. It made her appreciate him more, and she was grateful this part of their dynamic hadn't changed.

Scooting closer, she lifted his arm and brought it around her, then set her head on his shoulder. "I don't care who knows or how much they gossip about us."

He pressed his lips to the top of her head, lingering. "I only care about you."

Merciful heavens, this man. She'd known him her whole life, but had never witnessed this side of him.

Tilting her head to stare at him, she took in his features as if it were for the first time. She supposed this was a new Aden to her, anyway. His eyes were still a charismatic shade of blue, his face was still angular with sharp cheekbones and a wide jaw, and his hair was still a perpetual state of chaos with a barely finger-combed style. But he had a faint scar on his upper lip she'd not noticed before and he had the widest shoulders. Enough to block out the world if she needed them to, and he would if she asked. There was safety and security in his embrace she'd distinctly been lacking. Funny how she hadn't realized that.

"What's wrong?" His gaze darted between hers, his hand cupping her jaw. He caressed her cheek with his thumb, back and forth.

"Nothing. Just relaxed."

"If you're sure." He gazed at her a beat more. "I was going to wait until I walked you to your front door to do this, but..."

He closed the fractional distance between them, sealing his lips to hers. Their first kiss had been tentative, then ramping with interest. Their second had been hot and heavy. This one? Oh, boy. This one was tender, evoking both control and emotion that grabbed her by the trachea. Firm lips and deft experience proved he not only paid attention to detail, but cared how the product was presented. She felt it in every body part from her hairline to her toenails—a welcoming heat, an unparalleled ache, and the distinct sensation she was truly connecting to someone on a molecular level.

Want for want.

Need for need.

Anticipation for anticipation.

His arm closed tightly around her, cinching her closer, and he turned his head to press his lips to her ear. "I wish we were at home."

Her, too. "Yours or mine," she teased.

"I don't care. It could be the barn, for all the shits I don't give."

Laughing, she buried her face in the crook of his neck. He smelled so good.

He held her like that until the riverboat redocked and passengers began deboarding.

"Come on, darlin,' before your carriage turns into a pumpkin."

Cute.

Fingers entwined, they walked down the pier and toward the car.

She squeezed his hand. "That was fun. Thank you."

"You're very welcome. The food was better than I thought it would be."

"It was. I—"

Spinning her around, he backed her to the side of his truck and full-body pressed her against it. He held the back of her head with one hand, the other on her waist. Five distinct fingertips imprinted on her hip, and her girly bits got tingly. Holy bejezus, he had moves.

"This isn't first date behavior. You'll have to forgive me, babe." He kissed his way along her jaw, across her cheek, and stopped at the tip of her nose. "You are irresistible."

Aww.

A groan, and he shoved off, opening the passenger door. "In you go."

She climbed in and buckled her seatbelt, thinking she might need a metaphorical restraint for their newfound relationship. Or an ice water bath.

He got in the driver's side and cranked the engine, but instead of shifting gears and pulling away, he rested his arms on the wheel, hanging his head.

She wondered what was wrong, but he just seemed to be gathering his thoughts. Nothing in his posture indicated he was upset.

Without moving a muscle, he muttered, "We're not jumpin' in the sack tonight. Not on our first date. I sincerely want to take our time and not rush things. So, I mean this with the utmost amount of chivalry. Your house or mine?"

Rolling her lips over her teeth, she tried and failed to hide a smile.

Head still lowered, he turned it far enough to glance at her out of the corner of his eye. "Don't look at me like that."

A laugh bubbled from her throat. "Like what?"

"Like you're gonna do whatever you want, and damned what I think."

"Well, sure. That's a given." She batted her eyelashes.

Another groan.

"How about your house to pick up the dog, then we'll go to mine? I will present myself in a very ladylike fashion and behave."

His shoulders shook with a laugh. Slowly at first, but it gained velocity.

"Ah, man. That'll be the day." He glared at the roof of the truck. "You're such a liar. Alright." He shifted into gear. "Your place it is."

Chapter Twelve

A den woke with his face in Scarlett's hair and the cat on his feet. Color him surprised, but she'd behaved herself once they'd gotten back to the mansion, just as she'd promised. They'd watched a movie in her room and had fallen asleep, him in boxers and a tee, her in…what she called pajamas.

Though it was early, he'd slept pretty much the whole night. He'd like to thank her for the cure, but she was only a part of the puzzle. Ever since they'd crossed the proverbial friendship bridge into the uncharted territory of a romantic relationship, his mind had settled down. Mostly. She still drove him batshit, yet she was also a balm to his soul. Always had been. Having her near settled him in ways it shouldn't, considering the vast differences in their personalities.

He needed to get up and feed the horses since his staff was off. Dufus needed to be fed and let out, too. Rolling, he glanced over his shoulder. The dog was asleep on the settee in the corner.

A check of the clock on Scarlett's nightstand showed it was only five-thirty. He could probably go feed the horses and be back before she got up.

Carefully, he slipped from bed and padded into the bathroom to relieve himself, then sent her a text that he'd be back, in case she did wake up first. He got dressed the rest of the way and whispered for the dog. Downstairs, he turned off the alarm and stepped onto her porch.

On his way across the yard, he reset the alarm on his mobile app and took a deep breath. The sun was making its way past the horizon, casting golden light across the lawn and reflecting in the dewdrops. Everything was still. Quiet. Hushed. He wasn't much of a morning person, but he did cherish this time of day. No one to cater to or demand things from him. No customers to entertain. Just him, his dog, and the land.

Keying his way into the house, he fed Dufus and started coffee, then headed to his bedroom to change into work clothes. Coffee in hand and Dufus on his heels, he went back out and opened the barn doors.

Eclipse, one of his black male Percherons, was always the first to greet him with a loud whinny. Smiling, Aden strode to the stall door and ran a hand over his muzzle.

"One sec, and you can eat."

He greeted the other three—Obsidian, the other black male Percheron, then Honey and Caramel, the brown female Hackneys—and went to the tack room.

Once they'd all been fed and sent out to pasture with fresh water, he mucked the stalls and closed the barn doors. He'd made good time, as it was only seven, so he had a swift shower before throwing on clean jeans and a tee.

Frankly, he was pretty pleased to be out of the dress clothes he'd worn for dinner last night. Knowing Scarlett was going to be dressed to the nines, he'd figured he should, as well. Hanging around town or her place was one thing, but out on their first date was another.

It made him wonder if different expectations would be put on him now that they were dating. They were in a completely different social class, and he just didn't fit into that mold. She never left the house in anything but outfits that probably cost more than a month's worth of horse feed.

Doubt began to niggle through his mood, and he shook his head to clear it. She'd said yes. After knowing him, everything from personality to extra curriculars, she'd said yes to him. It was finally time to see where that led.

Dufus in tow, he made his way back to her place. Humidity was already clinging and there wasn't a breeze to be had. The trees were still with stagnant, heavy air.

Perfect day to stay inside. Her staff were off, and she didn't have an event until next weekend. Far as he knew, she didn't have any appointments this weekend, either.

Using his mobile app to turn off her alarm, he reentered and coded it again. If there was any doubt about the differences in their circumstances, the Taylor estate would set that to rights. The foyer was larger than his entire house. The chandelier cost more than a year of his earnings.

He'd been in this mansion more times than he had strands of hair on his head, but he'd never been truly comfortable here until after Miss Maureen had passed. She'd been kind and welcoming, but it had still been her place. He was the landscaper's kid. It was part of the reason he'd climbed up the rose trellis to hang out with Scarlett in her room as a boy. Hell, as a teenager and young man, too. Once Miss Maureen had died and a business arrangement had formed with Scarlett, it made more sense to use the door.

Trellis or door, friend or boyfriend, it still felt awkward, him being allowed here.

He glanced at Dufus. "We're going to be quiet." He petted soft black fur, giving an ear scratch for good measure.

Gentle brown eyes stared up at him in response. His forever companion.

"You're a good boy. Come on."

Tail wagging, Dufus followed him up the grand staircase and into Scarlett's bedroom. She was still asleep, exactly as he'd left her. Cotton had moved to the settee, where Dufus jumped up and laid down beside the cat.

Scarlett was not a morning person in the slightest, so waking her might be fun. Or deadly. He weighed his options, deciding to slip into bed and try his luck.

Toeing off his shoes, he stripped down to his boxers and t-shirt, then climbed under the duvet. She drew in a breath, rolled over, and never opened her eyes. Light snoring followed.

Grinning, he watched her while she slept. His little spitfire. Her sleek cocoa locks looked more like chestnut in the early sun streaming through her balcony doors. Dust motes clung to the rays directed at her. She had a flawless quality to her skin with warm undertones. Pouty pink lips. Arched brows. Oval face. She definitely had O'Hara characteristics, so her folks had done something right when they'd named her after the fictional character. Forest had said once that she looked like she'd been Photoshopped. Fitting. But she stole his oxygen like this. Sans makeup and without the weight of obligations.

He could do this every morning and never grow weary of watching her.

Thinking he'd catch more shut-eye, too, he slid closer and draped his arm around her slender waist. How many years had he wondered if he'd ever get to hold her? It didn't feel real. Or, better yet, like it could all be stolen from him. Tucking her head under his chin, he closed his eyes, lulled by her even breathing and the lingering scent of her perfume.

When he next stirred, the scent of mint hit his nostrils and fingers were stroking his chest. Soft brushes of...lips? Yes, lips were caressing his throat.

An inhale, and he opened his eyes. Honey-soaked eyes framed by thick black lashes stared back at him.

"Good morning." Her voice was like a smooth single malt.

More neck nuzzling, and other parts of him started to awaken. "Yes, it is."

She smiled against his throat. "I see you fed the horses and the dog."

"MmmHmm." She needed to quit touching him sometime in the realm of never. His muscles tightened in response to her limited exploration while his brain tried to scale back. He was only a mere mortal.

"So, you don't have anywhere to be?"

"Nope." He fisted the back of the silky blue garment she called a nightie, trying to restrain himself from going caveman.

Nuzzle, nuzzle. "And I don't have anywhere to be."

"That would be correct." Breathing was becoming a strain.

"Our date was last night."

Confused, he angled his head to meet her eyes. "We were both there, yes."

"Which means, this is a new day."

More riddles he couldn't solve. "Uh huh."

"Thus, this would be date number two."

He couldn't think straight. "I guess."

Sweet mercy, she swirled her tongue over the sensitive spot between his neck and shoulder, and he about climbed out of his skin. His pulse jacked to dangerous speed. He groaned, long and loud.

Lifting her head, she looked at him, the devil himself curving her lips. "Which means I no longer need to behave myself."

Last night's conversation in the truck after the riverboat cruise slammed into him with the force of a rocket booster. Oh shit. Were they doing this? Were they actually going to go there?

"Scarlett..." His tone grated like sandpaper.

Her hand trailed down his chest to the waistband of his boxers. "Aden."

That was it. He could only withstand so much.

He rolled, tucking her under him, and stretched out, aligning all their parts in glorious harmony. Lacing their fingers, he brought their arms up over her head to rest on the mattress, pinning her in place.

"Be sure, babe." He stared into her eyes, restraint a thin tether. "Be sure," he repeated for both their sakes. Admitting attraction, kissing, going on a public date? Baby steps compared to what came next. Sex would be the end all. He'd loved her for his entire life, and feared he'd plummet to the bottom of hearts-and-arrows afterward.

In her eyes was the same concern that had a chokehold on him. Understanding, coupled with anxiety and bravery, stared back at him. Her gaze swept over his face as if she were trying to figure out how they got here. He didn't know the answer, but he couldn't make himself be sorry.

"Yes." A shaky exhale escaped her lips. "Yes, Aden."

Ah, the way she said his name. Tender. Breathy. It wove around his windpipe and slithered to his chest, squeezing the resolve right out of him.

Bending his head, he lowered his lips to hers. She opened immediately, trusting him. It was something he'd never take for granted. She tasted like the mint he'd smelled when waking and met his strokes with her own. Slow, drugging, their tongues mated. Every fiber in his being connected with her in that moment. A fact he was only aware of because he'd assumed that had always been the case. But no. This was new. Different. Deeper.

Inching his way lower, he caressed the shell of her ear, kissed her neck, brushed his lips across her collarbone. So supple, her skin. She arched, wiggling her hands for freedom. He obliged, and she threaded her fingers in his hair, clenching the strands. A shiver of approval raised the fine hairs on his nape. He never realized how much of a turn-on that could be. Lower, he moved, until he found her full, perfect breasts behind the lace of her nightie. He slid the material down, exposing dark rosy nipples.

She writhed under him, but he kept the pace as he saw fit. He was going to take his time, hold her on the precipice of forever, and cherish her.

Sucking a peak between his tongue and the roof of his mouth, he circled her other nipple with his thumb. A strangled cry emitted from her, and he smiled. He switched to the other nipple and repeated the motions, determined to draw out her pleasure. The anticipation was killing him. Nudging the thin straps of her nightgown off her shoulders, he kissed his way to her navel, taking the garment with him. She threw her head back, breathing heavily, skin flushed. She smelled divine—after hints of roses and something sultry. He situated himself between her thighs, working the nightie to her ankles.

And, mercy, all she'd had on underneath was a thin band of panties that covered virtually nothing. He made quick work of those, too, and groaned. She only had a strip of dark curls on her mound, and the rest of her was bare. He glanced up at her, and found her watching him with hooded lids. Her pupils had all but swallowed her irises, and she bit her lip. Nothing in his warped imagination had prepared him for this. For her. She was utterly breathtaking.

For the moment, she was his. Finally.

He lay on his stomach, the sheets cool against his hot skin. His erection pressed into the mattress, but the pressure did little to alleviate his errant need to take her. It was never-ending, his desire for her.

Spreading her folds, he licked at path around her opening to her nub, and she arched off the mattress, head thrown, hair fanned out on her pillow. It was the most beautiful thing he'd ever laid eyes on. His little belle, a raging wildfire in his arms. His heart shifted ribs with a staccato beat. He repeated the motion, and she gasped. Again, and he earned a thready, needy moan.

Skin hot, muscles tight, hair on-end, he licked and sucked and teased her until she was trembling on the precipice with her pillow in her fists. Then he paused, she whimpered, and he started her all over again. Leading her to release, only to yank it back before she could tumble, extending her yearning and drilling holes in his restraint.

Again and again. Over and over until *he* could take no more.

Kneeling, he flipped her over, and up went her hips in a silent demand for more. He wouldn't just give her more. He'd give everything. All he owned, desired, and would ever accumulate. It was all hers. He didn't have riches or a trust fund, but he could give this—time, dedication, and pleasure.

Running his hands up the backs of her thighs, over her round backside, he drank in her warm skin tone, her response to his touch, and was about at his breaking point. He kissed and nipped his way up her spine to her neck, shifted himself between her legs, and swept her hair aside. Aligned perfectly, in full contact once more, he settled over her, propping on one arm to bear his weight.

It was too much and not enough. What had started as an ache had become a throbbing.

He brought his lips to her ear, sucking on her lobe. "Say my name, babe."

Maybe it was his leftover anxiety or utter disbelief at the moment, but he had an extreme need for her to reiterate that she knew it was him with her. Not another lover. Not a quick release. Not a plaything. But him, the guy who'd been here all along, waiting. For her. He half expected her to taunt him, but she didn't.

"Aden." She turned her head, offering her profile, eyes closed and lips parted. "Aden, please."

He unraveled. Her begging him with his name from her mouth unraveled him, one frayed string at a time.

A wedge in his throat, he adjusted himself, and from behind, he slowly, meticulously entered her.

If it were possible, he would've choked on his tongue.

Hot, firm, her body welcomed him. He couldn't remember how to breathe, but she moaned, and he felt the vibrations every damn where. To give himself a second, or to bring her closer yet, he slid an arm between her and the sheets, cradling her to him, and it gave him a better angle.

By God, he had Scarlett Taylor in his arms, was making love to her on a lazy Saturday morning after waking up beside her.

In sensory overload, he thrust.

Stars. Literal stars danced behind his lids.

Bringing her arm up, she reached behind her to hold the back of his neck. The position arched her spine and pulled him deeper.

Opening his mouth over her shoulder, he repeated the motion, and her hips jerked to meet his thrusts. It was a dance, one they'd not rehearsed, yet it was fluid and beautifully orchestrated. There was no awkward first pairing or wondering what the other needed. It was as if all the years they'd spent as friends had prepared them to anticipate what the other desired or wanted.

She felt so damn good. There were no words. Cradling him, even in such an intimate act, she felt so damn good wrapped around him.

Burying his face in her neck, he rolled his hips, and she trembled. A moment later, her entire body locked, and she quaked under him. Keeping the motion, lest she lose her vibe, he sucked on that sweet spot behind her ear. Her walls gripped him in a vice that had his eyes watering. She emitted the sexiest moan, a gasp, and then she relaxed.

Oh, she wasn't done yet, as she was about to learn. He would make her come again, but this time, he wanted to watch her fall off the cliff. Then, he'd follow.

A kiss to her shoulder, he pulled out and rolled her over, then plunged into her again in one deft stroke. It was like being lost and found in the same erratic beat.

She tilted her head back, lips parted, and her hair spread out on the pillow, a move he realized she did while in the throes and while just as lost as him. Utterly damn beautiful. Eyes closed, brows furrowed, she pressed her palms to the headboard as if to gain leverage. Her breasts jutted with the movement, her peaks brushing his chest. Her hips rocked in time with his thrusts, and he couldn't hold out much longer. She was annihilating him, one needy whimper at a time.

Grabbing one of her thighs, he brought her leg up and held her behind her knee to angle deeper. His pelvis nudged her clit with each thrust and...yeah. She was tensing up to tumble again. His muscles strained and sweat beaded on his brow, but he didn't let up. Resting his forehead to hers, he struggled to hold on, pistoning faster, rolling his hips.

"Come for me again, babe."

He kissed her, their tongues tangling in the same glorious way their bodies were, and she went rigid a second time. She let go of the headboard, wrapping her arms around him as if concerned he'd let go. Or stop. There wasn't a chance in hell. The world could burn down around them, but he'd be none the wiser. Again, her walls gripped him, pulsing, and she quaked. She let out a cry into his mouth, and he was done for.

A tingling shot up his spine as his balls tightened. With a bark of shocked pleasure, he came. Hard. Wild. It was as if his whole body had locked up in an unyielding cataclysm. A band that had been stretched too thin, eventually snapping.

While coming down, he slowly rocked his hips until they both went lax. He collapsed partly on top of her, panting. She threw an arm over her face, breaths soughing.

After hours, days, years, she turned her head and pressed her lips to his forehead. "Damn, Aden."

He chuckled, but even that took more effort than he had left. "My sentiments, exactly."

Sliding out from under him, she rolled on her side to face him. Her tender gaze swept over him as she brushed some hair from his damp brow. "I told you behaving is overrated."

Grinning, he draped his arm over her waist. "I concede to you being correct. This *one* time."

"Just this once, huh?"

"Yep." He sighed, happier than he'd been in he didn't know how long. She'd been partially right about something else, not that he'd admit it. Attraction was one thing, but chemistry was another. There was no telling if they had any together until they acted upon the first to investigate the second. Turned out, they had both. And if he thought she was gorgeous first thing in the morning with sunlight streaming through her hair and her skin aglow, then post-coital put that to shame. "You're beautiful, babe."

Her lower lip jutted as her gaze softened. "Thank you."

"I'm sure you hear that a lot." Understatement. She had her pick of admirers. "You really are beautiful." Inside and out. Even when they bickered each other into a corner, she always had his best interests at heart. She cared about others on a level most didn't see unless they were in her inner circle.

"It's nice to hear, no matter how often. Especially coming from you because I know it's not just a line to get me in bed."

"The guys around here need to get more clever if that's all they got." He'd rather they stay oblivious, all things considered. "I already have you in bed, anyway."

"Gonna keep me here?" She winked. *Winked*, the brat.

"Yep." At least, until he recuperated. "For the record, you're smart, too. Funny sometimes."

"Sometimes?" Up went her brows, challenge in the twist of her lips. "Just sometimes?"

"I said what I said."

Cotton jumped onto the bed, and Dufus went to Scarlett's side to rest his chin on the mattress.

"I forgot they were in here." He laughed and rolled to his back.

She laughed, patting the bed as an invitation. "Come on, you can join us."

Dufus wasted no time, launching onto the bed and laying between them. Cotton, not one to miss out on free cuddles, crawled up his chest and began kneading.

"Your cat thinks I'm a pillow."

"Your dog thinks I'm a blanket."

"Eh, at least they get along." He petted the white furball, who rewarded him with purring. Loud purring. He wasn't much of a cat person, but Cotton was okay in his book. "I'm not sure we're getting up anytime soon."

She didn't reply.

Turning his head, he glanced at her. Asleep. With the sheets tangled around her legs and the dog cuddled up to her chest, she'd fallen back asleep. It wasn't a half-bad idea.

He closed his eyes, too.

Chapter Thirteen

Butt parked on her kitchen island, Scarlett swung her legs, watching Aden cook at the stove. He had *the* hottest body she'd ever had the privilege to observe. Wearing worn jeans slung low on his narrow waist, he tapped his bare foot in time to his stirring. Why were bare feet so sexy? She'd stolen his shirt to come downstairs, so he was missing that article of clothing, too. Wide shoulders, sun-kissed skin, six-pack abs from manual farm labor, and biceps that could crack walnuts. His sandy blond hair was a cluster on his head from her repeatedly running her fingers through it, and probably from sleeping afterward.

He was making omelets because she couldn't cook, and her chef had sent all leftovers to the homeless shelter. It was either Aden do his thing, or they ate potato chips for sustenance. And they needed sustenance after that epic display of animalistic romping upstairs. Neither of them wanted to go out to forage for food. One, because of people and gossip. Two, they wanted time to themselves. And three, it required too much effort.

She'd enjoyed their lazy morning. Not just because of amazing sex. Sleeping in, waking up to him in her bed, and isolating themselves to have some chill time was just what she'd needed. It wouldn't always be like this, she knew, but it would be relaxing while it lasted. Normally, her staff would be around, she'd have appointments or events, he had the horses and his own sched-ule. But, for now, it was just them.

The scent of green peppers, tomatoes, and onions wafted through the room, and her belly rumbled. She could eat the entire pantry right now, she was so hungry. He whisked eggs and added them to the vegies in a skillet, then put heaps of cheese on top. Spatula in one hand, he flipped bacon in a different pan with the other.

"I'm wasting away over here, Aden."

His shoulders bounced with a laugh. "She who can't make toast without burning down the historic mansion shouldn't rush the guy cooking her food."

Yeah, yeah. "Is it almost done?" She lived for taunting him, but all joking aside... "I'm starving. Someone woke me up this morning and had me work up an appetite."

"Oh really? Where can I find this brute? I'll make him pay." He plated the bacon. "And for the record, *you* woke *me* up, and it was *your* idea to work up an appetite. Not that I'm complain-ing."

"Slaying my dragons?" She grinned, despite how he never let her get away with anything.

"Always."

As her grandmother liked to say, *her cup has runneth over.*

He was funny and handsome, and cooking her breakfast. Well, brunch, actually, seeing as it was almost lunchtime. It was still hard to wrap her mind around the fact that she'd slept with Aden. Her friend. The guy next door. A man who'd come in and out of her house so many times, she didn't have enough fingers and toes of the entire town's population to count the incidences. He was a staple not only at her estate, but in her friend group. How had this happened? A shift in their dynamic this fast?

And why the heck hadn't they done it sooner? Why hadn't she caught on to his feelings or wised up to her own? Admittedly, it had been jarring, somewhat strange, at first. It was Aden, after all. But, geez. Once they'd gone there, stepped over the line, they had enough sparks to set all of Vallantine ablaze.

She tilted her head. "Can I ask you a question?"

"No." He flipped the omelet, never missing a beat.

She rolled her eyes, not that he could see. "Good. You said before that you've had feelings for me for a while now. How long is awhile?"

His shoulders stiffened, and she regretted asking. He paused in motion, his back to her, then he plated the omelet and cut it in half, dividing it between two plates. Silently, he added strips of bacon to each. Turning, he walked to the other side of the island and set the dishes down.

"Come eat." He pulled out a stool.

Glancing over her shoulder at him, her belly clenched. She hadn't realized it was this much of a sensitive topic. His features had flattened to a blank canvas and were completely unreadable. Avoiding eye contact, he stared at the counter, waiting for her.

Hopping down, she rounded the island and took a seat. Only after she complied did he sit next to her.

"Thank you for cooking." Suddenly, she wasn't quite as hungry.

"You're welcome." He dug in, staring straight ahead.

Unnerved, she did the same. "This is good." And it was. What she could taste of it, anyhow. The abrupt change in the atmosphere had left her stomach in knots and her tastebuds absent.

Dufus came up and set his head in her lap.

Absently, she petted the sweet boy while eating and blankly staring around. Nothing new. Nothing she hadn't seen a million times. Black and white checkered tile, ornate white cabinets, and a coffered ceiling. Green granite countertops and stainless steel appliances. The window over the sink let in sunlight from the yard, and reflections from the pool scattered light on the backsplash. The only thing not ordinary was Aden.

"High school," he muttered, seemingly out of nowhere, and in such a low tone, she thought she'd misheard. Fork in hand, he stared ahead, his jaw ticking. "I first noticed feelings for you in high school."

What? Her utensils clattered to her plate.

Sighing, he closed his eyes a moment, then opened them and picked her fork back up, holding it out for her without making eye contact.

She wished he'd look at her, but she accepted the fork.

High school? They were twenty-eight years old. They'd graduated ten years ago. Not accounting for the four years they were actual students. That long? He'd had feelings that long? And she'd been oblivious. Just completely, stupidly unaware that the person she'd spent the most time with in this world and depended on had wanted more than friendship. How many times in how many ways had she inadvertently hurt him? Something she would never consciously do. Not ever. Romantic feelings often made a person more sensitive to rejection, and common phrases or behavior could be taken out of context. But she hadn't known. He hadn't said a word. Not one syllable *for a decade*.

He drank from his orange juice. "Your mother had put you in one of those damn beauty pageants again. The last one you ever did, in fact. Your besties weren't allowed backstage, so you were alone in the dressing room. I snuck back there between sets to check on you, knowing you hated those things and your mama was relentless."

Struggling to recall, she drank her own juice. "Sophomore year?"

"Yeah." He nudged his empty plate aside, pinching the bridge of his nose. "You were wearing this shimmering peach-colored evening gown, your makeup overdone and hair puffed up." He shook his head. "You looked nothing like yourself, but it hit me out of nowhere. This feeling of... I don't know. Awareness, I guess. It would come and go, but it wasn't constant. As the years tacked on, it got stronger."

A lump wedged in her throat and her eyes burned. She'd hurt him without knowing it by not acknowledging his feelings. He had to have felt so alone. It wasn't as if he could tell anyone, especially the person he trusted most. Her sweet, annoying Aden.

He glanced at her, and panic disrupted his features. "Ah, shit." His amazing blue eyes widened. "Don't do that."

"Do what?" A sob hitched her chest.

Reaching for a napkin, he spun her stool to face him, his feet on the rungs dragging her closer. "Cry, darlin'. Don't cry." He dabbed her cheeks like a gentle version of whack-a-mole. "Come on. You know damn well I can't hack your waterworks."

"I'm sorry." More tears welled and fell, until she couldn't see him through the haze. She attempted to take a few breaths, but emotion clogged her airway. "I'm sorry. I can't..." Frantically, she waved her hands. The harder she tried to quit, the worse it got.

"Alright. Okay." He lifted her from the stool and plopped her on the island, standing between her legs. Wrapping his arms around her, he held her to him, one hand smoothing her hair. "Let it out, then."

It had been a while since she'd had a bout of tears, so maybe she was overdue. If it was one thing she couldn't stand, it was her friends hurting. Rebecca and her fibromyalgia pain. Dorothy's desperation to start a family and being met with disparagement. Aden having to look at her, day in and day out, while living with the reality he'd never have those feelings returned. It had to have seemed like abandonment, and it was her fault.

Resting the side of her head on his shoulder, she buried her face in his neck. Such strong shoulders. They'd carried a lot of burdens. His whiskers tickled, but she didn't move, because she liked being held by him. Eventually, her tears subsided as fast as they'd appeared, and she let out an uneven breath.

"Ah, babe." He cinched his arms, kissing her temple. "One day, you're going to need to deal with this irrational guilt you carry around."

What was he talking about? She raised her head to look at him. Quiet resolve stared back at her through eyes as familiar as her own.

"You heard me." He dabbed at her cheeks again with the napkin, his gaze following the motion of his hand. "Irrational guilt. You wear it like a shroud. Always have."

"No, I don't."

His lopsided grin was a cheap shot. "Really? Why are you crying?"

"I'm not."

He gazed heavenward as if calling for patience from On High. "Why *were* you crying?"

Pouting, she stared over his shoulder at the adjacent wall. "I had no idea you felt that way, and for so long."

"Because I didn't tell you."

"It...made my heart hurt." She looked at him, and her stupid organ wanted to break again. For all her faults and his, they'd been a solid unit long before this recent shift. "I'd never want to do anything that would cause you a second of pain. But I did. For years, you held these feelings, and I brushed them off as if you didn't matter. You *do* matter."

"I didn't tell you." His smile was pained as he cupped her cheeks. "Thank you for that, but I know. The point is, I didn't tell you. Thus, you didn't have an inkling, so how can any of it be your fault? That's one point in a long line of things you claim responsibility for. It's irrational."

Maybe so, but emotions weren't always grounded in fact, nor did they always make sense.

Deflating, she stared at the dark blond curls on his chest. "Why didn't you tell me?" He'd hinted and circled around the topic a few times, yet never spit out an answer.

"There's not enough hours in the day to tackle that conversation."

She narrowed her eyes on him. "CliffsNotes version."

Resting his hands on the counter beside her hips, he leaned into them. "Your folks, for one."

"What about them?"

His expression dialed to pure *duh*. "They hate me."

"My father doesn't hate you, and my mother hates everyone and everything. She doesn't count."

He tilted his head as if to say, touché. "He'd still rather you wind up with anyone else."

"I'm not so sure about that." She gave him a short version of their talk at lunch last week. "What else you got?"

Seemingly wrestling with narrative in his head, he looked down as if ashamed. After a long pause, he sighed. "The point is, Scarlett, that night in the garden was the first time you ever looked at me as more than a friend. It's like I said before, there was no point in disrupting The Force."

"And if I'd not tried to kiss you? Would you have just gone on forever, wishing and hoping for change?"

"I don't know." He shrugged, straightening, and swiped his hand down his face. "Truth? I'd rather have you in my life, even if it was just as friends, than to mess up everything by opening my mouth."

For the first time since they'd crossed the line, she got a glimmer of the depths he'd gone through to preserve their working and ongoing friendship. And it sliced her in half.

"You're not going to cry again, are you?" The genuine concern etched in his features made her laugh.

"I'm not going to cry again."

"Good. You know it disrupts the Earth's rotational pull."

She threw her hands up. "For real, why am I labeled the dramatic one?"

He grinned, and her brain cells cindered to dust. "It makes me feel helpless. You don't cry often. I get that sometimes you just need to let go, but it guts me."

Because he cared about her, else he wouldn't have that reaction. She'd been blind a long time, but no more. She'd show him she cared, too.

Cupping the back of his head, she brought his lips to hers. He froze a fraction of a beat as if surprised, but then he relented and slanted his lips at a different angle. Sentiment and endearment entwined in the way he kissed, and it rocked her to the core. When she'd said she'd never been kissed like this before, she'd meant it. There was passion and there was interest, but she'd never encountered this kind of heart before. He gave everything, gave all, in the way he caressed her lips, stroked his tongue. The connection was both jarring and a comfort.

Breaking away, she trailed her lips across his jaw and down his neck. He had the most delicious tendons that popped when he was aroused or strained. Latching onto one where his shoulder met his neck, she swirled her tongue over his salty skin.

He groaned. "Don't start trouble, darlin'."

She laughed and shifted to the other side, repeating her motions. "Complain, complain."

"I'm not..." He tilted his head to assist in her ministrations. "Complaining. Shit, your mouth is a weapon."

"You say the sweetest things." Threading her fingers in his hair, she sucked on his earlobe.

"It makes up for my dirty thoughts." Another long groan. "We're in the kitchen."

"And?"

"And...I don't remember." Her hair around his fist, he tugged her head back and ate at her mouth. Hungry, desperate. His hands skimmed up her thighs until he reached her hips. Abruptly, he jerked his gaze to hers. "You're not wearing anything under my shirt."

"Nope." She unbuttoned his jeans and slid the zipper down. Each click of the teeth was an echo in the room. "You're overdressed." She slid his denim down his thighs with her toes and took him in hand.

A strangled sound arose from his throat. He'd made the noise a couple times upstairs earlier, and it amped her desire. He wanted her. Aden wanted her.

And gawd, how she loved the feel of him. Thick shaft, long, and velvet skin over hard muscle. He pulsed in her grasp, panting hard against her neck. She stroked him from base to tip, and relished the way his body tensed against her. The veins in his arms protruded. Another sexy thing she'd not paid any attention to until now. Huge hands, roughened from outside work, yet erringly gentle when he touched her.

His fingers dug into her hips. "You're killing me."

She grinned, nuzzling his cheek. "Want me to stop?"

"Don't you dare." The gruff desperation in his rough demand had her tingly.

Enjoying her exploration, she skimmed her fingers down his spine with one hand and kept up her ministrations with the other. Their first time, she hadn't had the chance to touch him as much, to find the places he liked, to pleasure him as he had to her.

She pulled out one of the stools with her foot. "Have a seat."

"I'm good right here."

"Suit yourself." She nudged him back a step, scooted off the counter, and dropped to her knees in front of him. Dipping her fingers in the waistband of his jeans, she slid them down his legs the rest of the way.

He stepped out of them, his jaw tense. "Scarlett..."

Cupping his balls, she massaged lightly, and his eyes pinched closed. Emboldened, she grabbed his base, made a circular motion, and stroked him again, swirling her thumb across the tip. He hissed through his teeth. His reactions had her so wet, so turned on, that by the time she swirled her tongue around the head, the juncture of her thighs was achy with need.

Closing her lips around him, she moaned.

"Damn, babe." He lunged forward, hands braced on the countertop behind her, and glared down at her through blue eyes radiating with deep desperation. Chest heaving, he watched her, not moving an inch.

Smiling, she returned to her task, lowering her gaze, and took more of him. He was above average in size, but not so much that she couldn't please him in immeasurable ways. He'd taunted and teased the hell out of her this morning, dragging out her pleasure until she'd thought she'd expire.

Tit for tat.

Base in hand, she bobbed her head until he hit the back of her throat. A string of expletives followed, and she created suction as she released him. She used her tongue to lick, her mouth to suck, and her hand to stroke. Just as he would tense to the point of ready, she did something else to set him up all over again.

After several elongated play rounds, he opened his eyes, frustrated fury in his depths. "Payback?"

A grin, and she shrugged.

"Alrighty." Hands under her arms, he lifted her to her feet.

She reeled, but he grabbed her behind the knees and hauled her up his body. She wrapped her legs around his waist as he pivoted. Her back pressed against the wall, and he held her in place with his weight. Her aching breasts throbbed, trapped between their bodies.

"Game on, darlin'."

He crushed his lips to hers, devouring her, as he aligned himself and plunged.

Yesss. Relishing him inside her, she gasped against his lips.

"All good?" He lifted his head to stare into her eyes, and one corner of his mouth curved in a conceited smile. "Oh, yeah. You're good."

Resting his forehead to hers, he eased out, so slowly, she wanted to weep. The empty sensation lasted mere seconds before he thrust, filling her anew. She gripped his shoulders, but she was still spiraling. Her body and the way it reacted to him was unlike any experience before. Like she had no control or choice but to respond. Heat furled in her belly, and she closed her eyes, overtaken by smoldering, dizzying need.

He buried his face in her neck as if they weren't close enough and he needed an all-points contact. Sometimes his responses seemed as if he was worried she'd disappear or change her mind. Ragged, desperate sounds rasped against her skin, proving he was just as delirious as her. Over and over, he pumped, and the way he rolled his hips at the end of each thrust had his pelvis bumping her clit to get her there faster.

Never mind. She was already there. A zinging electrical storm surged through her.

Somehow, he knew. "That's right, babe." He groaned against her ear, bit her lobe. "You feel so damn good."

She dug her nails into his shoulders, quaking. Convulsion after convulsion wracked her, until all she could manage was a strangled scream that died in her airway. He let out a quiet roar, palms pressed to the wall on either side of her, and thrust one last time. He stilled for a beat, jerked, grunted, and let out a heaving breath.

"We're going down." Arms around her, he about-faced, and slid down the wall to the floor.

She wasn't sure how, but his shirt wound up wrapped around her hair and shoulders. As she struggled with it, he laughed and pulled it off the rest of the way. It sailed across the kitchen.

She collapsed, head on his shoulder. "I'm hungry again."

His chest bounced with a laugh, the rumble vibrating her. "You only ate half of your food. No wonder."

"Well, you made me cry. I lost my appetite."

He went utterly still.

Crap. "I didn't mean that the way it came out." She stroked his arm. "I'm sorry."

Slowly, he wrapped his arms around her, his palms gliding up and down her back. It was soothing, a balm to the burn they'd just experienced. She'd never been much of a cuddler after sex, but in Aden's arms, she was safe. Contented. This other side of him, the one that went beyond his typical protective nature to a nurturing one, was something she'd not experienced from other lovers, and she hadn't expected it from him.

"This is nice." She smiled, breathing in his outdoor scent.

"Your butt's not on the cold tile."

She laughed, fingers toying with his chest air. "Want to move?"

"No." He adjusted the slightest bit, but she stayed dead weight. "Maybe in a minute."

Moving was stupid. They should stay put. "We're pretty good at this."

"We're pretty great at this."

Agreeing completely, she sighed, recalling the previous conversation. "I'm sorry it took me so long to realize your feelings or to make a move."

"No worries, Scarlett." He skimmed his hands over her back in a soothing motion. "Had we rushed things and you weren't there yet, it wouldn't have ended as well." He kissed her temple. "You were worth the wait."

"Aww." Well, geez. Emotion clogged her throat, and her chest heated.

"You better not be gearing up to cry again. I was just speaking the truth."

"Aww again." Criminy, this man. She'd had complements in her life, but he had a way of stating the simple to evoke a complicated response. Like reaching in her chest to personally pluck her heartstrings.

"Time to get up." He lightly smacked her butt. "The floor is unyielding, and we need to find clothes."

"Clothing is overrated."

"Fine. Make me manhandle you."

With her in his arms, he stood and strode across the kitchen with her legs and arms wrapped around him. He bent, snatching his shirt and jeans off the floor, somehow without dropping her, and pivoted for the hallway. He carried her all the way up the grand staircase, into her room, where he unceremoniously dropped her on the bed.

She bounced once, grinning at him.

He pointed at her. "Don't go getting any wild ideas. I need to recuperate."

"Okay." She glanced in the direction of her closet, then at her dresser. "I need to shower before getting dressed."

He groaned as if that conjured images.

"Hot, soapy water all over my—"

"Scarlett Taylor. Shut-up."

She grinned wider. "Make me."

He inhaled. Hard. "Woman…"

This was way more fun than it should be. "Wanna join me?"

"Yes, which is why I'm going downstairs to clean up the kitchen." Without further ado, he strode from the room.

Laughing, she rose and started the shower. While the water heated, she debated wardrobe options. She didn't think they were going anywhere, so she snatched a pair of baggy cotton bongo capris in a pretty peach color with a white V-neck shirt. Casual and comfortable.

Once she'd showered and dried her hair, she stared at her reflection in the mirror, debating cosmetics. It was just Aden, and he'd seen her without. There really was no need, so she decided to forgo it and went back downstairs.

Aden was leaning against the kitchen sink, phone to his ear. "Hold on, she just walked in." He pulled the phone away. "Forest and Graham want to know if we can get together tonight."

Unable to help it, she laughed. "Are you asking permission to go play with your friends?" Though she was disappointed because she wanted more time alone with him, she wasn't so needy and selfish as to keep him from his life.

Unamused by her reply, his expression flatlined. "I think they meant all of us. The whole group."

"Oh." Now that sounded like fun. They hadn't had a friend night in over a month.

Voices emitted through his speaker.

He put the phone back to his ear. "You know, your woman is BFFs with mine. She could just call… Hi, Rebecca. Uh-huh. Hold on." He pushed a button on the cell.

A squee emitted, loud and piercing. "So, the date went well? You're still over at Scarlett's?"

Aden stared at the ceiling. "Yes, and you're on speaker."

"I'm calling Dorothy. We're definitely getting together. You have to tell me everything, Scarlett."

He glanced at her. "Is that what y'all do? Share intimate details of..." He waved his hand. "Stuff."

"Duh." She walked closer and snatched his phone. "Why don't y'all come over here tonight? Six o'clock?"

"You're on. Bye, Aden!"

He waved as if Rebecca could see him. "Sure thing. Glad I could help." Sarcasm dripped from his pores. He gave Scarlett the hairy eyeball. "What kind of intimate details?"

Not a second passed, and both their phones blew up.

She pulled hers from her pocket and glanced at the screen.

Rebecca: 6:00 at Scarlett's.

Dorothy: Awesome. I'll bring the cocktail mixes.

Forest: I'll bring pizza.

Graham: Beer here. You can have your froufrou girly drinks.

Forest: Word.

Rebecca: I'll bring pretzels and cookies.

Laughing, Scarlett put her thumbs to work texting. *I have stuff here, too. Want me to make something?*

Dorothy: Oh God, no!

Rebecca: We're fine. Thanks.

A scary emoji followed the last text, to which laughing emojis poured in.

She sighed, glancing Aden's way. "No faith in me, I swear."

"You have many attributes, darlin', but cooking ain't one of 'em." He stared at his screen, shaking his head. "They're still going at it." He pocketed his phone. "No, really, what kind of intimate details?"

"Poor Aden." She wrapped her arms around his waist, smiling up at him. "Worried?"

His lids narrowed to slits. "Should I be?"

"Nope. You're good in bed. Multiple orgasms. Five stars."

He choked, eyes wide. "Seriously? You rate..." He sighed, nostrils flaring.

She rolled her lips over her teeth. He was so dang adorable. Wary blue eyes, whiskers covering his wide jaw, blond strands all a mess. Not accounting for his yummy body and great personality, she was quite smitten already.

"You were kidding." Nodding, he gave her a once-over, his features evening out. "You look nice. Typically, you wear dresses. I like this version of Scarlett."

She did, too, the few and far between instances she got to be her. "You didn't like the other one?"

"The contrary is apparent."

Huffing a laugh, she rose on her toes to kiss his nose. "I wore nothing at all earlier. You're seeing all kinds of versions today."

Gaze whimsical, he brushed a strand of hair from her cheek. "I'm very fond of all of them."

"Be still my heart." He slayed her. A sigh, and she eased out of his arms. "I guess I'll go change and put on makeup."

"Hold it." He grabbed her hand as she went to walk away. "Why?"

Um... "Because we're having company."

Seemingly perplexed, his brows furrowed. "The guests are our friends. You don't need to get all done up for them."

Staring over his shoulder, she debated. Whereas he was right, it just wasn't proper. One did not go out of the home or greet guests in the home without looking their best. Images had to be maintained at all times and...

She froze. That was her mother talking—the mantras and etiquette she'd verbally hammered into her for Scarlett's entire existence. How she'd despised having to be on-point all the time while other kids got to play on the swings or throw a ball. Instead, she'd been told to sit like a lady with her knees together, or what colors to wear in what season, to smile no matter what, and to never make a scene.

And she'd continued these rigid regulations into adulthood. Her parents no longer lived on the estate, Scarlett ran her own business she'd started from the ground up, and she answered to no one. Sure, she loved looking nice and professionalism was important, but why was she letting her mother dictate her life?

"Shit." Aden ran his hands up and down her arms. "I'm sorry. Far be it for me to tell you how or what to wear. Heck, babe, put on a paper bag. It doesn't matter to me. I just wanted you to be comfortable."

"Comfortable," she mimicked in a distant voice unlike her own. What exactly was comfortable? Did she even know?

"Yes." He looked down his nose at her. "To be yourself."

"Myself." She huffed a dry laugh devoid of humor. Did she even know who she was without the spit and polish? Without obligations and pleasantries?

"You're scaring me."

Her gaze darted to his, and she snapped out of the intrusive thoughts. They didn't belong here with him.

"I'm sorry." She smiled to ease his mind. "I was just thinking brownies sounded better than cookies. I'll text Rebecca." She kissed his cheek. "I'll stay dressed like this, thanks. How about a movie before they come over?"

Chapter Fourteen

"All right." Forest eyed the glass in his hand. "I'll give you this. Your Georgia Sunsets are actually damn good."

Dorothy smiled. "Told you. Now give it back and get your own."

Aden laughed at their back and forth, stretching his legs before him from his seat on the couch in Scarlett's upstairs living room. Him? He preferred beer, too, but the Bookish Belles' drink wasn't bad.

There was a stack of pizza boxes on the table, a pitcher of the cocktails on Scarlett's minibar in the corner, beer bottles in the cabinet fridge, a bowl of pretzels being passed around, and enough brownies on a platter to feed the Army. His friends were all gathered, laughing, carrying on, and he finally had Scarlett in a way he'd always assumed would never be possible. Life was pretty good right about now.

"Have to admit, Scarlett. I like your digs." Graham popped a pretzel in his mouth.

"Oh!" She pressed a palm to her forehead. "I forgot you've never been here. I'm so rude. We should show you around."

Graham, being the newest member of their circle, had just moved to Vallantine less than a year ago. He'd taken over as editor of the newspaper, where he'd met their Rebecca, and fallen in love. They now owned the Gazette together. Unless he actually joined book club soon or attended an event, there really would have been no need for him to come by.

"Not rude, at all." Graham glanced at him. "Aden, would you mind giving me a tour?"

"Sure." He lumbered to his feet, full from pizza. "Come on."

In the hallway, Graham ran his fingers through his dark brown strands. "Hope it's okay that you do the tour. I figured you're here nearly as much as her. I wanted to talk to you privately about something."

That sounded ominous. "Everything kosher?"

"Yes." Graham glanced over his shoulder. "I'll get into it away from prying ears."

"Okay." It left Aden curious, but he'd find out soon enough.

Graham eyed the family portraits along the dark-paneled hallway. "This is really something. Her family's owned it all this time?"

"Yeah." He spoke as they walked around the second floor, Aden showing Graham her kitchen, guestrooms, the master bedroom, and her library. "Many great-grandfathers ago, around when Vallantine was founded, the mansion was built shortly thereafter. Scarlett's done some renovations since she's inherited the place, mostly to accommodate the events she hosts."

They made their way downstairs, where they poked their heads into each of the four ballrooms, then Scarlett's office. They paused in the kitchen, then went out the back door so Graham could check out the pool and gardens. It was warm and muggy, and it appeared that the breeze had stayed gone. The air was so humid, breathing was a chore.

The pool was looking more welcoming by the second.

"Jeez." Hands on his hips, Graham shook his head. "You know, Rebecca said Scarlett was loaded, but I had no clue the scale of what she meant. I mean, this is the kind of estate they turn into museums."

Aden nodded. "It's rare that it's remained in the family all these years. Most don't. In fact, the other estates back here have had multiple owners. All except a couple."

"I never would've guessed it from her. She's so normal. Yeah, she's always well-dressed, but she sure doesn't flaunt her wealth." He shrugged, speaking under his breath. "I'm probably stereotyping here, but she's not..."

"A snob?" Aden chuckled. There was almost no one on planet Earth with a bigger heart than her. She cared, sometimes too much, and had umpteen causes. "She sure isn't. Her grandmother was pretty wonderful, too. Scarlett takes after her. She actually hates the elite culture."

Graham grinned. "So, you and Scarlett, eh?"

He supposed everyone in Vallantine knew by now. "Yep."

"I guessed that even before Rebecca and I started dating."

Aden scratched his jaw. "That makes one of us."

"Oh, come on." Graham crossed his arms, widening his stance. "The way you two go at one another? Plus, you're out here at the town limits all by yourself."

Aden sighed. The guy wasn't wrong. "We're very different, her and I, but despite that, I've had a thing for her for quite some time. Didn't mean she did, though."

"No kidding. Well, I'm glad she came around." Graham glanced over the yard. "I once dated a governor's daughter for a whole five minutes. Couldn't hack it. Aren't you intimidated?"

Every hour of every day of every week. "By Scarlett? No." Her family? More than he should. It was a beautiful estate and grounds, though, and it was familiar. He kept reminding himself this was Scarlett's domain now, not her family's.

"Good for you, man. All that matters is that you make each other happy." He shoved his hands in his pockets, seemingly wrestling with something in his mind. "Can I show you something?"

"It's not pervy, is it?"

"No." Graham laughed. "I told Forest earlier, but..." He shrugged. "Wanted your opinion, too."

"Okay, I'm curious. Lay it on me."

Extruding his hand from his pocket, he held it out. A small black jewelry box rested on his palm.

Well, shit. No way.

He gestured for Aden to take the box.

Hesitantly, he did, and flipped open the lid. Yup, there was an engagement ring in there, all right. White gold, at least a carat, a round-cut diamond cushioned in the center, and flanked by a halo of other smaller diamonds. It looked exactly like something Rebecca would wear. Old-fashioned, decent-sized, but not flashy, and unique in design.

He pressed a palm to his heart. "I'm flattered, but I'm into women. So are you."

"Funny." The poor guy looked nervous, rubbing his neck and gaze hyper-focused on the box.

"Seriously, it's perfect. She's going to love it."

"Yeah?" Graham blew out a breath.

"Absolutely. It's a good choice." Aden snapped the lid shut and passed the box back to Graham. "When you gonna pop the question?"

"I was going to do it during the Peach Festival, but things got crazy around here. Plus, after I talked it over with Forest this morning, he agrees it might mean more if the other two Belles are around. Not, like, a public show or anything, but something intimate."

And just like that, Aden connected the dots. "You're going to do it tonight. That's why y'all called."

Graham offered the most awkward smile Aden had ever born witness.

"Ha." He slapped Graham's arm. "That's awesome. Screw it. Come here." He dragged Graham to him, did a bro back slap/hug combination, and immediately stepped aside. "Knowing blondie, it would mean a lot to have her besties around." Rebecca had spent many years away from Vallantine in the pursuit of a career she thought she'd failed at, only to come home and find all she'd been seeking was right here. She'd missed her friends the most. This idea was the right call.

"Okay, good. She's just not into flashy crap or big gestures. Neither am I. Though I've been thinking about it for a couple months, I just got the ring two weeks ago. It's burning a hole in my pocket. We haven't been together that long, but when you know, you know. My parents love her, and her friends like me. She's it for me." Bending at the waist, he let out a nervous laugh. "I feel like puking. I'm so nervous."

"She's going to say yes."

"From your lips, man." He straightened. "Will you be a groomsman? If she says yes."

"I repeat, she's gonna say yes. I'd be honored to be a grooms-man." Now or never. "Ready to head in? It's hotter than blazes out here."

"Absolutely. Thanks for the tour, and the ear."

"Anytime."

They backtracked through the house and upstairs again, only to find all three ladies doing some strange dance in sync with one another, Dorothy begrudgingly, and Forest laughing so hard, he had tears in his eyes.

They stopped when they saw Aden and Graham, and burst into hysterics.

"We leave you alone for five minutes." Graham kissed Rebecca's cheek, then claimed a vacant chair.

Aden scratched his head. "The hell was that?"

Scarlett fanned her face. "Forest bet us we couldn't remember our choreographed dance number from the eighth grade talent show."

"Why, Forest?" Aden plopped on the couch. "Why, man? We already lived through that once."

Dorothy mumbled, "I'm still scarred."

Forest still hadn't caught his breath, wheezing and laughing. "I'm dead. *Dead*, I tell you."

It was good to see his old buddy enjoying himself again. Ever since Forest's divorce a couple years back, it seemed to Aden like Forest had just been going about the motions.

"I'm still mad we didn't win." Rebecca sat on Graham's lap. "We were way better than Suzy Genry's baton twirling."

"Eh." Dorothy shrugged. "She did tap-dance while twirling."

"Goodness." Scarlett sat beside Aden on the sofa, patting his thigh. "Just be glad I'm not doing beauty pageants anymore."

Amen. Aden swiped a hand down his face.

"Word." Rebecca lifted her glass like a toast. "Those were horrible."

"Agreed." Dorothy ran her fingers through her auburn strands. "Want me to put the leftover pizza in the fridge?"

"I'll do it later." Scarlet sighed in a dreamy tone and leaned against Aden. "I may eat another piece after that workout." She abruptly raised her hand. "Oh, Aden is building us a new treehouse."

He rested his head on the cushion, staring at the ceiling.

Forest chuckled. "He looks so happy about it, too."

"Wait." Graham looked at each of them. "You have a treehouse?"

"There's a story to that," Dorothy said. "I'll give you three guesses whose idea it was, and you won't need the last two guesses."

Graham laughed, gazing at Rebecca on his lap. "What did that mean ole Scarlett make you do?"

"Hey, now. It was a good idea at the time."

Aden whipped his attention to Scarlett. "The hell it was." He looked at Graham. "These three decided that treehouses were romantic, or some such shit, and raided the barns for scrap lumber. Then they marched their happy asses to the back of the estate and started building it themselves."

It was Graham's turn to fall into hysterics. "I can't picture Scarlett with a hammer. I can't picture any of you with a hammer."

"I'm not *that* bad," Dorothy added.

"Mmm hmm." Aden put his arm around Scarlett, tucking her to his side. "It looked like a rejected Tim Burton set. I wound up rebuilding the damn thing, so they didn't kill themselves using it."

Laughing, Forest covered his face.

"Remember how mad your mama was?" Dorothy hissed. "Fit to be tied. Even the staff hid from her."

"Proper ladies don't use tools," Scarlett mocked. "Proper ladies don't get dirty."

Rebecca and Dorothy finished the rant together. "And you are never to play with Aden Abner again!"

Huh. He hadn't heard that part. She obviously hadn't listened to her mother on many things.

"Joke's on her." Scarlett took a sip of her cocktail. "Look at me. No makeup today *and* I played with Aden Abner all day."

The girls laughed, but Forest's expression was somber. "I wasn't going to say anything, but since you brought it up, I sorta did a double-take there when I walked in. It's been some time since you haven't been all dolled up."

Graham grunted. "Actually, the first time we met was at the Tipsy Turtle. Remember? All three of you walked in while Forest and I were there. You had on PJs, but even then, you wore makeup."

"I had to talk her into slumming it today." Aden squeezed her shoulder.

Scarlett hummed. "I'm working on trying to be less of an actual southern belle." Her lips twisted. "That was the day of Gammy's funeral. Like besties do, we took Rebecca out for comfort food." She grinned. "Our girl didn't like you very much at first. She was fixin' to start a fight."

"Yeah." Graham smiled up at her, the big dope. "She had me at hello."

Scarlett "awed," but Dorothy corrected Graham. "Actually, she told Forest to mind the company he keeps."

Rebecca buffed her nails on her shirt.

"First time I met *you two* was at the bar." Graham kept his gaze on Rebecca, his smile slipping. "First time I met *her* was on the sidewalk outside our homes. She gave me advice on how to get our crotchety old mailman to quit tossing my letters in the grass."

Graham asked her to stand up, and Rebecca rose from his lap, confusion wrinkling her forehead.

Aden glanced at Forest and grinned.

Forest winked and refocused on the couple.

"You were the prettiest thing I ever laid eyes on." Graham took her hand. "Every day, you wake up and face your condition with grace and strength when most would crumble. You saved my career, you saved the Gazette, and you saved me. I don't know where I'd be without you."

He slid from the chair, getting down on one knee.

All three women gasped.

Rebecca covered her mouth with her hands.

With a shaking hand, Graham held out the box. "I love you. Marry me, Rebecca?"

She stood in seemingly stunned silence, eyes leaking, but after a few moments, she emphatically nodded. "Yes." She wiped her eyes. "God, yes."

Scarlet screamed loud enough to make Aden's ears bleed, and Dorothy clapped. Without taking their eyes off the couple, Forest fist-bumped Aden.

Poor Graham dropped his head in relief, then lumbered to his feet and wrapped his arms around Rebecca.

While Graham put a ring on it and the ladies screeched and bounced, Aden grinned from his seat, so damn happy for them. He'd grown up with Rebecca, and like the belles, he'd worried about her after she'd left Vallantine, especially after her fibromyalgia diagnosis. Once she'd returned, it was as if the unit had been completed again. She deserved a family since hers had been stolen from her, and Graham was it. And for a newcomer to their group, Graham had fit in well and loved their girl to no end. He'd had his career railroaded by scandal before moving to Vallantine. He deserved a second chance just as much.

All was right with the world tonight.

A bottle of champagne later, their friends left, and Aden went in search of the dog while Scarlett cleaned up. Unable to locate him on the second floor, he strode downstairs, only to come up empty.

Hands on his hips, he hollered up the stairs for Scarlett.

She didn't answer.

"Babe?"

Still nothing.

Sighing, he began the trek up the grand staircase. "House is too big."

She wasn't in the kitchen any longer, and all the lights were off. Heading into her bedroom, he found Cotton on the bed, but no Scarlett or Dufus. Just as he was about to walk out, movement on the balcony caught his attention.

Weaving around the bed, he glanced out. Scarlett sat in one of her white rocking chairs, phone to her ear, and hand flailing in angry gestures. Dufus, looking all kinds of nervous, had his head in her lap, pawing at her calf. Who the hell could she be talking to this late? It was nearly midnight.

Turning the knob, he eased the door open, but she didn't seem to notice. Waiting her out, he crossed his arms and leaned on the frame.

A crass female voice emitted from the phone, but he couldn't make out the words since it wasn't on speaker. Regardless, he recognized the tone.

Swell. Her mother had found out about their relationship. He supposed it was bound to happen one way or another.

Scarlett stiffened. "It's none of your business."

He felt like he was in the Peanuts cartoon with the *whaa, whaa, whaa* that followed.

"I've entertained this conversation long enough, and at an ungodly hour. I had the best day today, and I won't let you ruin it."

Whaa, whaa, whaa.

"No. Goodnight, Mother. Sleep well." Disconnecting, she dropped her head in her hands and made what would've been the cutest growl if not for the circumstances. Absently, she petted Dufus. "Sorry, buddy. She upsets me, too."

"You shouldn't let her."

She jumped and craned her head around. "Hey."

"Hi." He stepped the rest of the way onto the balcony, shutting the door behind him. Sitting in the chair beside her, he set it in motion. "You okay?"

"I will be." She sighed, leaning back in her seat.

It was still hot outside, and there still was no breeze, but higher up on the balcony and without the sun made being outdoors more tolerable. The view didn't hurt. Stars dotted the navy sky and a crescent moon had a wavering halo. Below them was her in-ground pool. Beyond was the vast gardens. Barely detectable, off to the right, was his house and barns.

A twisted sort of perspective washed over him as he sat on her pedestal instead of from the gallows. Just because he'd been welcomed into the castle didn't mean he would ever be royalty. He didn't want her mansion or her riches. He just wanted her. But with her came all the predetermined assets that some people, her folks included, would assume he was after.

Twenty-eight years, and they still assumed the worst of him.

He shook his head. "Have your attorney draft up a non-disclosure."

Her gaze whipped to his. "What? Why?"

"That's part of your mother's issue, isn't it? That I never signed one like the rest of your staff?"

Her lips firmed. "You are not my staff."

"She'll never see it that way, and though an NDA won't shut her up, it may show her I'm compromising." Having a legal piece of paper that said he couldn't talk about the family in a negative light or spout anything about the intimate dealings could simmer her mother down a bit. For a while.

"No." She stared ahead. "I'm a grown woman and this is my house. I will not treat you like a criminal. I trust you. I don't care if she doesn't. That's not my problem."

"Babe."

She didn't acknowledge him.

Reaching over, he took her hand in his. "I'm not getting between you and her. She may be a horrible human being sometimes, but she's your mother. She's your family."

A sneer twisted her lips. "I knew this was coming. I just knew it, but still, she gets under my skin."

Oh, how he knew that so very well. Time after time, year after year, Scarlett had come to him, or he to her, so she could vent or work through her anger, her wounds, inflicted by the very person who was supposed to love her the most. He thought of his own mom, quiet and humble. She had the patience of a saint. When angry, she could scare paint off the wall, but she'd never treat him like how Collette Taylor treated her daughter. As if she were a doll to be brought out for company, not someone with a mind and will of her own who had feelings.

Not for the first time, anger warred with hurt in his heart. Just once, for a solitary minute, he wished her mother could view Scarlett the way he did. Maybe she'd finally get over herself, finally love her daughter for the boisterous, witty, charismatic, beautiful creature she was instead of trying to constantly tear her down. It was easy for him or anyone else to advise her to cut the woman from her life, but that was a call for her to make, not him, and not because of him. Roots ran deep here, and especially in her lineage.

Truth was, he'd give her up if he thought it would make a difference. He'd sacrifice it all to mend this fence. Maybe then, Scarlett wouldn't walk around with this hole inside of her she could never fill, and guilt she could never appease, wouldn't constantly overcompensate for something she'd never lacked in the first place.

But he couldn't make her mother love her, and he couldn't turn her into a good person. What he could control and ensure was what he'd always done, which was be here. Day in and day out. Picking up the pieces and showing her that her mother was wrong. Showing her that she was loveable.

His stomach rolled, and his chest grew tight. Over two and a half decades collided inside his mind to reveal what he'd always known, even if denial had been his most loyal bedfellow.

He loved Scarlett.

Not just as her friend, or her shoulder to cry on, or the one she leaned on. Not as the guy next door and business liaison. Not as the thorn in her side or the one who came running whenever needed. It went so far beyond that. He loved her as the man whose heart she held in her nimble fingers, whose soul had somehow intertwined with hers despite social classes or personality rifts, and who couldn't imagine a life without her in it.

He was hopelessly, defiantly, and unequivocally in love with Scarlett Taylor.

Always had been.

Forever would be.

"I want to tell you something." He glanced at her a moment, at his best friend turned lover, then stared ahead, because she may love him, but he had no clue if it would ever be on the same level. There was just enough repudiation left in him to not want to find hesitation in her features.

"You can tell me anything."

He nodded, but acid ate away at his gut. "I love you."

Out of the corner of his eye, he caught her abrupt flinch. Maybe not a flinch, but she'd definitely reared. She was obviously surprised, but not in the oh-shit way he'd been preparing himself for.

"I love you, too." Her tone was part question, part confusion, and all truth.

But she wasn't getting it.

Letting go of her hand, he adjusted the chair so it faced more of her and less of the view. She was prettier to look at, anyway. "I have loved you for a very long time, and for that entire duration, I had myself convinced it was love. Just love. Like it was as simple or complicated as that. But I don't love you."

That adorable lower lip of hers poked out. "You just said you did."

"I know."

"But you don't love me?"

"No." He inhaled for courage and laced his fingers together. "I don't love you, Scarlett. I'm *in* love with you. For the squeaky noise you make when frustrated to the way you can argue yourself out of a corner. For the way you believe in me and stick up for me, sometimes at a detriment to yourself. For the way you let me look after you and protect you, despite being able to do it yourself, just so I feel like I'm contributing. I thought it was love. All this time, I figured it was love. Then this happened." He waved his hand between them and shrugged, leaning back in his seat. "It wasn't love. I'm batshit in love with you."

She stared at him several elongated minutes, mouth agape and very unlike her.

If this was all it took to shut her up, he should've tried it sooner. It would be nice if she formed thoughts into words this time, though.

Fine, he'd speak. "I realize we've only been at the physical part of our relationship for under forty-eight hours, and all of those were spent here in the house, but that's where I'm at. Seeing as you took longer to wise up to how amazing we are together, I don't expect you to be on the same page. Yet." Sarcasm, his friend.

More staring. He was either going to get a complex, or his heart shattered.

The dog's head shifted back and forth to stare at them, probably sensing the awkward tension.

"I'm thinking of dyeing my hair blue." He wasn't, but he was checking her level of catatonia to see how far down the rabbit hole she'd plummeted.

After the sun rotated the earth and four seasons came and went, she blissfully deigned to reply.

"You would look sexy no matter what color you put in your hair."

He blinked. Tilted his head. But, nope. She'd still ignored everything else he'd finally had the guts to spew. He wasn't sure if he should laugh or weep.

At least she thought he was attractive. He had that going for him. Leave it to her to drop a supportive note, as well, backing him in whatever he chose.

Just as he was about to call this a wash and leave, tail between his legs, she cleared her throat and grabbed his hand, sandwiching it between hers.

"I love you, too. I always have."

"But?" He didn't like where this was going, and his gut hollowed.

"But you're right." She exhaled ever so delicately, her gaze focused on their joined hands. "You've had romantic feelings a lot longer than I have, and to separate a love that was always there with something deeper isn't a switch that I can flip. I'm not sure I can separate them. You're Aden." She huffed a laugh, her expression reminiscent of melancholy mixed with endearment. "You're my Aden. We have incredible chemistry. I think I just need more time to go from love to *in*-love. You deserve better than an automatic response."

Okay. Alright. "That's fair."

For her, it had only been a weekend, but for him, it had been much longer, even if it was mere moments ago he'd realized.

"Are we okay?" Biting her lip, she peered at him.

"Yes." He brushed his thumb across her lip to stop her anxious habit and kissed her instead. "We're just fine."

Chapter Fifteen

"Wait." Rebecca paused in her motion of setting out chairs with Dorothy in the Myrtle Ballroom for book club, her expression incredulous. "Your mama said what?"

Scarlett, arranging cucumber sandwiches on a platter, nodded. "You heard me right. She ordered me to end the relationship with Aden."

That conversation had been a week ago, and she was still fuming. She'd taken the late night call out on the balcony, hoping to keep Aden from overhearing, and to let Mother have her say, then be done with the matter. Except, that's not how things had panned out. Mother had not only let out a string of insults about Scarlett's man, but she'd, in no uncertain terms, had demanded compliance.

Ah, and then her precious Aden had tried to offer a solution, had said the sweetest, most endearing things afterward. How could her mother not see how good a person he was, how much he wanted to take care of her, love her? The back and forth between swooning and livid rage was making her dizzy.

Dorothy, jaw dropping, plopped in a chair Rebecca had just placed. "My God, Scarlett."

"I know." Turning, Scarlett leaned against the table, her belly churning. "I don't know what to do. I mean, breaking up with

Aden is out of the question, but there has to be some middle ground here for Mother to be satisfied."

"She'll never be satisfied." Rebecca rubbed her forehead. She glanced at Dorothy as if seeking permission, then refocused on Scarlett. "I don't have any family left." Her breath hitched. "I would give anything to have them back. I would, but..."

Dorothy shot to her feet and stood beside her, rubbing Rebecca's arm for comfort.

Scarlett straightened to do the same, but Rebecca put her hand up and shook her head.

"I'm okay." She sniffed. "What I'm trying to say is, family is important. I have you guys and Graham's family now, but your mom will never be satisfied. She's been like this your whole life, and you know it. Some people are only happy when they are making everyone else as miserable as them. I don't think there is middle ground when it comes to her. I'd hate for you to lose something wonderful and lasting with Aden for the sake of appeasing her. Family comes in all forms. Aden has been yours for a long time."

Her words, though true, were like a sucker punch to the solar plexus. Scarlett stared at the ground, gaze wavering. Even without a romantic entanglement, Aden had more love for her in his pinky toe than her mother did in her entire being. What did that say about her that she feared her mother didn't even like her?

"She's right." Dorothy smoothed her auburn strands. "She may be your mom, but you're not five years old anymore. Perhaps ask yourself what *you* want, not what she wants. In the end, that's all that matters."

What *did* she want? It had been ages since she'd asked herself that question. Aden, in his current capacity, had not ever crossed her mind, but now that they were together, she wanted him. She did. She wanted to see where their relationship led and how amazing they could be together.

But at what cost?

She wished her grandmother was still alive. Without hesitation, Miss Maureen would bluntly tell her what's what, and then flip it back to Scarlett for reentry. She missed her advice and presence. More than anything, she missed the support.

Glancing down, she sighed. There was a white spot on her black dress, right above the cinched waist. Darn it. She must've bumped the sandwich platter. It looked like mayo.

"I need to go change before people get here." Which would be in about thirty minutes, including her mother and Aden. In the same room.

Her besties stared at her like they wanted to say more.

She smiled to appease them. They were just concerned about her, after all. "I'll think about what you said. Thank you."

"We're here for you." Dorothy twisted her lips. "Instead of changing dresses, what about something else?"

Rebecca nodded.

Scarlett stilled. Was this some kind of twisted social experiment?

"You said the other day you were trying to be less...formal. How about natural and relaxed?" Dorothy crossed her arms. "It's your call. You should be comfortable in your own skin. We're just trying to support your wishes. Book club might be a great start. None of us will judge you, and we're all normal people."

"Your mother notwithstanding."

Huffing a laugh, Scarlett ran through her options. Both of her friends were wearing capris and a blouse. The other people in club, mostly women from ages twenty to seventy, weren't pretentious. The few men involved were more the jeans and tee types.

"Okay." She checked her watch. "If I'm late coming down, can you let people in?"

"Absolutely." Rebecca smacked Scarlett's ass. "Go, girl."

Rushing up the stairs and into her bedroom, she kicked the door shut.

In her bathroom, she stared at herself in the mirror. She hadn't applied heavy cosmetics today, had gone on the more natural side, since she didn't have any appointments, and it was just book club tonight. Could she do it? Wash it all off? Hanging out with friends was one thing, but for book club with fifty plus people? She'd been wearing outfits and cosmetics as a shield for years, partly due to her breeding, and partly because of the mask. If she looked good, acted chipper, then everything was fine. Right?

But it wasn't fine. Things hadn't been okay in a long time. Her friends were right. She'd achieved her plan of opening an event business. It was thriving. She had her health, great friends, a promising relationship with Aden, and more money than she'd ever need in a lifetime. Yet obligations and responsibilities constantly weighed on her mind. Keeping up pretenses was wearing her thin. And for what? To please her mother? To ensure the Taylor name hadn't been synonymous with scandal?

Nerves in her belly and her heart heavy, she started the faucet and grabbed her facial wash. She scrubbed off the eye shadow, the lipstick, and the foundation, watching it go down the drain. After applying moisturizer, she brushed her hair, and headed for the dresser in her bedroom. Picking out a pair of jeans and a lavender swoop neck blouse, she got dressed, slipped into black flats, and went downstairs, not allowing herself the time to change her mind.

Outside the Myrtle Ballroom, voices floated toward her. Laughing. Chatting. Happy ambiance.

Her eyes grew hot, but she blew out a watery breath and cleared her throat. She could do this. She could be her natural self. She didn't need a shield. Most of the townsfolk have known her since infancy.

What if they saw through her without the barrier and didn't like her?

Someone called her name, and Rebecca replied. "She'll be right down."

Down, down. Indeed.

This was ridiculous. If Aden could be brave enough to tell her how he felt, then she could be brave enough to walk into a room full of people she knew to talk about books. Books didn't judge. Books were an escape. These were her like-minded peers.

A deep breath, and she rounded the corner. "How is everyone? Do we have enough food?"

There was a point five second pause, and then the chatter started.

These cookies are wonderful!

You look so refreshed, dear. New haircut?

I need the recipe for this divine pimento cheese dip.

I love your shirt. Wherever did you get it?

There were no hateful words to break her spirit or pitying looks because she'd let herself go. They asked how her day was and carried on as normal.

Hand to her chest, she glanced around for her besties. Near the front of the room, beside the table holding next week's book options, there they were. They smiled at her, understanding both her plight and relief.

Thank you, she mouthed.

Rebecca winked and Dorothy nodded.

She turned, intending to see about drinks, and ran smack into a wall. No, not a wall. Six feet of solid muscle wearing a button-down green plaid shirt and gray cargo shorts. Blue eyes smiled down at her.

Her Aden. Suddenly, she was okay. Air returned to the atmosphere and the lingering traces of oppression had fled.

"Hi," she breathed.

"Hello." Bending, he spoke against her ear. "You look beautiful."

Not caring who saw, she turned her head and kissed his cheek. "Thank you."

"I'm peeling those jeans off you later."

A laugh burst from her lips, her cheeks heated, and the room went several octaves quieter. Rolling her lips over her teeth, she peered around.

Yep, everyone was staring. She'd had inquisitive looks and a few questions all week while out in town. The gossip mill had been a'buzzin'. But this was different. It was a group of townsfolk, in one room, in her house. Perhaps it was time to crack the binding.

She slid her arms around his waist. "Y'all act like you've never seen two people in a relationship before."

That outta do it.

Aden groaned, but whispers started, which turned into murmuring, and then the whole room was having a say.

I knew it! I knew it!

Those two? Like oil and water.

Aren't they precious?

She rose on her toes. "Is my mother here yet?"

"I haven't seen her." He kissed her forehead and backed away. "I need food sustenance. I haven't eaten since breakfast. We had four carriage rounds today."

"Okay, y'all." Rebecca waved her arms. "Let's get started."

As patrons started taking a seat in the circle of chairs her besties had set up, Scarlett took a quick glance around. Just as she began to hope her mother wasn't going to grace them with her presence, she strode in.

Geez, she was like a fart in a fan factory. The whole room went almost silent. Some didn't dare look her in the eyes, others shifted uncomfortably in their seats. The rest outright ignored her.

In a rose-colored two-piece skirt suit with a white blouse, her black heels clacked as she walked deeper into the room. Handbag on her arm, she removed her oversized black sunglasses, her sharp gaze shifting like she was searching for something.

Crap. Or some*one*.

Scarlett wove behind a few stragglers claiming a seat, and plopped next to Dorothy. Cowardly? So what? Mother wouldn't have a chance to get ugly if Scarlett wasn't alone. Now, she'd have to wait until after the meeting to harp on Scarlett.

Rebecca leaned around Dorothy. "It's hotter than a goat's butt in a pepper patch, and she's wearing three layers?"

Scarlett shrugged. "Pretenses." Appearances over comfort.

Plate in hand, Aden sat beside Scarlett. "I'm assuming you noticed your mama's here. Have you eaten?"

She shook her head.

"Figured as much. Here." He held out a cucumber sandwich on a napkin.

She shook her head again. "Thanks, though."

"Don't make me force you," he joked.

She sighed and took it from him to alleviate his concerns. Since it was smaller than her palm, she popped the whole thing in her mouth. "Happy?"

"As a clam."

Rebecca started the meeting off with an open discussion about this week's book. As residents piped in with opinions, Scarlett attempted to look everywhere but at her mother directly across from her, but it was futile. Glaring daggers were pointed straight at her, lips firmed, and eyebrows so deeply furrowed, they formed one continuous line. Her mother was not pleased with her. When was she ever? Whether it be Scarlett's wardrobe, appearance, choice in boyfriend, climate change, the staff, or the state of world affairs, it didn't matter.

Her besties were right. Collette Taylor was never happy. Maybe it was high time Scarlett stopped trying, and focus on her own happiness.

Halfway through discussions on the book's subplot, Scarlett reached over to take Aden's hand in hers.

He squeezed it as a sign of support, to let her know he was there for her. One of the many things he did daily to quietly demonstrate he had her back, and she appreciated it.

Dorothy's mother pressed her hands to her chest over her navy blue t-shirt, smiling, her chubby cheeks aglow. "I, for one, really enjoyed the ending. The way he came to her and apologized in the pouring rain, then they kissed." She sighed dreamily, patting her pixie short red strands just shades deeper than her daughter's. "It was magical."

Murmurs of agreement rose from the circle.

This week's pick had been a newer contemporary romance by a southern author. It was the lady's debut book, and one of the other members had suggested it. They liked to switch genres to mix things up for club, but whereas cozy mystery was Dorothy's favorite and thriller was Rebecca's, romance had always been Scarlett's go-to. Give her a happily-ever-after any day. She'd truly enjoyed this read, as well.

"Honestly, Jean." Mother set one hand over the other on her lap, feet crossed at the ankles and spine straight. "How trite. The book was fluff. How any of you can read that drivel is beyond me."

An absolute and resounding silence encased the room. The kind where one could hear the heartbeat of the person sitting beside them.

Dorothy trembled beside Scarlett, her jaw ticking, eyes narrowed in anger.

Scarlett ran a hand down Dorothy's back, thinking of how best to handle the situation. She was the host, after all, but the perpetrator was her mother. Anger beat at her temples while embarrassment for Jean tumbled her stomach. That had been completely uncalled for, and in a room full of people, no less. While she grappled with what to say, Rebecca leaned forward.

"Romance is the number one selling fiction genre, and has been for over forty years." Rebecca laced her fingers. "It outsells mystery, horror, fantasy, and thrillers. It may not be your cup of tea, but it is for many. Inserting negative commentary is insulting millions of people."

Well said. Rebecca had a knack for stats and remaining calm in uprooting circumstances. She'd handled that better than Scarlett would have, and she dealt with crazy brides for a living.

Many of the members in the room nodded.

Gary from Plumber's Crack, one of a handful of gentlemen and small business owner in the group, cleared his throat. "Look, the gooey stuff ain't much my thing, neither, but some of those bedroom scenes were pretty darn great. My wife sure didn't complain."

A round of laughter filled the room, lightening the atmosphere.

"Thanks, Gary." Jean's reddened face began to recede to her normal tone. "I liked the one in the kitchen."

"And the shower," another called, but Scarlett couldn't tell who.

"This is crass." Mother's disapproving stare was directed above like she couldn't even bother to look down her nose any longer.

A sigh, and Scarlett rubbed her eyes. Enough was enough. "You're causing a scene, Mother."

Rule number eighty-five in Collette Taylor's distorted handbook of how to be proper. One mustn't cause a scene.

"I'm not the one making a spectacle of myself." Mother skimmed her gaze over Scarlett, and she felt it like a brand. Searing and sharp. "Look at yourself. You should be ashamed."

She guessed that meant her mother had noticed her lack of cosmetics and that her outfit wasn't designer. She'd like to be sorry, but she wasn't. She'd hit her give-a-damn limit.

Aden tensed beside her, his fingers gripping hers a little too tightly.

Subtlety, she shook her head to let him know she had this. Before she could wrangle a response from her lips, Jean slapped her palms to her thighs.

"What has happened to you, Collette? That is your daughter, and she's beautiful." Shaking her head, Jean focused on Scarlett. "I am so proud of you. Of all three of you." She glanced at Dorothy, Rebecca, and Scarlett. "So very proud."

"Thanks, Mom." Dorothy nodded.

Eyes burning, sinuses stinging, Scarlett smiled at Jean by way of thanks. It had been some time since she'd heard anyone say that to her. What's worse is it had to come from someone who used to be her mother's best friend. They'd been so close once. Inseparable, like Scarlett and her besties. No more. Mother had driven everyone out of her life, and Scarlett was about to be the last to depart the station.

Mother sniffed as if indifferent. "You're one to talk. You've let yourself go, Jean."

Dorothy shot to her feet while the rest of the room stared in stunned horror.

"Let's go, Mom. We're leaving."

Jean bent to collect her purse by her feet, visibly shaken.

"No, you're not leaving. Neither of you did anything wrong." Scarlett rose to stand beside Dorothy. She'd had enough. Fury had her shaking to the point of pain. Pinpricks of black dotted her vision. Her heart thundered. "She's leaving." Glaring at her mother, she clenched her teeth. "You're done. You are no longer welcome at book club."

Aden stood, but remained in place, like he was preparing to pounce and just waiting for permission. The fact that he never, not once, stepped between her and her mom, had not so much as spoken a word out of respect, and just last week said he wouldn't, only proved how concerned he was and how tense the room had become.

Slowly, her mother got to her feet and, in a move so meticulous it worried Scarlett, strode toward her. Each clack of her heels set Scarlett's teeth on edge. Not a soul so much as swallowed, but she could tell Dorothy was this close to losing her gourd for the first time in her life. Calm, patient, understanding Dorothy. Breathing erratic, her bestie's frame grew more rigid by the step.

Scarlett shifted in front of Dorothy, partially blocking her, lest her mother try something. She didn't think it would get that far, but her mother had never gone to these lengths.

She came to a stop mere inches from Scarlett, her expression devoid of emotion. Fine lines had turned to deeper wrinkles on her once pretty face, a testament to time marching on, but it was more an account of the hatred in her heart. True beauty came from within, and sadly, her mother was bankrupt in that regard. Scarlett looked at her, at this woman who'd raised her, and she suddenly seemed like a stranger. She had the same hair color as her, though Mother's was much shorter, and the same facial shape, but that was where the similarities ended.

Mother tapped her chin with her sunglasses. "You'll side with them over your family?"

She couldn't be serious. After insulting the entire book club and laying into Jean, a woman who had once been her closest friend, she had the gall to throw that at Scarlett's feet?

She said the first thing that came to mind. "Would you do the same for me?"

When no reaction came, her heart sank. Reality sluggishly filtered through her resolve, and left her hollow. It hurt. So bad, it hurt.

"Even if I was in the wrong, had caused a scene, had hurt those you cared about, would you ever defend me?" Useless, irritating tears threatened, her throat so tight, she couldn't swallow. "I've never done any those things. I've always done what you've asked of me. I've been your perfect puppet."

Mother inhaled, her lips a thin line. "Why would I bother?"

Scarlett's chest hitched, her lip quivering.

"You parade around in these clothes as if you have no means or self-respect for better ones." Mother adjusted her handbag on her forearm, the only indicator of a nervous tick. "You turned the family estate into a playground. You behave as if you had no proper upbringing. You spend time with these people who are beneath you. Worst of all, you spread your legs for filth. For the help."

A crack resonated through the room. Loud. Jarring.

Gasps followed.

It wasn't until Scarlett's palm began burning that she realized what had happened. She'd slapped her mother. In front of the townsfolk, in front of witnesses, she'd used violence. Shaking, she stared at her hand, horrified by her actions, then at her mother, whose expression never wavered. Her eyes were full of fury and a reddened mark had formed on her cheek, yet she didn't so much as flinch.

Everyone was staring.

Her besties had moved beside Scarlett, paused in an almost comical position with their arms out and seemingly unsure how to move them.

Jean had her fingers over her lips, tears in her eyes.

But Aden. Oh, Aden. Brows wrenched and hand pressed to his abdomen, he watched her, his jaw ticking and fervent distress in his eyes. Pain twisted his features into someone she almost didn't recognize.

And that was it. His pain and her friends' fear was the anvil that grounded her. Because they'd done that her whole life. Supported, encouraged, and grounded her. *Them*, not her mother.

"I will no longer cater to your warped whims." Scarlett's voice quivered, was clogged with emotion, but she cleared it. Still shaking, she wrapped her arms around herself as if that would be enough to hold herself together. "These people aren't beneath me. They're beside me. They have more integrity and decency than you could ever strive to emulate." The more she spoke, the stronger her voice became. "This might be the family estate, but it's not your kin's history. You are the outsider. It's my home, I did whatever the hell I wanted with it, and it was with Miss Maureen's blessing. Lastly, the only filth in this room is your attitude. Aden is kind, and smart, and hard-working, and funny, and he is selfless. He loves me in a way..."

Abruptly, she straightened, trembling to her core at the stark realization. A horrible, twisted agony echoed through her midsection until it became difficult to stand. Hot tears splashed onto her cheeks, and in the distance, Aden made a sound of distress.

Her gaze drifted from the ground, up her mother's body, to her face. "Did you ever love me at all?" The fact she had to ask was eviscerating. "You were around for recitals and swareys. You had your persona on point for an audience, but you weren't ever there when I needed you behind the curtain. I can't recall you ever having a kind word for me. Was there *ever* a time when you actually loved me?"

Mother tilted her head back to look down her nose at Scarlett. Painful seconds ticked by. Then, she wove around her, heels clacking toward the door.

The question hung in the air, but the answer was written in Mother's silence.

The front door slammed, and Scarlett bent at the waist, attempting to stay upright. Raw grief tore at her chest as she held back sobs. Her throat hurt and the pressure in her face was horrible.

Her own mother didn't love her. Perhaps, she never had. What did that say about Scarlett?

Chatter piqued around her, the voices loud.

Hands took her by the arms, directing her somewhere, but in her haze of confusion and shock, she didn't know where.

Then, someone picked her up, and she was in their lap, her face pressed against a cool shirt. Soothing circular motions slid across her back. The scent of the outdoors invaded, and the weight in her chest lessened. Relief released the chokehold on her muscles.

Familiar arms held her.

Aden had her. She'd be okay. She wasn't alone.

"Scarlett." Rebecca smoothed her strands, her expression sympathetic as she squatted in front of Scarlett. "I'm going to send everyone home."

She nodded, not sure of what else was supposed to do. She was hosting a book club. She needed to...

She didn't know.

"Thank you, everyone." Dorothy's voice rose above the others in the room. "Please, take some of the food home. Yes, we'll email everyone next week's book pick."

After Scarlett didn't know how long, the chatter became murmurs. Dizzy, drained, she lifted her head from Aden's shoulder. Jean was tidying the food table, putting leftovers into containers. Dorothy and Rebecca were folding chairs, stacking them in the closet rack. Everyone else had gone.

Aden offered a tight smile, jaw tight in concern. "How are you doing, babe?"

She wracked her brain, but it had shut off. "I don't know."

He nodded. "Understandable. How about we go upstairs? You can rest."

"Dorothy, I'm going to head home." Jean lifted her arms to hug her daughter.

Panic clutched Scarlett's airway for some unfathomable reason. Maybe because Jean was the last maternal figure remaining in her life. She didn't know, but Scarlett didn't want her to go.

"Please, don't." She tried to swallow past the lump in her throat, but couldn't. She straightened, shifting off Aden's lap to stand on shaking legs. "Stay."

Walking over, Jean cupped Scarlett's shoulders, a comforting smile curving her lips that didn't reach her eyes. "Are you sure? You've had a rough evening. I don't want to be a burden."

"You're never a burden," Scarlett said, ferocity in her tone. That was the sort of thing her mother would tell people. Scarlett would be different. Everyone was welcome here.

"Okay, but your handsome young man is right. Let's go upstairs and get you comfortable."

Aden called for Rebecca. "I have something I need to do. Are you all right for a bit?"

"Sure, you—"

"You're leaving?" Scarlett's alarm began anew. Her stomach shifted to somewhere near her knees. "Why?"

"Hey, it's okay." He wrapped his arms around her and kissed her forehead. "Your besties are here, and I'll be back in an hour."

What was so important that he had to leave *now*? He had a determined set to his jaw, but compassion radiated in his eyes. Remnants of concern were still etched in the bracketing around his mouth.

"Okay." If he said it was important, then it must be important. "Thanks for having my back."

"I didn't do anything but stand there."

"Exactly." Dear Aden, letting her fight her own battles, but lingering close just in case to pick up the pieces. She wondered if he realized how strong that made him. "Thank you."

One corner of his mouth lifted. "If you say so."

Chapter Sixteen

Teeth clenched, temples pounding, Aden drove through the middle of town to the outskirts where the offices were located a few streets behind the main square. Cast iron lampposts were just coming on, casting a yellowish glow over the awnings and cobblestone road. A pink and purple sky across the horizon blended with navy for a tranquil sunset. If he wasn't in a murderous rage, he might appreciate the beauty more. Leaving the square where lampposts switched to streetlights and cobblestones changed to concrete only amped his irritation.

The evening's events filtered through his head, and it was all he could do to not break something. That woman had gone too far. Let Collette Taylor shun him, stick her nose up, say crappy things. She'd done it Aden's entire existence. He'd dealt with it. But to go after the book club, after Mrs. Wilson, after his Scarlett?

Mercy, the knot in his gut just kept clenching. He'd stood there, like he'd done time after time, letting her handle her mother. He'd stayed out of it, respected Scarlett's space, and not inserted himself into family business, but damn. It had killed him. *Killed him* to just stand there, hyperventilating, avid anxiety cutting off his airway, and scared shitless the woman would cross that line he always assumed she'd step over someday.

Today had been that day.

That look on Scarlett's face, the wrenching and absolute grief, would play through his mind's memory loop until the day he died. He'd suspected all along her mother was incapable of love. Most narcissists weren't able to love anyone but themselves, but to hear it aloud? In front of a room full of people? It had to have been not only embarrassing and confusing, but gutting.

And he was going to do something about it.

He didn't give a rat's ass if the Taylors did everything in their power to ruin him. Take his business, his land. Take everything. He was not going to sit idle anymore, waiting for the day they finally stole all the will from Scarlett's beautiful spirit. Money didn't replace affection. And it didn't give permission to treat their daughter like a nuisance to be squashed.

He pulled his truck into an office lot, staring ahead as he put it in Park. A row of single-story white stucco buildings, all connected, were dark. The parking spaces were empty. It was past business hours, after all. One black-framed window was illuminated, though, and one spot had a car, just as he'd expected. A burgundy Rolls-Royce sat one space away from his, the price tag on the thing starting at more than his property and his folks' combined.

He'd never thought he'd wind up here, of all places. Of all *people*. Then again, he'd never thought he'd have Scarlett on a romantic level. He might lose her if he walked through that office door, but at least someone would stand up for her and call these bastards out on their BS.

Screw it.

Climbing from the truck, he strode toward the door and wrenched it open. The scent of cleaner filled his nose, and a blast of AC from an overhead vent ruffled his hair. A short hallway with thin gray carpet and pristine white walls lay before him with inner offices on either side. The one on the left was closed, but it was the one on the right he was after. LED light illuminated from the sidewall windows flanking the door.

Trying the handle, he found it unlocked, and stepped inside. A waiting room with brown leather chairs, an empty secretary desk, and fake palmetto plants greeted him. Nondescript art hung on the walls above a chair rail. Paint splashes on canvas that any five-year-old could have created. Beyond the waiting room was another door, open, and with a warmer light spilling onto the carpet.

"Can I help you?"

Gerald Taylor filled the doorway seconds after his voice, wearing part of an expensive gray suit. The coat had been removed, paisley tie loosened, and white shirtsleeves rolled to his elbows. He emitted the slightest reaction of surprise, a minor straightening of his spine, unnoticeable had someone not been paying attention.

"Mr. Abner?" A wrinkle formed between his brows. "Is Scarlett all right?"

"Yes." Since the guy actually appeared concerned, Aden alleviated him of that. "Physically, she's fine. Have you seen your wife today?"

"No." Mr. Taylor went to smooth his tie, a motion Aden assumed was habitual, only to realize it was askew. "She has book club on Friday evenings." He frowned. "So do you, I thought."

Some of Aden's irritation began to flee, which was probably a good thing. His heart no longer rattled an incessant beat behind his ribs. "I need a moment please."

"All right." Mr. Taylor pivoted. "Come on in. I was just finishing something before heading home."

Aden followed him inside the spacious room. Floor to ceiling mahogany shelving lined the wall to his left, a window to the parking lot ahead, and a matching mahogany desk that wouldn't fit in Aden's kitchen to the right. Unsure why, he went to the shelves, glancing over golfing trophies, crystal baubles, and pictures. It was the photos that surprised him. They were all of Scarlett through various stages in her life. Dance recitals, beauty pageants, a couple with Miss Maureen, prom, and a more recent one of her by a weeping willow tree on the estate. It was the depiction she used for her event business.

"I forgot you've never been here." Mr. Taylor stepped beside him, gaze on the shelves. "I don't golf much anymore."

"Seemed you were pretty good at it." Aden hadn't known.

Frankly, he'd not had much correspondence with the man at all, but it was apparent he cared about his daughter. Yes, these were trophies for display, but most of the unit held tributes to Scarlett.

"Long time ago now, but I try to get out for exercise once in a blue moon."

Aden nodded as two sudden realizations smacked him upside the head. One, Mr. Taylor was having a cordial conversation with him, without witnesses, and there were zero signs of the dismissal Aden had been expecting. And two, his assumptions about Mr. Taylor viewing Scarlett as an obligation had been false. Actually, if Aden had bothered to think beyond the superficial, the guy and his daughter had lunch together once a month, and he couldn't recall Mr. Taylor ever saying an unkind word about her in the few and far between instances Aden had witnessed them together. None of the automatic corrections about posture or impressions or appearances. If anything, he'd acted more aloof than judgmental.

"This is my favorite picture." Mr. Taylor smiled, removing a framed photo of Scarlett and Miss Maureen on the front porch swing. "They both have that up-to-no-good expression."

Huffing a laugh, Aden took the offered photo, studying it. It had to have been taken roughly five years ago. "She's a lot like her grandmother."

"I thank God for that." Mr. Taylor took the picture back and replaced it on the shelf. "Scarlett told me you two were seeing one another."

And here it came. The lectures, the veiled threats.

"Yes. That's part of why I'm here."

"Okay." Mr. Taylor gestured to his desk. "Have a seat."

Aden claimed a brown leather chair across from the desk, glancing at an enlarged framed painting on the wall behind it. It was an aerial of the Taylor estate from sometime around The Depression. Buildings that no longer existed were present.

"What can I do for you, Mr. Abner?"

"You can call me Aden, for starters. Mr. Abner's my dad."

The guy nodded, amusement in his faint smile as he sat behind the desk. He had dark hair like Scarlett's, interlaced with gray, and strong facial features. His face was clean-shaven, always proper, but he had slight shadows under his eyes that was a testament of someone world-weary. Maybe life had gotten to him, too.

"Something happened at book club this evening I thought you should hear about from me before the rumor mill started churning out its rhetoric." Scarlett wouldn't tell him unless her father directly asked, and Aden knew that was part of the problem. For years, she'd taken her mama's psychological warfare in silence.

Lacing his fingers on his desk, Mr. Taylor leaned forward. A deep frown intensified the wrinkles on his forehead. "I thought you said Scarlett was all right."

"I said she's physically okay. Emotionally, she's a wreck."

Leaning back in his seat, Aden crossed his arms and rehashed what had gone down at the book club meeting. The way Mrs.

Taylor had laid into Jean Wilson. How she'd insulted members for enjoying this week's selection. That she'd gone after Scarlett's BFFs and Aden via her daughter. He spared no ugly detail. The more he relayed, the harsher Mr. Taylor's expression became.

"Scarlett told her to leave." Aden's chest hurt, but the guy had to know. "She asked your wife if she ever loved her. Your wife didn't reply, and left the house with Scarlett in tears."

Mr. Taylor inhaled, nostrils flaring, and glared into Aden's eyes with a barely controlled wrath he was beginning to respect. Not a muscle twitched except a tick of the man's jaw. Several elongated moments dragged by where Aden didn't dare shift in his seat.

"I will take care of this."

Aden had no clue what *take care of this* meant, but he hated to be on the other end of the man's thinly veiled rage. "I trust you will. Look, I don't meddle in your family affairs. Scarlett may be my friend, and I know more than I should about the Taylor dynamic, but I've never gotten involved. It's been difficult to keep my trap shut sometimes because of how badly Scarlett's been hurt. Lately, it seems as if Mrs. Taylor has lost any semblance of a filter. This wasn't the first instance, which is why I'm bringing it to you."

"I appreciate it. Sincerely." Finally, Mr. Taylor broke the intense stare-down to focus on his hands. "Do I need to go see Scarlett?"

"I would, yes, but perhaps in the morning. Jean Wilson is there with her, along with Dorothy and Rebecca. Give her time to process."

A stiff nod was his only reply.

Time to go for broke. "I would like you to please have your attorney draw up a non-disclosure agreement and a pre-nuptial."

Dark brown eyes widened and landed on Aden. He stared a long beat. "I was under the impression you two just began dating."

"You're correct, and no, I'm not proposing anytime soon. The legal paperwork is a formality."

Mr. Taylor picked up a pen, running it through his fingers while still hyper-focused on Aden. "Does Scarlett know about this? Why don't you ask her to file the paperwork?"

"She doesn't know I'm here, and if I asked her, she wouldn't agree. In fact, she'd outright refuse."

"So, you're going behind her back?"

Drawing a deep breath for courage, Aden crossed one leg over the other. "I've been in love with your daughter since farther back than I can recall. I don't have enough adjectives to list all the reasons why or to describe her attributes. It took until recently for her to realize my feelings, and potentially hers. I don't know if we'll get down the aisle or if she'll change her mind about me and call it quits. I want to be prepared, in case."

Aden tapped his fingers on the arm of the chair. "The paperwork isn't for her. It's for you. Scarlett knows I don't want anything except her, but you don't know that. You barely know me at all, aside from me being the landscaper's kid who hung around your daughter. I'm more than that. I'm her friend, a business owner, her constant champion, and the man who'd die for her if it came to that. I can financially support her, but she doesn't need me. I don't want the estate or the money."

Aden leaned forward in his seat, determined to ram the rest home. "The non-disclosure is to prove to you that can trust me, because I'd never violate her privacy, and the pre-nup is to ensure you whole-heartedly understand that I didn't stick around this long in her life for a shot at the pie. I did it because I love her."

Sighing, he eased back in his seat once again, hoping like hell he didn't just blow up his and Scarlett's world by trying to eliminate a threat. Or, rather, by proving he wasn't one.

Mr. Taylor stared at him, expression unreadable. "I see why she likes you."

Wait. What?

The guy removed his tie and set it on top of the suitcoat at the edge of his desk. "You're right. I don't know you, but any young man who pounces into my office ready to slay my daughter's foe, even if that foe is her own mother, is okay in my book. No, I don't know you, Aden, but I'd like to change that."

Aden didn't dare speak. Or move. Or so much as breathe.

"She's not going to like the legalities, but I'll have my lawyer draw up the papers." Mr. Taylor rocked his chair. "I'll leave it up to you and her on whether you sign them. I'm a cynical bastard, so I would rather you sign them, but the estate is hers. The fact you're even asking for her protection says a lot about your character."

This couldn't possibly be his reality right now. Aden kept mum, lest this was a prank.

Up went Mr. Taylor's brows. "Was there anything else?"

Lumbering to his feet, Aden glanced around. "Yeah," he said, eyes on the trophies. "You should go golfing more often, sir. I think Mr. Wilson would enjoy that." Dorothy's father had once been as close with Scarlett's as their mothers. It would be a shame to waste a good friendship.

"I just might."

Nodding, Aden headed for the door.

"Oh, and Aden?"

Knowing it was too good to be true, Aden turned, glancing at the love of his life's old man, wondering about the other shoe that was about to drop.

"Please call me Gerald. Mr. Taylor was my dad's name."

Dumbstruck, Aden laughed. "Yessir."

Once he was in his truck and heading back to Scarlett's, he pulled a deep breath and released it. Perhaps he should've requested a meeting with Mr. Taylor sooner, but it probably wouldn't have had the same outcome. Aden always assumed Mr. Taylor had known about his wife's attitude and behavior, especially toward Scarlett, and had chosen to stay mute. Looking back on it, he hadn't been around as much as Mrs. Taylor, so maybe she'd had him fooled, too. Could be he just hadn't realized her elitist garbage had spilled onto Scarlett or the level of perfectionism she'd demanded from her daughter.

Regardless, he was aware now. Aden was shocked at how upset the man had been when he'd offered details. He had no doubt Mr. Taylor would handle it.

It wasn't Aden's business anymore.

He turned in Scarlett's driveway and keyed in the code for the gate. Once open, he drove the long, winding path to her estate lined with mature gnarled oaks and parked by the fountain. Rebecca and Dorothy's cars were still there. He was pretty certain Jean Wilson had ridden to club with her daughter. He hoped their presence had helped Scarlett in his absence.

He'd hated leaving her after such a cataclysmic unveiling, and while she'd been sobbing, no less. He knew her so well, every idiosyncrasy, and this evening had to be in the top five worst days of her life. Even through the anger, he'd had to force one foot in front of the other to leave her in the capable hands of her BFFs. Her pain was his pain. Her joy was his joy. It had always been that way between them.

For him.

Which was why it had been high time for him to change things. First, by going directly to her father to man up. Second, to walk away from her during a peak emotional event. It hadn't been planned, but to him, it was a necessity.

He wasn't going to rush her. She would come to realize her true feelings in time, whatever they were. Yet something she'd said when he'd professed his love had been wiggling around in his mind. She'd claimed she wasn't sure if she could separate love from in-love. He'd always figured he'd accept her affection, no matter what, if she ever offered it. To a degree, he had and would, but he couldn't be in a permanent romantic relationship where the woman wasn't with him for the right reasons. Even if that woman was Scarlett.

Hard truth was, he didn't know if she loved him because he was her friend, because he'd always been a rock for her, or because she genuinely had a soul connection like him. And she'd been correct. She may never be able to separate them unless he dialed back on the first two issues to dig at the third. It might kill him, but they both deserved a shot at the real deal.

Exhaling, he climbed from the truck and stared at the giant, looming mansion. White pillars and siding. Black shutters and a wrap-around balcony. Symmetrical. Antebellum. He'd had a love/hate relationship with it for his whole life. It represented a culture he'd never be a part of as someone on the outside always looking in. A wealth he'd never accumulate. A status he'd never reach. Scarlett's mother had fed into that mindset, and it was time to let that go.

It was just a house. Wood and nails. Best to let it quit intimidating him.

He ascended the porch steps and went inside. At the top of the grand staircase, voices came from the direction of the living room. Heading that way, he padded down the hall. The ladies were huddled on the couch, their backs to him. Leaning on the doorframe, he waited, not wanting to disturb them.

Mrs. Wilson had Scarlett in an embrace, her cheek resting on Scarlett's head. "The thing to remember through all of this is that she's wrong. She's bitter, and taking it out on you. There are lots of people around you who care about you."

"Was she always like this?" Scarlett sniffed. "I don't understand."

"I think the fact you don't understand is proof you're nothing like her, but to answer your question, no. She wasn't always this bad. Looking back on it, I'm not sure why I tried to stay friends so long, other than nostalgia or obligation." Mrs. Wilson looked over Scarlett's head at Rebecca. "Your parents' passing was hard on all of us, especially you. Ever since, she's just gotten worse. No one's fault but hers, and certainly not yours." She squeezed Scarlett. "There were moments, genuine moments, when you girls were little that I look back on fondly."

Scarlett heaved a sigh. "I don't know whether to be relieved she's gone or mortified about how she left."

"Both are reasonable." Dorothy leaned her head back on the cushion. "Everyone was appalled, and no one blames you. What you said to her was brave. I don't know about you, but I feel like a weight's been lifted from my shoulders, and she wasn't even my mother."

"Same." Rebecca stretched. "Do you want a refill, Mrs. Wilson?"

"No, thank you. I should get going."

Aden knocked on the doorframe to let them know he was here since there was a pause in the conversation. They turned to look at him.

"You're back." Scarlett smiled. Her eyes were red and puffy, but dry.

"I am. How are you?" He leaned over the back of the couch, kissing her forehead upside down.

"Better, thanks."

He nodded, glancing at the others as they stood. "Are you staying?"

Rebecca slid her purse over her shoulder. "Now that you've returned, I'm going to head home to let Graham know what went down before he hears it elsewhere."

Good plan.

"I'm just going to go home." Dorothy smiled. "Ready, Mom?"

Aden walked them out and locked up. When he got back upstairs, Scarlett had switched from the living room to her bedroom. He found her at the edge of the bed, staring blankly out the balcony doors. Moonlight cast her in ethereal hues, amping the despondence in her expression.

Sick to his stomach, he shook his head. He would've gone to see her mother tonight, too, lay into her, but it wouldn't have done any good. She wouldn't ever change. He hated what she'd done to his Scarlett, though.

Sitting beside her, he laced his fingers with hers, running his thumb across the soft skin on the back of her hand. "How are you really?"

She kept staring out the window. "Numb."

Her monotone was worrisome, but maybe this was normal when the waterworks were over and reality set in. His folks would never do this to him, so he couldn't exactly relate, but he did know her, and she was probably questioning her entire existence.

"I just don't get it, Aden. I don't. I have my flaws, and I didn't live up to her expectations, but..."

He waited for her to finish that thought, but she let it hang, and he feared he knew exactly where she was heading with it. "But how can a mother never have loved her own daughter?"

He wondered about that often, especially because that daughter was Scarlett, and a person had to try exponentially hard not to love her. He'd attempted the feat, and never got close.

"Yeah," she breathed, finally looking at him. It was as if her honey-infused eyes had lost all remnants of their spark. "What could I have possibly done to deserve that?"

Oh, hell no. "Nothing. Not a damn thing. Do you hear me? Absolutely nothing. Even if you'd been everything her twisted heart desired, the outcome would've been the same. *She's* the defective one, not you."

"Mrs. Wilson said the same thing." She turned her face toward the balcony again. "I know that in here," she tapped her temple, "but not here," she finished, pressing her hand to her chest.

Suddenly, she looked at him as if a thought bloomed. "Where did you go earlier?"

"It was something I had to take care of, that's all." Now was not the time to get into it.

"You're not going to tell me, are you?'

"Not tonight." He would later, because he kept nothing from her, but she had enough swirling around in her head. Which was why he needed to skedaddle. "I'm going to sleep at home tonight. Dufus needs to go out, too." The dog had a great bladder, but it had been a few hours.

"Why? You can't stay?" Panic tinged her tone, radiated in her eyes.

One day, she'd stop making him bleed. Or not.

"I can stay, but I'm choosing not to." He shifted on the bed to face her, hoping she'd understand. "I've been thinking about something you said, about how it's hard to separate the current relationship with the friendship we always had. I've been here for you whenever you've needed me. The same as you have for me. I will continue to do that tomorrow, and the day after, and the day after that, because I love you."

"So will I," she argued.

He took a breath to summon patience. "You took a blow tonight. Normal operating procedure is for me to be with you. Years from now, I want to look back on this and know you love me because of what we are and have been together, not out of gratitude or habit."

"That's ridiculous." Fury infused her gorgeous eyes. "You aren't a habit."

Maybe, maybe not. It was a difficult task to see beyond a common routine to what happened when that was interrupted. The disruption was required in order to be certain. All this time, all these years, they'd not tested the theory.

"You have your BFFs. You have me. Tonight, I want you to have *you*. No distractions or crutches. Process what happened and think about what you want without radio interference."

Glaring at him, she opened her mouth, but quickly shut it again. Her irritation was fizzling, but remnants were still present in the way she pressed her lips tightly together and went unblinking.

Terror and anxiety wrestled in his gut, but he didn't want to be something she regretted later. Giving her a chance alone to figure it out would mean they'd never live a lie.

Swallowing hard, he tucked her silky cocoa strands behind her ears and cupped her face. He kissed her, pouring everything he had left into it so she knew he hadn't changed his mind.

She sighed against his lips, resting her forehead to his. "You're going to feel silly when I'm right."

He grinned. "Doubtful." Rising, he kissed her forehead. "Goodnight, babe."

Chapter Seventeen

After a few hours of restless sleep at best, Scarlett padded down the hall in her PJs and a robe toward the upstairs kitchen. She'd bumped her mid-afternoon appointment to tomorrow and had told her staff to take today off. All she wanted was coffee, a tank-sized box of chocolates, and to be left alone.

While her pot brewed, she stood in front of it, glaring. It was taking an eternity. Why had she not noticed how slow it was before? And the sun through the window was frying her retinas. Maybe this was like the watched pot never boils thing?

She fed the cat instead of stalking the coffeemaker.

Finally finished percolating, she poured herself a cup of coffee, added too much cream and sugar, because, why not, then went out onto the rear balcony. The sun wouldn't be on this side of the house yet, so she could pout in peace and quiet.

Plopping in a rocker, she set her feet on the railing and crossed her ankles. Birds chirped, the happy assholes, and crickets sang an obnoxious tune. It was hot, but the humidity was tempered by a breeze carrying the scents of blooms from the gardens and chlorine from the pool. Maybe she'd go for a swim later, if she felt like it.

Probably not.

Damn her mother, anyway. Scarlett had devoted too much of her time and energy to giving the woman what she wanted, while still trying to stay true to herself. She'd offered her mother benefit of the doubt for her sniping and had even made excuses for her behavior. Over and over, Scarlett had defended her own choices, her friends, and Aden to deaf ears.

Last night had proven Collette Taylor was never going to change, never accept Scarlett or the people in her life, and...

Never love her.

Sinuses stinging, she took a sip of coffee.

Her mother was never going to love her. It was something she'd repeated over and over in her mind while trying to sleep so it would sink in. The shock had left her mostly numb, but today, she was raw. Angry, hurt, and raw. Mrs. Wilson, her besties, and Aden were right. It was her mother's flaw, not Scarlett's.

Still, it was difficult to contend with. Why wasn't she loveable? Could she have done more? Deep in the recesses of her mind, she understood there was nothing she could've done or said, but it wasn't natural. A mother was supposed to love her children.

Normally, she'd hash such things out with her besties or Aden. They had a little after the situation, she supposed, first with the girls, then with Aden. But none of them had stayed. Which was strange in and of itself. Aden, especially. He'd always stuck around when she'd had a bad day, even as friends, or he'd come to her when he'd needed it. He'd been acting weird since her mother had stormed out, slamming the door in her wake.

What had been so important that he'd had to take off after Mother's outburst? And why hadn't he stayed when he'd returned? Ever since their first date, they'd spent every night together. Making love. Waking next to one another. Daily routines and talking about anything.

His spiel about her needing time for herself was on-point, but that never meant not having him here. He'd seemed incredibly focused on the aspects of their love, too. She didn't get why it mattered. They loved each other. Period.

Their conversation from when he'd professed his feelings poked at her memory. At the time, she'd been leveled by the sweet, endearing things he'd said. It had taken her awhile to recover, but as her synopsis threaded again, she'd realized the words were stuck in her throat. She just wasn't sure about the differences. To her, love was love. Yes, it came in many forms, and yes, romantic love was different, but how was she supposed to separate years of caring about someone from the actual man it involved?

She'd also gotten the impression he was at a crossroads, and the wrong decision from her could make or break their relationship.

Her phone dinged. Twice.

Aggravated, she pulled it from the pocket of her robe and glanced at the screen.

Rebecca: Checking in. How are you, Scarlett?

Dorothy: What she said. Need us over?

Did she want her friends right now? They've always been a comfort, and talking it out might help.

But, no. She wanted to lick her wounds alone, and Aden was right. Being by herself and in her own headspace would probably be the key to unlocking the storm inside her. Though she was an independent woman, she was almost never left to her own devices. Between her staff, her besties, her family, her former lovers, her guests, and Aden, it was rare she actually had any unaided moments. Only she could give herself answers.

She thumbed a text to them. *Thank you, but I'm okay.*

Just as she was about to head in to refill her coffee, the doorbell rang.

For crying out loud. The staff were off, her besties would call first, there were no appointments, and Aden wouldn't ring. Pulling up her doorbell camera, she was surprised to find her father on the porch. He had a key, but never used it. He didn't visit much, either. What was he doing here?

Oh, gosh. Had the rumor mill alerted him to what had happened at book club? Her belly cramped.

Clicking the mic icon, she spoke through her phone. "Hi, Daddy. Come on in. I'm upstairs."

"Will do."

Crap, she wasn't dressed, but she was at least somewhat presentable. There was no time to change. Rushing inside, she wove through her bedroom and to the top of the grand staircase.

Her father stepped into the foyer and closed the door behind him. He was dressed in casual khaki slacks and a white polo, indicating he didn't have business today. Without glancing up, he climbed the steps. Halfway, he spotted her.

"Hi, there. Did I wake you?"

She waved her hand, dismissing the thought. "No, just slow to get moving this morning. Let me get dressed."

"No, you're fine." He reached the top and offered a tight smile. "I'm intruding, and it's your house. Stay as you are."

What an odd thing for him to say. She gave him a brief welcome hug and pointed to the hallway. "Let's go in the living room. Do you want coffee?"

"If you have some made."

"I do. Make yourself comfortable. I'll be right back."

Cinching the belt of her robe tighter, she went into the kitchen and poured both of them some coffee. Remembering he took it black, she left it at that and strode down the hallway, into the living room. He'd claimed one of the vacant chairs that flanked the fireplace, staring idly at his hands.

"Here you go." She passed him a mug.

"Thank you."

"Is everything okay?" She sat in the other chair, facing him, and tucked her legs under her, adjusting her robe to cover her legs. "You don't normally visit."

"I probably should've called first." His expression was troubled as he stared into his cup.

"You don't ever need to call first. It's the family home."

His eyes twinkled like he'd found the response amusing. "I appreciate that." He puffed his cheeks, obviously gearing up for a tough topic. "Aden came by my office to see me last night."

It took her a few seconds to process his words, and then her stomach bottomed out. That's where Aden went after leaving here? Why? He and her father didn't exactly have a chummy relationship.

"He mentioned what happened at your book club."

Oh, boy. She probably should've made it a point to call him, knowing how fast gossip spread in Vallantine. Since this particular gossip involved Mother, he would be directly affected. Why had Aden taken that initiative, though? He never got involved in family business.

"I'm sorry. I didn't think to call."

Father set his coffee on the table. "Why didn't you? Furthermore, why didn't you tell me how bad she'd become?"

Honestly, she hadn't seen the point. He'd not ever stepped in, except to tell Mother to simmer down sometimes, and had usually taken a passive approach like dealing with her exuded too much effort. He wasn't active in her day-to-day life or in Vallantine all that much. It was Scarlett's problem. Wouldn't that be like tattling, anyway?

"I didn't realize it would upset you this much." She took a sip of her coffee, but it only made her stomach queasier, so she set it down.

"Of course, it upsets me. Her behavior was reprehensible, and I had to hear it from Aden."

And, here they go. She could anticipate what came next. Aden wasn't a good match for her. Aden has no right to involve himself in their lives. Aden...

"That man cares about you an awful lot."

Alrighty. Had she accidentally spiked her coffee?

Father sighed, leaning back in his chair. "I didn't know how bad it was, and that's partly my fault. While you were growing up, your mother did most of your activities. I worked a lot. You never complained. I figured..." He shook his head. "I don't know what I figured. I'm sorry you felt like you couldn't come to me."

Dang. Her eyes watered, and she blinked repeatedly to clear the impending waterworks.

"Aden was right to bring it to my attention." He glanced away, seemingly lost in thought. "I haven't taken the time to get to know him, but I'd like to change that. He's been as important a figure in your life as Dorothy and Rebecca. It wasn't until we talked last night that I realized how much he loves you." He smirked. "Pretty protective fellow."

Breathing a laugh, she pressed a palm to her chest, eyes leaking like a faucet. "Yes, he is, but he also lets me fight my own battles."

He nodded, his gaze scanning her features. "You don't have to fight them alone. That's all I'm trying to say."

And here she thought she'd cried herself into dehydration last night. Guess she was wrong. "Thank you," she mustered.

To calm down, she reached for her cup, hoping to swallow some of her emotion.

Leaning forward, he took a sip of coffee, too, and returned it to the table. "I've filed for divorce."

She choked, coughing violently. "I'm sorry." She grabbed a tissue, covering her mouth as the residual coughing subsided. "You did what?"

Her father stared at her, unblinking.

"Oh God, Daddy. It's not because of me, is it?" Overwhelming grief and guilt compressed her chest, had her belly threatening to revolt.

Gaze on his lap, he pulled a breath. "It is, in part, because of you, but not for the reasons you think. This isn't your fault. I've been posturing the idea for some time, and now was the point to act. What your mother said to you was uncalled for, and something no daughter should ever hear."

She waited him out since he seemed to have more to say, but everything in her wanted to barrage him with questions and demands.

Finally, he looked at her. "I should've listened to your grandmother all those years ago. She had your mother pegged from the start. Alas, it can't be undone." Another smirk curved his lips. "The conversation with Aden is what made me quit dragging my feet. Your mother and I never made each other happy, not like the two of you. It was time to leave."

Wow. Talk about a whack upside the head with the Stunned Stick.

"Does Mother know?"

"Yes. I went home last night and informed her. She's being served any minute now."

Yikes. She wanted desperately to ask how Mother had taken the news, but Father wasn't one of her besties, and this wasn't fodder for gossip. Still, the hurting side of her hoped Mother was stewing in her own choices, miserable and alone.

"What will you do?" Coffee now cold, she set it aside.

"I'm going to look for a place in Vallantine, I suppose. I'm letting her keep the house there."

Generous of him, and more than Mother deserved. "You could stay here until you find something."

He blinked at her in surprise.

She shrugged. "It *is* the family estate. I have three gue-strooms."

He tilted his head as if to say, touché. "I might take you up on that until I find something appropriate. I don't want to stay long-term. It's your home now, and you have a business to run. Plus, you and Aden are going to want privacy."

Interesting how he didn't seem to have any qualms about Aden being here. That must've been some chat they'd had last night. An idea niggled in the back of her mind about her predicament with Aden, but she shoved it aside to deal with later.

"You can stay as long as you like, Daddy." Thinking about Vallantine and the properties, nothing seemed appropriate for him unless he found another estate back here by all the older ones.

Oh. Hold on. "Build here."

He reared. "What do you mean, here?"

"On the estate." She leaned forward, her mind whirling. "Think about it. I sold the north side of the property to Aden for his home and business, including the barns and pastures. The whole south side is nothing but grass and trees. Miss Maureen's gardens and my pool are behind the mansion. There's nothing unencumbering. That has to be at least ten acres, and if cordoned off correctly, rectangular in shape."

"I never thought of that." He immediately shook his head. "No, though. I can't do that."

"Why not?"

Seemingly flustered, he opened his mouth and swiftly shut it again. "It would be breaking up the estate."

A few weeks ago, she'd asked him at lunch if he was upset she'd inherited the estate. What she hadn't dared ask him was… "Are you angry I sold part of it to Aden?"

His gaze flew to hers. "No. You never had much interest in the stables, and Aden had a solid business plan. He worked hard and earned it."

Slowly, she nodded, erringly relieved, not only that he wasn't mad, but because he respected Aden. "So, why would selling off a chunk of the other side, which goes unused, bother you? It's staying in the family, and it would be nice to have my father next door."

His expression said he was running out of excuses, and a glimmer of hope had his dark eyes alight. "The Historical Society will never go for it."

"The Historical Society can only butt in if we do something to the mansion's structure, and that would be pushing it because it's private land. It's a gray area that favors us. Besides, you can design something that goes with the time period, such as a Victorian or a smaller scale Antebellum."

"Well, um…" He cleared his throat and reached for his coffee.

It was a rare day she saw her father flustered.

"This was your home, too. You grew up here." He and Mother had moved out not long after Scarlett turned eighteen, buying a generous house in a neighboring county. Mother and her grandmother routinely knocked skulls, and it was no secret Miss Maureen had planned to leave it all to Scarlett. For the first time, it dawned on her how hard that must've been on him. "Don't let Mother take this away from you like she did when you relocated. Come back home, Daddy."

Obviously having a difficult time meeting her gaze, he stared at his lap, lips twitching as if practicing what to say. Eventually, he closed his eyes and raised his chin. When he looked at her, pride and gratitude shone in his firm smile.

"Okay, sweetheart. Let's do it."

She clapped like she was an excited thirteen year old again who'd been given the green light to roam a bookstore and buy whatever she desired.

They chatted a little longer and made an appointment for Monday to see the attorney to transfer land to her father. Starting tomorrow, he'd stay with her until a new home could be built on the southern property. It released a lot of the weight she'd been carrying around and made her heart happy. Mother had ruined their lives long enough.

Once her father left, Scarlett got dressed and decided to visit the cemetery. Her grandmother was no longer alive, but maybe the act of talking to her would help her work out the other issues she faced. Not having her around for support or to bounce ideas off of had left a vacant hole.

Turning out of her driveway, she drove the two blocks through the historic district to the cemetery gate and through it. Ginormous hundred year old oaks created a canopy, gnarled branches reaching out to shield the beloved. Gray-green Spanish moss hung from them, swaying in the breeze, and added a dated timestamp to the grounds. Tree roots jutted from the earth, twisting, and disrupting some of the land around them.

To the right was the newer part. Simple inlaid headstones with markers. Some had flowers. Most didn't. Rebecca's parents and her Gammy were buried in that section. To the left was the older part. Tombstones were large, baroque, and darkly weathered by time. There weren't many newer graves, as only a few original families had plots remaining, but they dated all the way back to the original founders, William and Katherine Vallantine. Scarlett's lineage, Miss Maureen included, were buried there.

Turning left, she drove the bumpy brick-laid path at a crawling speed that cut through the older section, sunlight scattering through the leaves. Near the end, just two rows down from the Vallantines, was the Taylor plot. The family name marker was a twelve-foot angel statue, dark mildew trapped in the various crevices. It would probably be incredibly creepy at night, but Scarlett had never tested the theory. Surrounding it were all headstones from her line.

Climbing out of her car, she was met with a wall of heat and humidity. The scent of peat moss and damp clung to the air as she made her way to Miss Maureen's grave. Due to the trees and shade, there wasn't much grass, so she squatted by the headstone.

"I forgot to bring you flowers, but I'll pick some from your garden next time I come."

Feeling silly, she glanced around, but no one else was here. And her legs were uncomfortable, so she said screw it and plopped in the dirt. A sigh, and she tried to think of what to say. If her grandmother were still alive, that wouldn't have been an issue. They'd chit-chat and gossip and laugh.

"Mother and Father are getting a divorce." Hand to her forehead, she let out a loud, awkward laugh. "Never thought I'd say that, but they really are. Mother has gone looney tunes lately. Far worse than she's ever been. She flipped her gourd at book club. I miss you. You would've put her in place."

Chewing her lip, she picked at a blade of grass. "She never loved me. I bet you knew that already, but it was a shock to me." Staring at the headstone, her gaze wavered. "Aden and I have been seeing each other. He said he loves me, but wants me to think about whether I love him in the same way. This is one of those times I could really use your insight. I wonder what you would think of all this. I mean, you always liked Aden, but this is different."

She could envision her grandmother's voice in her head, the thick southern dialect and no-nonsense tone. But she couldn't conjure what Miss Maureen would've said, and a weight bore down on her chest. She didn't feel her grandmother in this place. She was buried here, laid to rest, yet Scarlett felt her presence and legacy more at the estate. In the garden, specifically.

Perhaps this hadn't been the best idea. Regardless, she was glad she came, and got to her feet, brushing dirt off her butt.

While walking back to her car, Aden texted.

How are you this morning?

Part irritated, part relieved, she thumbed a reply. *Fine, thanks. Daddy came by. You might've told me you went to see him last night.*

Getting behind the wheel, she started the car and drove out the way she came. She hadn't made it twenty feet, and Aden called.

Rolling her eyes, she connected him to the car's Bluetooth. "Hi."

"What did he say?"

Really? What were they, ten years old? "Hi, Scarlett. Good to hear your voice. I missed you," she mocked.

A long groan filled the line. "Hi, Scarlett. It *is* good to hear your voice. I *did* miss you. Now, what did he say?"

"He said you went to see him and told him about Mother's hissy fit at book club." Pulling to the gate, she checked for oncoming cars. "That is what you did, right? Left my house and went to my father?"

"Yes." He paused. "I told you I'd tell you later."

Rounding the corner, she pulled into her driveway. "It's later, Aden."

"You're mad."

She took a second to decide if she was, in fact, mad or simply irritated. "I'm slightly miffed. Not because you went to him, but the timing of when you did, and then wouldn't tell me."

"It couldn't wait, Scarlett. That hissy fit, as you called it, went way beyond shit she's pulled before."

No kidding. "You could have given me the chance to tell him." She pulled into the garage, leaving the door open and the car running for the AC. "And your timing sucked."

He went quiet long enough for her to check the connection. "You wouldn't have told him."

Glaring ahead, she strummed her fingers on the wheel, hating that he was correct.

"I'll take that as an admission." He sighed heavily. "He needed to know, Scarlett. For Christ sakes, she all but told you she didn't love you in front of half the town. He's not her. He does love you. I never, not once, put myself between you and them, but it was high time someone defended you."

A long, strenuous pause followed where she didn't know what to say and his breathing was labored.

He had always defended her, even if it was from the sidelines, and protected her every chance that warranted a response. They weren't actions seeking the limelight or accreditation. Just him taking care of her. Truly, this was no different.

"Since you're *slightly miffed* anyway, there's more."

Closing her eyes, she took a deep breath. "What's that?"

He cleared his throat. "I asked him to draft an NDA and pre-nup. The second part is in case we get that far."

She gnashed her teeth. "What the hell, Aden? I—"

"It was for him, not you, and I told him as much." He sighed. "Look, he doesn't know jack about me. I thought it was time he learned where I stood."

Glaring at the car's ceiling, she couldn't argue with that, either, but there were other ways to prove his trust. "Another thing you should've told me."

"I'm telling you now."

She chewed her lip, contemplating all he'd done and said. It was as if he was laying the groundwork after many months of planning. "You really want to marry me?"

He paused, and she could picture his dumbstruck, is-this-a-trick expression.

"I'm busy today, but how about next week?" he joked.

She grinned. The smartass.

"Yes, I want to marry you someday, assuming you figure out if I'm really what you want, and yes, I wanted your father's understanding about my intentions."

He was exactly what she wanted, but she still wasn't grasping his ultimatum.

"Okay, Aden." She shook her head, her heart lifting. "I have news also."

She relayed Father's announcement of filing for divorce and their decision to plot out land on the estate to build. Afterward, she could all but hear the crackling thoughts in Aden's head.

"Holy crap. Busy morning."

She huffed a laugh. "A little bit."

"In seriousness, I'm glad he's getting away from her, and I love the idea of you having your dad next door."

"Me, too."

He went quiet again for a beat. "I have to go, but think about it, darlin'. I'll stay home again tonight to give you space."

"I don't need space, I—"

"No, babe. You don't *want* space, but you do *need* space. Two separate things. You know where to find me."

Chapter
Eighteen

From the couch in his parents' living room, Aden stared numbly at the ball game on the television. Dufus was asleep at his feet, snoring. He'd only been partly watching because all the info Scarlett had told him kept ramming against the inside of his skull.

He was still trying to process the fact that the Taylors were getting a divorce. He wouldn't wish the decline of a marriage on any couple. It had to be difficult. Yet, he couldn't recall either of them ever being happy. No hand-holding or secret smiles when they thought people weren't watching. He rarely saw them in the same room. And based off Mr. Taylor's reactions to Aden's info bombs, maybe it would be a fresh start for the guy. He might be a tad stiff and proper, but he seemed to love Scarlett. The way Aden viewed it, moving back to the estate was a good step.

"Yes," Dad cheered, popping a peanut in his mouth, face glued to the game.

He sat a cushion away from Aden on the floral-printed sofa wearing a baseball jersey and jeans. He had darker skin tones like Aden from years of working in the sun. Stark white hair and deep crow's feet around his eyes. Retirement looked good on him.

They'd purchased a small bungalow home just a couple blocks away from Rebecca in an older subdivision. Cookie cutters with varying exterior colors. It suited them, though. Mom could have a small flower garden out back, and Dad had just enough grass to cut to keep him busy. Even though they'd owned the place about four years, it still seemed weird to Aden to have to drive to visit. He'd always pictured them in the ranch house on the Taylor estate where he still lived.

Above the TV on the beige walls were several family photographs. He hadn't paid them much mind, but it looked like Mom put up a few new ones. Him with his horses in a pasture. He was betting Scarlett had sent them to her.

"I like the new pictures, Mama."

She glanced up from her crocheting in a corner chair that matched the couch, a smile on her lips. "Thanks, baby." She'd been cutting her dark blonde hair shorter the past couple years. It rested on her shoulders and curved at the ends. "Scarlett dropped those off a month back. Said she took 'em for your brochures?"

At the mention of Scarlett's name, Dufus lifted his head, but Aden was stuck on what his mother had said.

"Yeah," he mumbled. Did Scarlett visit them often? She'd never said anything. "She's good at that sort of thing."

"Sure is." Mom adjusted the green yarn in her lap. "I'm glad that event business of hers is doing well. Such a big ole house for one woman. She's a social butterfly, that one."

Truth. "That was nice of her to bring them," he fished, seeing if his mother would say more.

"Mmhmm." Stitch, stitch. "In her case, that apple *did* fall far from the tree. Nothing like her mama, bless her heart. She checks up on us ever since your daddy had the knee replacement. She brings us some of that chicken salad her chef, George, makes." Mom shook her head. "I could eat the whole tub myself."

"Um… Dad's surgery was three years ago."

"Oh, I know. She still comes by, anyway. She tells me all the good gossip."

"Huh." Aden looked at his dad and did a double-take, finding him smirking. "What?"

"We like her."

"Yessir," Mom added.

Something smelled fishy in here. They were acting strange.

"She's hard not to like," he hedged. They got along with her, far as he knew. He couldn't recall a time they didn't, but then again, he'd had zero clue she dropped by for visits.

Dad's brows pinged his hairline. "Things going good between you two?"

He should've kept his trap shut and stuck to the game. "Yes."

Mom nodded, still crocheting. "Tell her you love her yet?"

Idly tapping his fingers on the arm of the sofa, he darted his gaze between them. "My love's not in question."

"Hogwash." Dad set his bowl of peanuts on the end table. "What's that girl gotta do to prove it to you?"

Saying it would be a great start. At least, in relation to what he was seeking.

"Way I hear it," his mother piped in, "she defended you in front of everyone the other night. Stuck it right to her mama."

Dad crossed his arms. "Sold you the land for your business and helped with all the marketing."

"Took care of ya last fall when you had the flu."

Back and forth, they went, making Aden's head hurt. He knew all this, and that was partly the point. Yes, she loved him. As a friend. Yes, she'd done all these and more. Because she cared about him. But was that in-love? Couldn't breathe without him, wanting him to have and hold, no matter what?

"Sounds to me like this is a *you* problem, son." Dad resumed his peanut popping, leaning back on the couch.

"It's the money, isn't it?" Mom set her hooks down, frowning at Aden. "It's because she's rich? You're intimidated?"

Dad pointed at Mom. "Thinks he's not good enough."

"He's worried what people are going to say."

Again, they went back and forth, and Aden rubbed his forehead.

"Stop. Just...stop." He sighed in irritation. "I don't care if she has pennies to her name or entire vaults in all fifty states. I could care less what other people say, and I *am* good enough."

Huffing, he stared ahead as a strange fist unfurled in his chest. Claws retracted from knotting his shoulders. It suddenly became easier to breathe. He hadn't realized the weight he'd been carrying around, the anxiety and fear.

But what had caused it to let up now? Ever since he'd acknowledged his feelings for Scarlett, he'd been worried she'd find out, and more worried that if she did, those feelings wouldn't be returned. An anarchy sword to their friendship would ensue. For years, this cycle culminated. Then, it happened. She'd figured it out, but hadn't dismissed him. The opposite. She'd nurtured the chemistry, and they'd slid right into a relationship. It had almost been too easy. Perhaps that was the issue. He'd wrongly assumed it would be more dramatic.

His folks might've been on to something. Though he and Scarlett had been close for decades, he'd always had the mentality of being an outsider. Wrong side of the tracks. Rich girl vs poor boy. The town, though surprised, hadn't tried to create a wedge. They'd supported the idea. His parents hadn't attempted to talk him out of it. And Scarlett had never, not once, treated him any different.

The only obstacle had been her mother and…well, himself. Realization dealt a one-two punch to his ribs. It wasn't just Scarlett who'd let her mother invade their mindset. He'd done it, too. Not on purpose, and while completely unaware, but the results were the same. Collette Taylor had placed doubt and insecurities in his head this entire time, and made Aden think he was less than.

The issue hadn't been whether Scarlett loved him the right way. The issue had been him believing he wasn't good enough. He *was* good enough. No one would ever love her as deeply, take care of her as well as him, or support her in the ways she actually needed it.

Damn, and he'd told her to think about it, to separate what was from what could be to decide if she loved him. She *had* loved him all along. She'd shown it every hour of every day. Their whole lives.

Reaching for his phone, he thumbed a text to her. *Never mind what I said. I'll be over tonight.*

He'd fix it then.

For now, he lumbered to his feet and called for the dog. "I'm going to take off. Love you guys."

After shaking Dad's hand and kissing his mama's cheek, he strode to his truck in their driveway. Scarlett's reply pinged his phone as he started the engine.

Okay.

That was it. Just *okay*? He narrowed his eyes at the screen and typed. *I'll bring dinner.*

The icon whirled, indicating she was replying. Seconds later, it went through.

Okay, thanks.

He sighed. Either she was distracted or peeved. Whatever, they'd work it out soon. Backing out of the driveway, Dufus in the passenger seat, he headed toward town.

Dusk was descending, casting the cobblestone streets and storefronts in pink and red hues. The lampposts flickered on, adding a yellowish glow. Tourists bustled about, popping in and out of shops. He had his choice of dinner options, but after Scarlett's tumultuous couple of days, he figured she'd want comfort food.

He parked outside the Tipsy Turtle, put Dufus on a leash, and went in. They were busy as all get-out, and his order was going to take thirty minutes, so he decided to walk a bit to waste time.

Heading toward the end of the strip, he pulled in a deep breath and relished the breeze. Humidity clung, but the unrelenting heat had abated now that the sun wasn't beating down. The jingle of Dufus's collar was background noise to the chatter of people as the dog walked in step with him. The scents of various food vendors blended with blooms from the curbside flower boxes, and his stomach rumbled. He'd only eaten snack food at his folks' place.

He paused outside the courtyard for Miss Katie. Brick was laid around the courtyard's circumference with a black wrought iron fence around the tree, which sat on a slight grassy noll. Shorter lampposts encased the perimeter. Spotlights were aimed up at the trunk. A few benches were scattered and iron signs telling the myth were posted.

"Wanna visit Miss Katie?" he asked Dufus.

The dog's tongue lolled by way of an answer as he gazed up at Aden through brown, expression-filled eyes. His loyal black lab rarely barked and was the best companion. They moved to an empty bench, where Aden took a seat and Dufus plopped by his feet.

Tourists and townsfolk mingled, some reading the signs, others just staring at the tree or catching a rest on the benches. Through the years, he'd not given much thought to Miss Katie or her legend, despite it being one of Vallantine's staples. The thing was almost twice as big as others of its variety, and ten times as old. Branches grew upward, reaching, and the shape neared a rounded crown. More decorative and ornamental if not for the size. Dark green deciduous leaves encased the branches. Red blooms would cover the tree in spring, but they were gone now. It had stopped producing fruit years before, yet good ole Miss Katie was still here.

One of the legends was that she granted wishes. He wasn't sure of that any more than he was about Katherine Vallantine's ghost in the library, but eh. Who was he to judge? Scarlett would come by the tree a lot as a teenager, casting wishes into the void, her hopeful heart open. He wondered if she still did that. He never had, but he got a kick out of her optimism.

Bending, he pet Dufus's soft fur, contemplating. What would he have wished for back then? A good baseball season? Relief from the heat? Passing grades? A good summer job to save up? Better parties? World peace?

Scarlett. He shook his head, no longer denying his greatest wish would've been for her. That she would view him as more. That she'd cross the line and kiss him. That their bickering was just a preamble to chemistry. He'd never dare say so aloud, but in the deepest recesses of his mind and heart, he'd had all he ever wanted or needed except her.

And now he did. He had her, and she had him. Heart, body, soul. It was the damn strangest thing, having a connection to someone so deeply that he could anticipate their needs, their desires, and realize they'd wanted the same things all along.

"What do you wish for when you have everything you dreamed about?"

The dog didn't answer, leaving Aden at a loss. He should count his lucky stars this wasn't some kind of mirage to taunt him, that it wasn't a trick of his imagination or whimsy of fate that Scarlett Taylor actually loved him back.

And there it was, his answer. "I wish it was true."

Smiling, he figured it couldn't hurt, casting a wish just in case. He'd leave the rest to Miss Katie to work her magic.

He patted the dog's flank. "Come on, boy. Let's get food and go see Scarlett."

But she wasn't home. He searched the whole mansion, which was a feat in and of itself, but there was no Scarlett. Sighing, he set the food on the kitchen island and shot off a text.

I'm here. Where are you?

The icon whirled. *Had to take care of something. Can you look in my dresser drawers under the TV?*

He stared at his screen, but nope. That was still a weird request.

Regardless, he climbed the grand staircase and pivoted for her bedroom. She had two dressers—a wide, shorter one under the wall-mounted flatscreen and a tall one on the other side of the room beside the settee. He'd never looked in them, and was uncomfortable doing it now.

Opening the top left drawer, he froze. Her clothes weren't in there. *His* were. The white tees he often wore while feeding horses or with his boxers around the house. The hell?

He opened several more, and it was all his clothes. Every drawer, his clothes.

Pulling his phone from his pocket, he texted her five question marks.

Her response? *Look in the upstairs hallway.*

He glared at the ceiling. Shook his head. Clenched his teeth.

Finally, he strode from her bedroom. She had no furniture along the dark, wood-paneled hallway, just photographs on the wall of her ancestors.

Oh, shit. Not anymore, though.

There were still dated images, but she'd taken down the one of her mother and father, having replaced it with one of just her and her father. His heart did a strange, worrisome flutter as he stared at the rest she'd added. One of her and her besties. Another of *his* mother and father. The last was a picture of him and her from he didn't know how long ago. A few years, maybe. They were outside his house, looking at one another, caught mid-laugh. Sun streamed through her cocoa locks and she had on a yellow sundress. Come to think of it, that might've been the day he'd closed on the land she'd sold him.

She'd...added him and his family to her wall. In her mansion. He ran his shaking hands through his hair, clenching the strands. As always, Scarlett had gone above and beyond to include him. Somehow, she'd caught on to the fact that he'd felt like an outsider, and had bent over backwards to ensure that wasn't the case.

Damn, but his sinuses stung.

His phone dinged a text alert. He checked it, not at all surprised it was her again.

Now look in the living room.

He couldn't take much more of this. She was fileting him, one gesture at a time.

Poking his head in the living room, he fumbled for the switch. Light illuminated from...*his* lamps. The ones from his living room at the ranch house. She'd put a couple pieces of his baseball memorabilia on the mantle, and some of his books on the shelves flanking the fireplace. A throw blanket from his bedroom laid over the back of her couch. She'd also set a new dog bed next to the cat tree.

Hands on his knees, he bent over, trying to get a grip. She'd loved him all along. In the way he feared she hadn't, she'd proved to him the opposite, like she'd done all their damn lives. She accepted him, included him, wanted him, and loved him.

A grin, and he straightened, thumbing a text. *Theft is a crime.*

Her response took less than five seconds. *Nah. What's yours is mine and what's mine is yours. Welcome home.*

Chapter Nineteen

Inside the dark library, Scarlett sat on the dusty floorboards, thinking that if coming here had worked for Rebecca last spring, maybe it would for her, too. Katherine Vallantine's ghost had conjured hundreds of Rebecca's old blog pages for her, seemingly from out of thin air, to remind her of childhood aspirations. As a result, Rebecca not only co-owned The Gazette, but had her own popular blog called "Because, Becca!"

Throughout history, many generations of Vallantine descendants or townsfolk would have unusual experiences in the library. A book or something would appear just when they'd needed it most from out of nowhere. An answer to what they'd been searching for. Legend was Katherine assisted all who entered seeking knowledge.

What Scarlett needed wasn't necessarily knowledge, but guidance.

Aden had texted to never mind what he'd said, that he would come over tonight with dinner. Did that mean he no longer sought some strange kind of separation for their love or a definition that didn't require one? She sure hoped so, darn it. She'd been wracking her brain, attempting to give him peace of mind in order for them to move on. It was why she'd brought over some of his things, hoping he'd feel more at home, that he'd know it was his place, too. Incorporating and merging their lives into one.

After he'd found her surprises at the mansion, his responses made her smile as her cell illuminated the dark confines of the library. She'd head home in a minute. First, she wanted to have a quiet moment with the ghosts of the past.

Dismal light in the library from very few windows as a natural source had shadows creating shadows. The tall, vaulted ceiling and empty shelves made the slightest shift become a reverberating echo. Pieces of equipment were everywhere from the work crews. Tarps and lumber and paint cans. For some, it might be a scene for a spooky horror flick, but to her, it was safety. The silence was both cumbersome and welcome.

The place had been built out of love, and love had kept it standing. She and her besties would take care of the rest. They'd finish restoring it to glory again.

Her grandmother had been like that with the family estate. They'd never run a plantation, nor had any crops ever been planted on the grounds, but she'd respected history, even the ugly parts. Her ancestors had settled in Vallantine almost twenty years after slavery had been abolished, same as the others in Vallantine's historical district. But her grandmother had made certain the upkeep of the mansion had been maintained, and had instilled in Scarlett to do the same. Miss Maureen had been a strong, unapologetic woman who'd done her best to be fair.

Again, she wished her grandmother were still here to offer advice on how to navigate life and love, or how to come to terms with her mother's behavior. The past two days have been like treading water in a hurricane. Pointless and exhausting. Without a positive outcome.

But no, that wasn't completely true. Daddy had taken measures to remove himself from a situation where he hadn't been happy, and was coming home to start fresh. She and her besties had gotten so far in library restorations—a dream of theirs. She had a thriving business venture. She and Aden had found one another on a level she'd never considered until finally opening her eyes one night in the garden.

So, what was her problem? Why the state of unrest?

A noise came from behind her. Delicate. A rustling or shooshing. Noticeable only because the library was vastly somber. Like something being slid across a table.

The fine hairs on her arms rose, and she slowly turned around. An envelope lay next to her purse that hadn't been there before. There was only one entrance and exit to the library, and she was facing it. No one had come in. Besides, it was so quiet in here, she could hear her own exhalations. She would've remembered bringing an envelope with her. Plus, she knew the contents of her handbag.

The envelope had materialized out of thin air.

Katherine? Had Katherine Vallantine done this?

Goodness, the rumors were true, after all.

Nothing dramatic. Just an envelope. No white mist, shadows shifting, or spooky vibe. No loud music for momentum. She was alone, just as she'd been before, and she didn't sense any sort of malice. In fact, traces of a lingering scent of roses wafted over that of dust and mildew.

She reached for the envelope with a shaking hand. It had the family attorney's logo on the upper left-hand side, and her name centered on the front. It was still sealed.

And she recognized what it was in an instant.

When her grandmother had died, after the funeral and during the reading of the will, both she and her father had received one. The estate lawyer had said it was a letter from her grandmother, penned the year before when her health had started failing. Overcome with grief, Scarlett had set it in her office to read later when she was in a better headspace. The loss had been too raw.

Dear God, she'd forgotten all about it. How had it gotten here?

Breaking the seal, she pulled out a single sheet of paper. Her grandmother had stationery sets, but this design had been her favorite. Delicate etched irises in the right-hand corner, lined paper, with swirls. Seeing Miss Maureen's handwriting lodged a wedge of emotion in Scarlett's throat. It somehow even smelled like her gardenia perfume.

Dearest Granddaughter,

You'll be receiving this after my arrangements, and I urge you not to be sad. I'm with my love again, and you have a wonderfully blessed life ahead of you, Scarlett.

You have been the genuine light of my life. I love your father, but I fear he can be a stick in the mud sometimes. Do try to cure him of that after I'm gone, please. There's hope for him yet. I will not mention your mother, other than to say the only thing she did right was to conceive you. Some individuals are born without soul, without grace, and it is not the responsibility of those around them to make up for what they lack. You mustn't either.

It is my hope that you pursue your ideas of opening the Taylor estate to events like we discussed many times. This grand ole place could use some excitement and cheer as it once had in days of yore. Dancing and gathering among family and friends.

While I'm on that subject, hold those two dear friends of yours close, as friends are the family we choose to have, not the ones we're obligated to indulge. Dorothy and Rebecca are wonderful darlings. Grow with them and learn from one another.

My last note is about love. It's the most important. It is infinite, and can sometimes be found in the most obvious of places, right under our noses. We often don't have to travel far to find it. I suggest you take a walk across a pasture to find your prince. I'm pretty certain he was always there waiting.

Be happy, Scarlett.

All my love,

Miss Maureen

Eyes wet, Scarlett closed the letter and replaced it in the envelope. She should've read this sooner, should've remembered it existed. She'd missed Miss Maureen fiercely since her passing, especially the support her grandmother had always freely given.

"You're pretty good at this, Katherine." She huffed a laugh, the sound echoing. She hoped the ghost heard.

What her grandmother had written about Mother had been simple, succinct, and eloquently put. And she was correct. Scarlett shouldn't blame herself or waste another minute of her energy on someone who didn't deserve it, or who would ever return the sentiments. It had been something she'd waffled about, but hearing it from someone she admired and respected somehow gave it weight.

And she guessed that closed the book on Aden. How funny her grandmother suspected he'd had feelings for Scarlett beyond friendship, even back then. She'd wondered off and on what Miss Maureen would think of the relationship. She had her answer, and her grandmother's blessing.

Aden was waiting for her. It was time to go.

Rising, she brushed dirt off her butt and glanced around, smiling. Soon, this wonderful building would be finished, and they'd reopen. She hoped Katherine Vallantine stuck around to see it.

With a wave of thanks, she locked up and walked to her car. On the ride home, she thought about what she'd say to Aden, how to profess a love that had always been fervent. They'd not changed things by growing intimate, had not altered the relationship. They'd evolved into something she believed would always find them right back here. To one another.

Instead of pulling in the garage, she parked beside the fountain, thinking she'd move the car later. Climbing out, she glanced up at the stars, stark against an ebony sky, and a crescent moon. An owl hooted in the distance and cicadas buzzed. It was still warm, still muggy, but there was a pleasant breeze that ruffled her stands.

"You look like a nymph in the moonlight."

Hand to her chest, she whirled.

Aden stood on the porch, leaning against one of the columns, arms crossed over his chest. All six feet of him. Biceps bulged under the sleeves of his t-shirt. Wide shoulders. Lean waist. Sandy blond hair all askew. Strong jaw dusted with whiskers. Beautifully muscled and...barefoot.

Rawr.

"Food's cold." He stepped down, walking to stand in front of her. He lifted his arms, setting them against the car on either side of her and caging her in.

"Sorry. I was at the library."

He frowned. "So late? Everything okay?"

"Yeah." She brushed her hair out her face. "Just having a chat with Katherine Vallantine."

Up went his brows. "Talking to ghosts?"

"Something like that." She relayed what happened, how the letter had appeared out nowhere.

He tilted his head. "So, the place is haunted."

"Maybe. I wouldn't be the first person she helped." She dug in her purse. "Here, read it."

Shaking his head, he shoved off the car. "That's private, babe."

On her insistence, he took it from her. She watched his expression go from sad to impressed to endeared to surprised as he read her grandmother's letter. Afterword, he carefully folded it and placed it back in the envelope.

"Wow." He passed it back to her. "Lots in there to process. She had a way with words."

"It was as if she'd known just what I'd needed to hear." She chewed her lip. "This thing with my mother threw me for a loop. What Miss Maureen said put it in perspective. I'm going to stop letting that woman dictate my life."

"Good plan. Funny you should say that." He scratched the back of his head, disrupting the strands further. "I came to a realization of my own. To a degree, she's been manipulating my mental status also. The constant rhetoric of not being good enough for you is something in particular I let her control. I believed it. Even if I didn't realize it, I believed her."

Her heart sank. "That's ridiculous." She cupped his jaw, dipping to look in his remarkable blue eyes. "You're an amazing man, Aden."

"Thank you." His aw-shucks grin had her belly flip-flopping. "I choose not to let her get in my head anymore."

"Good for you. She was wrong, anyhow." Smiling, she rose on her toes to offer a brief kiss. "I thought that last part of the letter was very interesting."

"Yeah." He chuckled, expression dialed to no-kidding. "I had no clue she felt that way about me. About us. It's almost like she's giving us her blessing."

"Exactly how I felt." She wrapped her arms around his waist. "So, are we done knit picking about variations of love? Because, for the record, I love you, I'm in love with you, and that's not going to change. I told you so."

He rolled his eyes. "I'm sorry. I have no excuse except to say that, once I got everything I wanted, I kept waiting for it all to be taken away. A cosmic joke at my expense or something. I just..." He let out a breath. "It's a bit much, finding out the woman you've loved forever actually loves you back."

"Aww." Dang, her heart. "That was the sweetest thing to ever come out of your mouth."

His expression flatlined. "Don't get used to it."

"Oh, I'm gonna get used to it. In fact, say something else."

"Shut up, Scarlett."

"Make me, Aden."

"Game on."

He backed her up against the car, a full body press, and grabbed the luggage bars on the roof, caging her between two solid biceps. His kiss was potent, drugging, and literally had her knees weak. He seemed to pour all his caged, pent up frustration into the kiss. From the slant of his lips to the stroke of his tongue, he dominated, until it was either come up for air or perish.

"You win." She nibbled his neck, soughing oxygen.

He groaned at her exploration. "Come again? Did you just admit—"

"You heard wrong." She laughed, tingling from her head to her toenails. "Take me to bed."

"With pleasure." He did an abrupt about-face, her hand in his as he dragged her. At the top of the porch steps, he halted, eyeing her. "By the way, real slick, moving me into the mansion while I was away."

That was pretty clever, if she did say so herself. "I didn't move you in. I relocated a few of your things to make my home feel more like our home."

Eyes narrowed, grin amped, he opened the door and swept her into his arms.

Breath in her throat, she stared at him in utter awe. "Ooh. I like this. Very romantic, Aden, but what if I want to walk?"

"Don't give a damn."

"You forgot the *frankly, my dear* part." That's what Rhett had said in *Gone With the Wind*, which Aden often quoted whenever he taunted her. A lot.

"No, I didn't." He stepped over the threshold and kicked the door shut behind them. "They didn't get a happy ending. We are. So, no, I didn't forget."

Pig Pickin' Cake Recipe
Cake:

- 1 box of yellow cake mix

- 1 can of mandarin oranges with juice

- 3 large eggs

- ¼ cup vegetable oil

Frosting:

- 1 tub of Cool Whip, thawed

- 1 can of crushed pineapple, drained

- 1 box instant vanilla pudding mix

Prepare:

- Preheat oven to 350 degrees

- Beat cake mix, juice from the oranges, oil, and eggs with an electric mixer until smooth.

- Fold in ½ the oranges.

- Pour batter into 2 round 9 inch greased cake pans.

- Bake for 15-20 minutes, or until centers no longer jiggle.

- Cool on a wire rack.

- In a separate bowl, beat Cool Whip, vanilla pudding packet, and drained pineapple until blended. Batter will be lumpy.

- Spread frosting onto one cake.

- Top with the other cake.

- Spread the remainder of the frosting over the sides and top of both stacked cakes.

- Decorate the top with the remaining oranges.

Enjoy!
(Store in a tight container in the refrigerator).

Want to help an author? Please consider leaving a review
and tell others about the great romance you just read!
Continue to read more about Kelly!

ABOUT THE AUTHOR:

Kelly Moran is an international bestselling author of enchanting ever-afters. She gets her ideas from everyone and everything around her and there's always a book playing out in her head. She is a RITA® Finalist, RONE Award-Winner, Catherine Award-Winner, Reader's Choice Finalist, Holt Medallion Finalist, Book Excellence Award Finalist, Amor Book Award-Winner, and landed on the "Must Read" & "10 Best Reads" lists in USA Today's Lifestyle section. She is a former Romance Writers of America® member, where she was an Award of Excellence Finalist. Her books have foreign translation rights in Germany (where she is a Spiegel Bestseller), the Czech Republic, Romania, Russia, France, and the Netherlands. She is the owner and founder of Rowan Prose Publishing. She also writes horror under the name Kelly Covic. Her interests include: scary movies, all kinds of art, driving others insane, and sleeping when she can. She is a closet coffee junkie and chocoholic. Tell no one. She's originally from Wisconsin, but she resides in South Carolina with her significant other, her three sons, their wily dogs, a bearded dragon, tree frogs, and their sassy cats. She loves hea ring from her readers.
www.AuthorKellyMoran.com